Tangled Chances

TANGLED SERIES

SOPHIE ANDREWS

 Created with Vellum

Content Note

Tangled Chances is a fake dating, workplace romance between the goldenest of all golden retriever boyfriends and the librarian he is obsessed with. But if you are for book banning, against supporting teachers, and don't feel like it's important to protect ALL children, then this book ain't for you. Everyone else, enjoy!

Teachers and librarians are saving the world. And they definitely deserve some good lovin'.

CHAPTER ONE

Jimmy

Pleasure was pain. That was what some people said.

And those people were full of shit.

Everything burned. My lower back, calves, and especially my abs—it all burned so bad. I grunted, nearly unable to hold myself up anymore.

"Keep going."

"I can't," I moaned, my entire body quaking with effort.

"Almost there."

"Oh my god," I whined.

"I can hear you, Jimmy," my brother snapped from his place on the other side of the Zoom chat.

I clenched my teeth. "I'm on mute."

Mike bear-crawled closer to the screen like it was nothing, even after he'd led this virtual workout class through forty-five minutes of high-intensity cardio and bodyweight exercises. "Come on, Jimmy. Keep that core tight."

I sneered at the screen as the faces of the others in the class grinned. This was their usual entertainment.

Lifting one single finger to the screen, I made my nonverbal response clear a moment before I dropped to the floor from my plank position.

"Hey, nice job, everybody," Mike said, wiping his forehead with the hem of his T-shirt. "Susan, I can see you really working hard. You didn't take any breaks during the cardio portion, good for you. Kai, man, that push-up challenge you're doing? Amazing. Lori, you worked up quite a sweat today, love to see it. And, Jimmy."

I lifted my head, expecting some smartass remark.

"Thanks for showing up." Older by three years, he still got his kicks in 300 miles away.

Using what little strength I had left, I slithered to my laptop and unmuted myself. "Have I told you your new haircut makes you look like a potato?"

He ignored me. "Make sure you guys hydrate. Drop any questions or comments in our Facebook group, and I'll see you all on Friday." With that, Mike waved a big bear paw at the screen and ended the Zoom.

Three times a week, for some stupid reason like familial loyalty and "health," I showed up to his online workout class. My brother had gone from a guy depressed and living in our parents' basement to a thriving business owner of an online gym and social media influencer. Although, most of Mike's Instagram audience was thirsty women.

I still thought he looked like a potato.

Rolling over, I grabbed my phone and typed out a text.

Sam, your boyfriend is picking on me again.

POTATO HEAD

She's not going to answer.

POTATO HEAD

You know she's not a morning person.

Of course, I knew Sam wasn't a morning person. She'd been my best friend since we were practically babies. The three of us Ewing boys grew up next door to the Kohler family, but I'd only learned about Sam's crush on Mike two years ago. She'd moved home for a few weeks, and they fell in love. I was over the moon about it. They were two of my favorite people.

> I'm the only one who shows up to your workouts. If that doesn't say anything about how the rest of the family feels about you, I don't know what does.

Mike responded with the middle finger emoji.

I trudged upstairs to grab a shower and get ready for work. In the kitchen, I filled up a glass of water and took a moment to check out the sunrise through the window above the sink.

Mornings were my favorite time of day, a new opportunity to do better. That was why I didn't mind attending my brother's classes. Because I was a morning person. I had always liked to run, needing an outlet for my excess energy, but I'd gotten used to working out with him while he was home. Now that he had these virtual classes, I tried to keep up with it, though I had yet to see any major improvements. I wasn't disciplined enough, according to Mike.

Then again, I had no interest in eating three dozen eggs a day or whatever my brother did to take after Gaston, minus the whole misogyny thing. At least I was stronger than Adam, our older brother. I could definitely take that dweeb in a fight.

Speaking of...

> I signed us up for a 5K.

BROSEPH

No thank you.

> It's for kids with cancer.

> You gonna say no to kids with cancer?

He texted me the middle finger emoji.

An hour later, I bopped along to Hootie & The Blowfish as I parked in my regular spot on the far side of Lincoln Elementary. While everyone else on staff fought for those spaces close to the front door, I didn't mind getting more steps in every day.

With my coffee in hand, I slung my backpack over my left shoulder and waved to Aggie, the frizzy-haired gym teacher in her white polo shirt and shorts, who was in the middle of dragging a couple of nets to the side door from a big shed just outside of the grassy area where the kids had recess. "Indoor soccer?"

She pointed to the sky, gray clouds coming our way. "We'll be stuck inside."

I puffed up my cheeks. Indoor recess meant I'd lose some of my planning time. *Again.*

"What's the song of the day today?" she asked.

"'Only Want To Be With You.'"

"Hootie?" She sent me a thumbs-up, her graying hair bouncing as she nodded in approval.

Aggie was two decades older than me, but we had a lot in common, including our mutual love of nineties music and sweets. She always brought in some kind of delightful concoction from her oven to every staff meeting, and as luck would have it, we had one this afternoon.

"Save me a seat later?" I asked, crossing to the sidewalk.

"Of course. I got cheesecake brownies."

"If you weren't already married, I'd ask you," I said.

"If I weren't already married, I'd say yes."

Sipping my venti chocolate chip Frappuccino with extra whip, I made my way inside and through the maze of halls to the main office for my mail. I shot a grin to the administrative assistant. "Morning!"

"Oh, Jimmy, hold on!" Greta called. "Mrs. Kaplan wanted to speak with you."

When I raised my brow in question, she merely smiled in response and tipped her head back toward the principal's door. I knocked on the doorframe and stuck my head in. "Hey, Mrs. Kaplan."

Short but with a long face and dark hair cut to her chin, she reminded me a little of Lord Farquaad from *Shrek*. She stood up from behind her desk, her ever-present walkie-talkie in her hand. "Jim, how are you this morning?"

"Great. I was hoping you could spare me a few minutes during the meeting this afternoon to see if anyone is interested in joining our softball team?"

"Absolutely. Anything for a finalist for Teacher of the Year."

I reflexively accepted the envelope she held out. "You're kidding."

She shook her head.

"Thank you," I said, rather shocked.

"This isn't my doing. This is all you."

I was gobsmacked into silence.

"I thought you'd be shouting down the halls about this," she said with a chuckle.

I blinked back into awareness and smiled at her. "Oh, you know I will." I nodded my thanks. "I really appreciate everything you've done for me."

I'd completed my student teaching here, and Mrs. Kaplan hired me immediately. It was the smoothest transition a first-year teacher could ask for. Now, seven years later, I was up for Teacher of the Year.

"Well deserved." She patted my arm and walked with me out into the hall, where a giant bulletin board with die-cut letters spelled out *April Showers Bring May Flowers*. With two months of school left, the kids were starting to get antsy. Hell, so were the teachers. Me included.

Especially after this news.

After a check of the time on her watch, Mrs. Kaplan parted ways with me at the end of the hall, heading toward the doors to greet the kids as they got off the buses. "Have a great day, Mr. Ewing!"

"It always is!" I turned down the left hall, where my classroom was across from the library. I caught the red hair of the librarian as she moved across it. "Good morning, Miss Hart," I droned because I knew she hated it. When she reversed two paces to stand in her doorway, I saluted her with my coffee.

Claire rolled her eyes, mumbling a quiet, "Morning," as she spun away from me.

I smiled at her back and unlocked my room, smacking the *Welcome, Second Graders!* sign on the way in. As usual, I hit the lights, powered on the projector with today's schedule, and cued up a playlist. With the volume as loud as it would go, I made a loop around the classroom, preparing the different learning centers.

But a minute later, the song stopped, and I whirled around to find Claire's index finger on my laptop. She was like a cat. Silent in her break-in to mute my music. "Could you pick a more annoying song?"

"'Walking on Sunshine' is a classic."

"Everything's a classic to you," she said with a sigh and readjusted her headband. Today's selection was pale pink with little pearls all over it.

I circled back to the front of the room, where she was slumped against my desk, eyeing my coffee. "How much sugar's in there?"

"Not enough," I said then sucked down about a third of it. Claire Hart, librarian extraordinaire, wasn't exactly known around these parts for her jolly personality, but she seemed down today. "What's with the sad face?"

She deliberately focused her attention to the windows. "Recess will be inside today. Try to keep it down, huh?"

Then she strutted out of my room, her black skirt swaying, her long hair that was more orange than red falling in gentle waves halfway down her back.

"Anything for you, Miss Hart!"

She didn't acknowledge me, only shut the library room door behind her. As much as she pretended to dislike me, I knew she didn't. I'd caught her biting her lip, holding in a smile more than a time or two. I'd get her to crack one of these days.

I plopped into my chair and thumbed my cell phone awake to find a text from the owner of my rental.

LANDLADY LUCY

Hey, Jim. I wanted to let you know we're moving my mom into a personal care facility and need to sell her house to pay for it.

I read it twice to understand. Lucy was a friend of my mom's, and when I was looking for a rental home, she'd offered her mother's house after Lucy and her husband decided to move her mom in with them. I supposed her dementia had progressed enough that they needed extra help.

Damn.

I loved that house. I'd really come to think of it as mine this last year. I didn't want to lose it.

Talk about a bad turn of luck. Went from award finalist to future itinerant.

That must've been a tough decision. I'm sorry.

LANDLADY LUCY

And I'm sorry that I'm giving you bad news.
You were an excellent tenant. We just made
the decision this morning. It'll be a few weeks
until we get everything in order, so you'll have
time to find another place.

What if I said I wanted to buy it? Would you
sell it to me instead of putting it on the
market?

LANDLADY LUCY

Do you have the money for it?

I answered without thinking or knowing how. Only that I
didn't want to lose my house.

I'll get it.

CHAPTER TWO

Claire

Staff meetings were always held in the library, and I walked over to the table in the corner where a student had left their book. No matter how many times I reminded them, there was always one who left their books.

"Tell me again what this shithead said to you."

I glanced over my shoulder to my friend as she lounged in one of the tiny blue chairs. "Why do you insist on making me relive my mortification?"

"So I can properly prepare what I will say when I see this motherfucker."

"Meredith!" I darted my eyes to the open doors, where our colleagues would start pouring in at any moment.

She shrugged, waiting on my answer. She might've looked like Elle Woods, but she had the personality of a bulldog. "What?"

I ignored her and stalked off to the adjoining computer lab to shut down the computers before dropping into the seat next to Meredith. A trio of fourth-grade teachers strolled in, smiling at us. Meredith waved at them while lowering her voice, which wasn't much quieter than her usual earsplitting volume. "If my boyfriend told me I was boring and grumpy, I would quite literally stab him in the neck with a high heel then stand over him while he bled out, asking, 'Am I boring now, bitch?'"

"Oh my god," I mumbled. "You need to be quiet."

She snorted. "I can't believe you let him get away with that."

"I didn't let him get away with it," I said, dropping my head into my hands like it weighed fifty pounds. "I broke up with him and—"

"And he acted like you slighted him. *Him*. If I ever run across that jackass in real life, he's done. *Done*."

I rubbed at my temples. Eric, my boyfriend of a year, did, in fact, call me grumpy and boring. Or, more accurately, said, "You're always so grumpy all the time. Maybe you should talk to your doctor to get on something." And, "Why don't you ever want to go out? All you ever wanna do is sit here on the couch. My friends think you're afraid of them. Little do they know you're actually just boring."

In the moment, all I could do was sit there, staring. Over the last few months, I'd gotten used to his backhanded compliments and passive-aggressive comments, although he'd never come right out and said anything so hurtful and offensive. I didn't know what his aim was, but once I shook myself out of my stupor, I'd immediately asked him to leave.

Less than twenty-four hours later, I felt like a kicked puppy.

Not that I didn't already know these things about myself. People often mistook my silence as judgment and misunderstood my being introverted as disliking people. I'd just never expected someone I had been dating to lay out my insecurities so plainly.

"He's an asshole. Forget about him," Meredith said, her bracelets clacking on the table when she slapped her hand down. Everything about my best friend was loud, including her jewelry. The only other person who had her beat in volume was Jimmy Ewing.

"Hey, everybody!" He grinned, entering the library with his usual swagger, though I couldn't help but notice his grin wasn't up to its typical ten. It was dimmed, somewhere around a five.

"Digging the new haircut, Leslie," he said to one of the fifth-grade teachers. "There she is! My work wife. I need your treats today." He slumped into a chair next to Aggie, the gym teacher, and she immediately opened up a Tupperware of brownies. He snagged himself two then passed them around the room. I sighed and got up to retrieve napkins from the back. I didn't want to have to come in early tomorrow morning to vacuum crumbs. I tossed a couple of napkins down on each table, nodding at Jimmy.

"Your classroom was abnormally quiet today."

He shrugged, his mouth full of brownie.

Ordinarily, his students were singing or dancing or playing basketball with the hoop above his door. There was always something going on across the hall.

When he didn't offer me an answer, I didn't push—unlike him—and slid back into my seat as Mrs. Kaplan entered the library, flicking off her walkie-talkie. She had a few papers in her hand, and after accepting a brownie "for later," she opened up the meeting with her customary welcome then got right into her agenda of monthly reminders and upcoming events for Spring Fling week, which I was often utilized for. Besides being the school librarian, I was also a sort of catchall, like the library itself.

"And now, I have some super-exciting news. Mr. Ewing, if you'll join me up here."

He grinned—closer to a ten—as he stood next to her, rocking back on his heels, his hands in his pockets, pastel-purple button-down rolled to his elbows. That Easter egg color shouldn't have looked so good on him, especially with the khakis, but he pulled it off. Along with his unruly curly hair that was in constant need of a trim and his slightly gapped front teeth that he often whistled through.

He was always desperate for attention, nagging until he got it, yet no one ever seemed to be mad at him for it. In fact, most people encouraged it.

Like a puppy.

"Our own Mr. Ewing is a finalist for Teacher of the Year," Mrs. Kaplan said, and whoops of glee shot up from the faculty, including a hoot from Hassan Zawahiri, the school psychologist and one of the few other males on staff. In a field dominated by females, Jimmy stood out and not only because of his gender. But because he sucked up all the air in the room whenever he was around. He wasn't even that big, probably not even six feet tall, and not all that muscular, yet there was something about him. The way he always greeted everyone like they were best friends and how he always threw back his head and clapped twice when he laughed.

Everyone loved him—teachers, parents, and, of course, his students. He somehow recalled all of their names, even years later when they ran to him for a high five or hug as they moved on to middle school. I supposed it was only a matter of time until Mr. Popular received some kind of recognition for his work.

Jimmy held up his hands. "Thank you, really. It's surprising and amazing, and I hate to sound like a pretentious tool, but it really is an honor to be nominated."

Mrs. Kaplan smiled. "It's an honor for the school as well. As we know, a success for one is a success for all. Now, I do believe you had something you wanted to announce."

He nodded and gestured to Hassan. "Our rec softball

league resumes next week, and we still have a spot open. A few of you are on it already, but since Marla went on maternity leave, we have to fill her position."

Hassan twisted in his seat, his eyes coasting over the rest of us. "It's a lot of fun, and we always grab a drink somewhere after every game."

Meredith snatched my forearm, forcing my hand up. "Claire will do it!"

"What are you doing?" I hissed.

"She loves softball."

"I do not."

Jimmy tipped his head to the side, his lips pouting, brows narrowed as he watched my ex-best friend and me argue.

"You need to get out of your funk," she said.

"I'm not in a funk."

"Oh, so you're just grumpy and boring, then? You're going to let him win?"

I huffed as Hassan stood, cell phone in hand, making his way toward me.

"You are not grumpy and boring," Meredith declared. "Let's go have fun."

"*Let's*? You volunteered me. You do it. I have no coordination."

Hassan caught the tail end of that sentence and grinned. "Hey, Claire, it's okay. It's all for fun."

"Well, not *all* for fun," Jimmy corrected good-naturedly since everyone knew he was the king of competitions. If there was a pool, he was running it. If there was a race, he was in it. If there was an award up for grabs, he wanted it. Which was why I was positive he'd be Teacher of the Year, no problem.

"Put your contact info in here, and I'll add you to the group chat," Hassan told me.

"I'll be there at every game, supporting you," Meredith told me then smiled sweetly up at Hassan, and suddenly it all made sense. He was recently divorced, and she hoped this was her chance to move in. She'd had the hots for him forever. But why did I have to be the sacrificial lamb so she could spend more time with him?

With an inward sigh, I accepted his phone and typed my name and number after kicking Meredith's foot. She grinned at me like she'd won Teacher of the Year.

Hassan and Jimmy both sat back down, and Mrs. Kaplan finished with the meeting. Once we were dismissed, I hung back behind the circulation desk, waiting until everyone was gone to lock up.

"I'll text you later," Hassan called to me as he walked out with Meredith in tow. Jimmy pulled up the rear, the last one out. He leaned against the counter, his backpack slung over one shoulder, his left hand holding the strap so I could see the black marks on the side of his palm.

I handed him a wet wipe, since I had them stationed all over the library for the walking germs in this place, and motioned to his hand. "Expo marker?"

He rubbed off the marks and balled up the wipe, tossing it in the trash can. "Yeah. Haven't quite mastered how to show the kids how to write better without battle wounds. Life of a lefty."

"That's what teaching is to you? A war?"

He shrugged. "Feels like it some days."

I hitched my purse over my shoulder. "But you earned the equivalent of a Purple Heart. I'm surprised you aren't shouting it from the rooftops."

He sighed and followed me out after I locked up. We made our way to the back exit. "It's a good news, bad news kind of day. The award was real good news, but I found out my land-lady is selling my house, so I have to figure out a way to come up with the money to buy the place or find somewhere else to live."

"Ah, that really sucks. What are you going to do?"

He huffed. "Search for buried treasure, I guess."

"Or," I said, dragging out the word. "You could get a loan."

He eyed me. "I bet you're one of those people who has an emergency fund and always pays down the principal on credit cards."

"And I suppose you are not one of those people." When he shook his head, I raised my brow. "*Shocking.*"

I gazed up at the gray sky, a few raindrops landing on my outstretched palm as Jimmy situated his backpack in front of him to pull out an umbrella. I liked the rain and strolled out into the parking lot.

"Hey, wait." He jogged to catch up to me and held the umbrella up over both of us. "Here. Don't get wet."

"I don't mind getting wet," I said, and his lips curled, doing something funny to my stomach. Like some lasciviously inappropriate comment was on the tip of his tongue.

I shot my eyes ahead of me, trying to ignore how our arms rubbed against each other as we huddled together under his umbrella.

"So, you going to tell me whatever's bothering you?" he asked, guiding us to where our cars were parked next to each other.

"Nothing's bothering me."

"No? Meredith forced you to be on our softball team for no reason?"

"She wants Hassan. I'm supposed to be her wingwoman."

"Really?" His brown eyes lit with curiosity. "Well now, that's interesting. Miss Frank and Mr. Z, speech pathologist and school psychologist, a match made in heaven. What?" He elbowed me. "What's that face for now?"

"You know as well as I do it wouldn't work out. You and she are basically the same person."

He toggled his head back and forth, weighing the idea. "Well, I do enjoy wearing pink."

I rolled my eyes. "You both couldn't stay in a relationship to save your lives."

He held up his finger between us. "I will have you know I was with a girl from Christmas to Valentine's Day this year, which was basically one step short of an engagement."

"Right," I said flatly. Jimmy had the attention span of a gnat. Between his personality and good looks, I was sure he had a different woman every weekend.

Stopped between our cars, I tipped my chin toward his rusted Mustang. "When are you getting rid of this hunk of junk?"

He gasped and placed his hand over the side mirror. "Not so loud. You'll hurt her feelings."

"Her?"

"Her name's Mariah." He tossed his bag into the passenger seat, then turned, waiting until I opened my driver's side door and slid behind the wheel, keeping me dry under his umbrella. "Like Carey," he clarified as if I couldn't guess. "And don't worry, we're going to have a lot of fun at softball." Then he shut the door for me and strode around to his driver's side, beaming a smile my way that split the gray clouds. "See you tomorrow."

Moments later, he drove away with a wave in my direction, blasting Mariah's "Fantasy."

CHAPTER THREE

Claire

"I can't believe I'm doing this," I mumbled to myself, tying my hair up in a ponytail while the other players on the softball team—all teachers from either our school or another elementary school a few miles away—tossed a ball back and forth or laughed in pairs. I didn't even have a mitt and had to order one online. My younger brother told me to oil it, but I didn't know what that meant.

Sticking my hand inside the leather glove, I wiggled my fingers, not particularly fond of how it felt, rough yet somehow sticky and damp.

"Look at you," Meredith cheered from behind me, and I swung around on her.

"Don't start."

"What? I was going to say you look so cute."

I didn't look cute. Cute were my playful skirts and headbands I wore to work every day. This morning, I'd thrown on leggings and an oversized T-shirt I needed to knot at my waist, the only clothes I owned to pretend I had any idea I knew what I was doing. I squinted around the field. Was I supposed to warm up or something?

"Oh hey, Mr. Z," Meredith said while setting her folding

chair up with her Yeti, which most likely contained a White Claw.

Our tall, dark, and handsome colleague jogged over, an easy smile on his face. "We're not in school. You can call me Hassan."

Meredith lifted one shoulder. "What if I like calling you Mr. Z?"

"Oh god," I muttered as Hassan stilled next to me, clearly not sure what to do with Meredith unleashed from the confines of our school building.

"Uh, so... Claire, if it's all right with you, we'll put you over in left midfield."

I peered out in the direction he pointed. "Left mid?"

He patted my shoulder with a laugh. "Come on, I'll show you where. Give you a quick rundown of what you'll need to do."

I followed him out to the grassy section of the field, to the area left of the middle. Who would've guessed? Then he demonstrated how to catch and throw a ball but informed me that Aggie would be on my left, and someone else named Lou would be on my right. Both of whom were experienced and would help cover for me.

"Got it?"

Nope. Not at all. "Yeah, sure."

"Great. We're going to get started in a few minutes." He took off in the direction of the other team, and my gaze wandered over to the opposing players, all in matching navy T-shirts with a name on the back.

"Oh my god." I ducked my head, realizing the other team was Eric's advertising and media company. "Oh no. No, no, no, no."

I'd known he played softball for his work team, but it never occurred to me that *I* would be playing against him. Staring down at the ground, I hustled toward the fence, intending to hide behind the row of bats or the stacked coolers or a tree very, very, *very* far away. Instead, I smacked into someone.

"Oof."

I lifted my head at the soft grunt. "Sorry."

Jimmy rubbed at his stomach, where I'd plowed into him. "What's the hurry?"

"Nothing."

"The game hasn't started yet, and already you're trying to take off."

"No, I, uh..." I darted my gaze around, but it ended on Eric as he hopped up to catch a throw that went just above his head. He effortlessly landed on his feet. Of course.

Jimmy followed my line of sight. "You know him?"

I swallowed, unsure if I wanted to divulge the embarrassing truth.

When I didn't answer, he linked his hand on the fence, grinning. "Oh, uh-huh. I see. He's who you were running from, eh? Is he an ex-boyfriend or something?"

"Actually, yes."

"Oh." He turned big eyes on me. "I'm really sorry, Claire. I didn't mean anything—"

"I know. It's recent and..."

"Claire!" Meredith screeched from yards away, drawing everyone's attention, including Eric's, and I leaped behind Jimmy.

"Hey, whoa. What's happening right now?" He held up his hands as I clutched the back of his T-shirt, forcibly spinning him around, hopefully hiding me from Eric.

"I don't want him to see me," I said.

"Claire!"

"Will you shut up?" I shushed my best friend when she was within whisper-shouting distance.

"Did you know Eric is on the other team?" she squawked.

Honestly. I didn't know why I was friends with her.

Jimmy glanced over his shoulder at me before looking to Meredith. "Yeah, that's why I'm playing the part of a wall this afternoon."

"Both of you shut up. Oh my god, he's coming over here. Oh my god. I hate you both."

"Claire," Eric said in his deep timbre. "What're you doing here?"

I slowly slunk out from behind my wall. "I'm, uh..."

Meredith crossed her arms, hip cocked out to the side, her lips pursed, ready to fire off some snark in my defense, but I clamped my hand around her bicep.

"I'm playing softball," I told him.

"Since when?"

Jimmy studied Eric and then me with a curious expression before smiling at Eric. He whacked my back a few times. "Since now. Star outfielder right here."

Eric laughed, all douchebag-like. "No way."

Jimmy sniffed, shouldering in front of me, less puppy and more guard dog. "Yeah."

"If you say so." Eric raised his brow, studying me from top to bottom, maybe wondering if I'd suddenly had a lobotomy and was Ms. Sunshine. Because Ms. Grump would never play in a softball league for fun. She didn't even know what fun was.

Hurt and anger had my shoulders curling in, and Meredith threw her arm around me as Eric pivoted away.

Jimmy whirled around on me. "*He* was your boyfriend?"

I nodded.

"Is he always such a dick?"

Meredith butted in. "Yeah. He called her boring and grumpy."

I sighed and rubbed my hand over my forehead, ashamed.

"Did he really?" Jimmy asked.

I nodded again.

"Well, he's a real asshole. Come on, let's go kill his team."

I slumped down against the bench as Hassan grabbed a bat and headed out to the batter's box. Eric was at first base, shouting encouragements to the pitcher, and I couldn't help but watch him. He wasn't conventionally attractive, although neither was I, so I'd thought we made a good match. Him with his long nose and Coke bottle glasses, and me with my too-wide smile and too-bright hair that I had tried dyeing, but with such pale skin and so many freckles, no other color quite fit. I liked that Eric was quirky and confident, but at some point that confidence tipped into narcissism. It was a gradual change, red flags I kept ignoring about what he wanted being more important than what I wanted.

"All right, good hit!" Jimmy yelled as Hassan smacked the ball to the outfield, and Meredith cheered from her chair while the rest of my team clapped. I did too since it seemed like the appropriate thing to do. Then someone else took their place up to bat. I prayed I wouldn't have to and kept my gaze on the dirt, zoning out.

For a long time, because Jimmy eventually bumped my shoulder.

"Hey, look alive now. We're on defense."

I shook myself back into the present and grabbed my glove. "Defense? There's defense in baseball?"

"Softball."

"Whatever."

He adjusted the bill of his cap. "There's defense and offense in every game. You just gotta know what you're playing."

"Right," I murmured, my eyes on him as he ran to the mound. I should've guessed he'd be the pitcher.

As I lumbered past him, he held up his hand for a high five, and when I lazily slapped his palm, he clutched my hand in a vise grip and towed me into him. "Show this loser what he's missing."

"What's that supposed to mean?"

"It means don't let him get to you."

I huffed. "Easier said than done."

"You can do it."

I pushed away from him. "How many more sportsball platitudes do I have to endure?"

He threw back his head and laughed, exposing the grainy skin of his jaw with a day's worth of stubble on it. "So many, Claire. So many."

Taking my place in midfield, I shifted from foot to foot, still completely unprepared for this. I shook out my arms, sweating from nerves.

I wasn't built for this. I should've been home painting my nails and reading a book.

"Hey, just keep your glove up," Aggie called from her spot next to me. "You'll be great!"

I waved at her, keeping my glove at my side. It was weirdly heavy. Like my fist was inserted into a raw sourdough loaf.

The first player up to bat was a woman with her hair braided and a bandanna around her head. She had muscles for days, and I inwardly cringed, hoping she didn't hit anything my way. She didn't, but the ball did go crashing straight to Nancy, at third base, who bobbled the catch. And before I knew it, the bases were loaded, and Eric was up to bat.

My stomach clenched, worried he'd hit it right to me. As if he could hear my thoughts, my ex-boyfriend nodded to me with a smirk on his face.

I couldn't believe we were together for a whole year. That I let him get into my head and convince me I wasn't good enough to be with anyone else, let alone him.

Jimmy pivoted toward me. "You got this," he told me, holding his left hand toward the ground in a staying motion. "We'll get him out."

I nodded and blew out a breath.

Offering me one last encouraging smile, he spun on his heel, readying himself for his pitch, and since I was positioned almost directly behind him, it was hard to ignore how his white shirt fit him snugly. His gray mesh shorts were loose but showed off his legs, sprinkled with dark hair, and mismatched socks. One was slightly higher than the other, with a ring of navy around it.

He wound up, slinging his arm back so the sleeve of his T-shirt curved along his triceps, and released the ball straight to Eric, who swung and missed. Meredith jumped up, clapping, as Jimmy turned over his shoulder to me, smiling like we were in on some inside joke.

Eric dropped his chin to his chest, fixed his glasses, then held his bat up once again, ready for Jimmy's next pitch. And there was something about the set of his shoulders that had me trembling with nervous energy.

Seconds later, Jimmy threw out his next pitch, and Eric sent the ball flying right at me.

Everything happened in slow motion.

"Get it! Get it!" Meredith shouted.

Out of the corner of my eye, I saw Aggie was running full bore toward me. Though with the sun right in my eyes, I couldn't see anything above me, and I held up my hand, attempting to block it, while I kept my glove out, hoping the ball would miraculously land in it.

It didn't.

It landed somewhere behind me, and I twisted around to grab it, trying to decipher everyone's directions.

"Throw it home!"

"Throw to me!"

"Hurry up!"

"She's headed home!"

I jerked my head right to left, having no idea where to throw, until Jimmy waved his arms. "Claire! Throw it to me!"

I followed his direction, but like a nightmare straight out of fifth grade, the ball was nowhere close to Jimmy, and he sprinted to pick it up off the ground before leaping sideways, aiming the ball at the catcher.

But he was too late. Eric crossed home plate a moment before.

"Hey, it's all right. It's all right!" Hassan called as Aggie slapped my back a few times.

"We'll get them back."

I nodded, my throat working on a swallow. My eyes stung, and I couldn't believe I was upset over a stupid softball game.

Jimmy removed his hat, smacking it against his leg in frustration before swiping his wrist over his forehead.

Embarrassed, I pivoted away, shuffling a few feet back so no one could see when I blinked tears away. It wasn't enough to embarrass me by calling me boring and grumpy, but Eric had to make me look a fool too.

A soft hand landed on my shoulder. "Hey, it's okay."

I shook my head and cleared my throat. "You're mad."

"No, I'm not," Jimmy said.

"I saw you slap your hat. You're frustrated."

"Yeah, with myself. Not with you. Hey, come on. We're only down by three and have the whole game to play. It's fine," he told me, his fingers warming my skin even through my shirt.

Forcing me to turn toward him, he dropped his voice to a murmur. "Don't cry."

"I'm not crying."

"No? Just allergies, then," he said, a tiny curl to his lips as he swiped his thumb under my eye. He fit his hat on my head, threading my ponytail through the back, and tugged the bill down on my forehead. "It'll help with the sun."

"What are you going to use?"

"I have an extra." Then he winked as he walked backward toward his spot. "If there's one thing you should know about me, it's that I never lose."

Which was, apparently, true.

I never got any better, but Aggie and Lou helped me out any time a ball came within a few yards of me, and our team ended up to be full of pretty good hitters. Except for me, obviously.

We beat Eric's team by one and celebrated with a team cheer, all of us putting our hands in the middle. I had never played sports in school and didn't understand the desire until now.

It was nice to be part of something. Part of a team.

And no one was angry with me for being so bad. It really was all for fun.

"Let's get together for a picture," Aggie said, handing off her phone to Meredith, as my gaze snagged on Eric, his brows narrowed in my direction.

When Jimmy noticed, he deliberately threw his arm around me. "Get on in here, slugger."

I gratefully moved closer to my protector, ignoring the glare coming from my left side.

"You did great today," Jimmy said.

"You don't have to patronize me."

"I'm not." He tugged on my ponytail. "You had fun, didn't

you?"

Surprisingly, I had, and I nodded.

"Good. That's all that matters."

"That so, Mr. I-Don't-Lose?"

He dragged me into him, my shoulder right against his ribs, forcing my arm around his waist. He smelled of pine deodorant, fresh air, and a little tang of sweat. "I do love to win. Especially when I'm playing against dickheads like him."

"Thank you," I said quietly, and he dipped his chin down to me. I was a few inches shorter than him, but I'd never quite noticed how much of a difference there was until this moment. When I was pressed along his side, his twinkling brown eyes staring down at me.

"Truly. It was my pleasure."

I laughed.

Jimmy's grin spread wide. "Did you just snort?"

"No."

"You did. You snorted."

"I did no such thing."

He tightened his arm around my neck, jostling me. "I love it. You should laugh more often."

"All right, everybody!" Hassan clapped a few times as Aggie accepted her phone back from Meredith. "Let's go grab a beer."

Cheers went up, and when Jimmy tilted his head in silent question at me. I smiled. "Yeah. I'll come."

"Wait for me!" Meredith hollered as she packed up her chair and Yeti. "I'd love a cold one!"

Meredith hated "cold ones."

But I gave in to the warmth spreading through my belly and tipped my head back to the clear sky, inhaling deeply. In the matter of one afternoon, I'd gone from grumpy and boring to showing up my terrible ex and being part of a team.

It felt damn good.

CHAPTER FOUR

Jimmy

I was making copies of math worksheets when Mrs. Monahan-Healy walked into the workroom.

"Hey, Jimmy. How're you doing?"

"Fine. How are you?"

She cocked her head at me, her ever-present cardigan slipping off her shoulder. "Fine? What's wrong?"

I huffed out a laugh. Mrs. Monahan-Healy was Sam's mom and a kindergarten teacher. I'd known Carol as long as I'd known Sam, so there was no fooling her. Removing my papers from the copier, I slid them into a manila folder. "I've got a lot on my mind."

She took her place in front of the copier, pressing a few buttons before facing me. "Lay it on me. What's up?"

Sam and Carol were a lot alike. Both problem-solvers. Both kind people.

"My landlord decided to sell the house. I've been there for over a year."

Carol frowned. "What are you going to do?"

"I asked her if she would sell it to me, and she said yes, but I don't have the money for a down payment. I can't get a loan without it."

"Hmm. That's a tough one. I'm sorry." She squeezed my arm. "I'll think on it, see if I can come up with any solutions."

I nodded, though I didn't feel real confident that she could come up with anything I hadn't already considered. It had been a week since Lucy gave me the news, and each morning I woke up in my bed was one day closer to the day I'd have to move if I couldn't get some money quick.

I offered Carol a sad smile before making my way out of the workroom and back down the hall to my classroom. I paused at the door of the library, where Claire was in the middle of some lesson about using an index. People often thought all librarians did was harass kids to be quiet and take care of books, but they did so much more. Especially Miss Hart.

She was responsible for teaching our students how to use media and technology, which was often challenging when this generation of kids was growing up with the entire world at their fingertips. They came into elementary school already knowing more about tech than those before them but were emotionally illiterate when it came to how to properly use it. And Claire had to balance all of it.

Not to mention, organizing the library and generally being the jack-of-all trades when it came to school activities. It also accounted for why she had four thousand keys on her lanyard because she had so many special jobs and permissions and doors to be able to open.

I caught her attention with a wave, and she tossed me a quick tip of her chin before going back to the kids in front of her. I stayed rooted in place for another minute, watching as she spoke with fluttering hands, her fingernails short and petal pink, her hair down, as usual, with her headband matching her dark-purple shirt. Her skin was pale and covered—I mean *covered*—in freckles. One day, I'd overheard her complaining to Meredith about them, but I thought they gave her character.

Not many people could pull them off, but she could. Her freckles and her headbands and her cute little skirts, they never failed to make me smile.

And her ex was a real asshole. I hoped wherever he was, he was contracting gangrene.

I didn't consider myself a violent person, but I wouldn't mind if someone else, say a biker with an anger problem, crossed paths with him and taught him what it meant to be humiliated.

I wasn't great at romantic relationships with women and would never think I had even one clue about the fairer sex to give advice, but I knew enough not to insult them.

Some people were just miserable assholes and wanted everyone else around them to be miserable too.

But Claire didn't deserve that.

Inside my classroom, I placed a worksheet on each of the kids' desks and then dropped down into my chair, turning on some white noise. It helped me to concentrate. I loved music and played it a lot during school hours, but when I needed to get work done, I couldn't listen to anything with lyrics. That screwed me all up, my brain spinning off in a bunch of different directions. But the low-frequency white noise, that was like someone giving my brain a massage, relaxing each part of me so I could focus on what was in front of me. I worked for the next twenty minutes until my alarm went off, signaling me to get my class from gym.

I waited outside the auditorium, fist-bumping each of them as they crossed the threshold then led them back to our room. I explained we were going to start our math lesson and complete the worksheet on their desks. "But first," I said, "it's dance break time."

I cued up "Summer Girls" by LFO, and we all danced like nutballs, shouting the ridiculous lyrics to one of my favorite songs. The students always seemed to have a lot of restless energy after specials, even after skipping around the gym, and a song break helped to ease them back into learning. I was only good to work for about twenty or thirty minutes at a time—unless I was hyperfocused on a task at home—so teaching elementary school really suited me.

The kids got me.

And I got them.

We hammered out math with the worksheet and then practiced understanding graphs using their iPads before we had a quick recap of today's word of the day. "All right, who can come up with a sentence for 'deter'? Remember, it means trying to make someone not do something."

Deter was not a second-grade word, but I liked to use "adult" words. They didn't have to know how to spell these words or even remember them, but it was a good brain challenge.

Elliot shot his arm up.

"All right, go for it," I said, pointing at him.

"Miss Hart deter you for playing music," he said with a grin, his sentence structure needing work, but he comprehended the meaning all the same, and the class broke up into giggles.

I grinned. "Miss Hart does deter me from playing music."

"Yeah, she always rolls her eyes at you," Shandi called out, and I headed to the door of the classroom.

"Miss Hart does always roll her eyes at me. You're right."

The library door was open, and I knew my words would reach her. A moment later, her red hair popped around the doorframe, her brows narrowed, her lips pursed in a playful angry pout. "Could you at least pick something better than LFO?"

"What would you prefer?" I asked, leaning against the

doorframe as I waved my kids to get in line. "You're probably a Swiftie, huh?"

She arched one eyebrow then ducked away again.

"Bet she would like the new Taylor Swift song you played the other day," Anya said quietly, from her position at the head of the line.

"You're right. Miss Hart is definitely in her cottagecore era."

"What's cottagecore?" Zeke asked.

"It's an aesthetic, which means a lot of things that are similar in feelings. Cottagecore are all things that..." I lifted my gaze up to the ceiling, thinking. "Things that make you feel... maybe warm and cozy, a fuzzy blanket while it snows or pretty pink roses in the summer or fresh bread and hot chocolate."

"I love hot chocolate," Colton said, and I agreed.

"Me too."

"What's your asstick?" Braxton asked.

"Aesthetic," I corrected with a chuckle. "Mine is whatever is clean or smells clean."

The kids all tittered with laughter, and I held up my hand for one of our callbacks. "Oops."

"I did it again!" my class answered.

"Everybody have what they need for lunch? Glen, I see you sneaking your Pokémon cards into your pocket. Don't make me be a snitch to your mom." I tipped my chin to his desk, silently instructing him to put them back in his desk where they belonged, because if I had another email from his mother about him losing those godforsaken cards, I'd burn them.

With my class lined up, we headed to the lunchroom, where I dropped them off then made my way to the teacher's lounge. I unpacked my turkey sandwich and stretched out my legs, scrolling through my family text thread, all messages about Mike and Sam's cat, Tangerine, needing surgery. I bobbed my head along to the radio playing softly in the corner of the room as I typed out a get-well text for their cat, but I stopped midsentence as the radio DJ announced something about a contest.

Jumping up from my seat, I held my half-eaten sandwich in one hand while I turned the volume up with the other.

"Ten thousand dollars to the winners, sponsored by Buckeye Home Décor, your locally owned and operated home goods store, for all your furnishing needs. Head to our website for contest rules, and stay right here for all of today's hits. You're listening to 99.1 KISS-FM. Back in two."

"What?" I asked the radio, straight out of the last century, hitting it like I could rewind. "Ten thousand dollars. Did anybody hear that?"

The other teachers in the room all shook their heads at me, and I shoved my sandwich into my mouth with a growl. Ten grand? That was enough for a down payment with a first-time homebuyer loan.

This could be my Hail Mary pass.

I hustled back down to my room and shook my computer awake, typing in the website for the radio station, too nervous to sit down. When the page finally populated, a big contest graphic appeared. **Do you want to win ten grand?**

Yes. Yes, I do.

I immediately clicked on the link and started typing my name, address, and phone number before finally reading the rules and regulations.

This contest was in honor of the radio station's tenth anniversary, and they wanted to give away ten thousand dollars to one lucky couple.

Lucky couple.

Couple.

Which I was not.

I slumped down into my chair, arms folded across my chest, as I lolled my head back against the rest.

My miracle solution was now back to selling pictures of my feet.

"Great," I muttered to my empty room.

I didn't know how long it was until my cell phone buzzed with an alert on our softball group chat. Aggie texted the pictures we'd taken last weekend with an apology for taking so long to send them out.

In the middle of my pity party for one, I didn't care and tossed my phone down to my desk, only to pick it up a moment later, thumbing through the photos, all of us in various stages of smiling or squinting.

I was about to close out the screen when the last picture caught my eye. I was on the end with Claire, my arm slung around her shoulders, her long red hair trailing out of the back of my baseball cap. We were looking at each other, smiling, obviously in the middle of a joke or something.

Sure, I'd always thought Claire was cute. Like freckle-faced bunnies were cute. Little animals you wanted to give a scratch on the back of the neck. It was part of the reason why I enjoyed annoying her so much, to see the flush in her cheeks as she heaved out a sigh in my direction. Adorable.

But this photo highlighted the curve of her generous hips with her hand on her waist, her foot popped up on the opposite ankle. I'd never noticed her body before. I mean, I had in a way all heterosexual men interested in sex noticed woman. But she so rarely wore pants, especially those skintight ones that left nothing to the imagination. In this photo, they were bright blue, in opposition to her bright-orange hair.

God, I really hated her ex.

There was nothing boring about her.

How could he not see that?

Without thinking, I downloaded the picture and cropped it so only she and I were in it then I uploaded it to my computer to complete the contest form.

No, I wasn't a couple. But I could be.

With one sure double-click, I was officially entered into the competition.

If only Claire would agree.

But that was ADHD for you. Impulsiveness for the literal win.

CHAPTER FIVE

Claire

I was in early to get some organizing done when Jimmy sauntered into the library, two drinks—or more accurately, ice cream sundaes—in his hands.

"Morning," he said, sliding one of the concoctions to me. "I didn't know what you liked in your coffee, so I got you one of mine. Chocolate chip Frappuccino."

"Because?"

He shrugged, and I eyed him. Not that it was unusual for him to be nice just to be nice, but he'd never once brought me something to eat or drink before. "Is there any coffee in here? Or is it all chocolate?"

He tipped his head, his lips curving up into a grin even as he stuck the straw between his lips, sucking it down. "It's delicious."

"It's dessert."

"If you say so. Try it."

I gave him a dubious look but took a sip of the iced "coffee" anyway. It was delicious. But I couldn't taste any coffee. Like, at all. "Thanks for the diabetic coma."

He saluted me with his drink then leaned his elbows on the counter as I added another book to the pile to be trashed. Some of these books were falling apart, unable for me or Mrs. Franklin, the library volunteer and unofficial book rebinder, to save them.

"What are you doing?" he asked.

"Getting a head start on summer cleaning."

He hummed around his straw, watching me for a quiet minute. Which was completely out of the ordinary.

I quirked an eyebrow in his direction. "Are you okay?"

He wagged his head back and forth, his mop of dark curls flopping side to side. "I could be. But I need your help."

"My help?" When he nodded seriously, I took my hand off the computer mouse and focused solely on him. "What can I do?"

He let a smile loose. "Before I start, I just want to say I really appreciate you hearing me out. You're going to think this is nuts, but let me get it all out before you tell me no, okay?"

"Uh... Okay."

"All right." He clapped his hands and rubbed them together. "You know how I told you I was trying to figure out a way to get money to buy my house? Well, I found a way. It's a radio competition, have you heard of it? It's 99.1. They're giving away ten thousand dollars. So, I entered."

He spoke so fast and barely paused for me to interject. "That's great."

"But that's where you come in. See, they're giving away the money because it's their tenth anniversary, and they want to give the prize to a couple. I'm obviously not part of a couple, but I entered anyway. No, don't look at me like that, Claire. I'm not even done explaining yet."

"Well, what are you going to do? You entered a contest for couples and—"

"I told them I was in a relationship with you."

I reared back. A record might have even scratched. "You *what?*"

"I didn't know what else to do. I really need that money."

The audacity of this man. "Anything else." I slapped my hand on the counter. "You could have done literally anything else. Sold a kidney on the black market. Got a second job as a rideshare driver."

He looked at me as if I had sprouted another head. "Number one, Mariah is very sensitive, and I couldn't let strangers have a ride in her. And secondly, I'm afraid of needles. I can't go under the knife."

I shook my head, my jaw flapping like a fish, at a complete loss for what to say to the absurd man standing in front of me.

"I read about the contest and then saw the softball picture and—"

"Softball picture? What does that have to do with anything?"

He lifted his hand like it should have been clear. "We were standing next to each other. It was a cute picture. The only one of me and you, so I sent it in when I entered. And they loved our story. We made it past the first round. All we have to do is—"

"Our story?" I huffed. "What are you— This is— I can't even—" I tugged at my blouse, sweating, as I started to pace. "We don't have a *story.*"

"Yeah, we do. I told them all about how we met here at school, and that we had a slow little progression."

"Oh my god." I faced him. "What is wrong with you?"

"Nothing," he said as if making up a fake relationship was an everyday occurrence for him. "They loved it. We made it past the first cut."

I clasped my hands around my head, shock and anger warring for the top emotional spot. Sure, I'd known Jimmy was a little...whimsical, but this was a straight-up fairy tale. "I can't believe you did this."

"All we have to do is go in for an interview live on air, and then—"

"Absolutely not. No."

"The finalists will all be listed on their website, and—"

"How could you do this without asking me?"

"Listeners will vote for their favorite couple, and I know we can win."

"Jimmy!" My shout stilled him, his hands frozen in midair, mid-explanation. "No. No. Not only are you distinctly breaking the rules of the contest—"

"I'm not breaking the rules," he said, deliberately misinterpreting me.

"This is for couples, and *we* are not a couple." I flicked two fingers between us. "Besides, no one would ever believe we'd date."

He wrenched back. "I know I can be...loud and whatever, but, I mean, that's—"

I cut him off with a sigh and sagged down to the chair. He had to be misinterpreting me again. Then again, he truly seemed miffed that I'd suggest I wouldn't like him. "This isn't about you. Well, it is, but not in the way that you think. You're fine. You're more than fine. Everyone loves you."

He inclined his head in that puppy-dog way of his. "Then why do you think people would never believe we'd date?"

I crossed my arms and legs, focusing my attention out to the corner of the library. It was too early in the morning to dissect the *why*, and I especially wasn't doing it with him.

"Hey, come on, talk to me," he said, quietly making his way around the worn wooden counter to forcibly spin my rolling chair so I had to meet his gaze. "Did I tell you I really like that headband?"

"Don't."

He offered me a small smile, one that felt more genuine than the megawatt one he wore most of the day. "I used to play a game with my grandad when we were at their house at night. We'd bet a nickel on what color Vanna White's dress would be on *Wheel of Fortune*, and every morning, I play the same game with myself, but about your headbands."

He admitted that so honestly, without any prompting, my stomach swooped. "You just say anything that's on your mind, don't you?"

"Yeah. So tell me what's on yours."

"Besides that you did this without asking me? And entering this contest as a fake couple is totally unethical?"

He moved his foot outside of mine and nodded. "Well, yeah, besides that."

I pinned him with an annoyed glare. He was really going to make me say it out loud.

"What?" he prodded, knocking his knee into mine, and I didn't know when he'd gotten so close, but I couldn't stand to look at him while I admitted it.

I dropped my gaze to my lap. "You're...you, and I...was dumped because I'm boring and the human equivalent of a rain cloud."

Jimmy leaned forward, his hands clasped between his knees, his head and shoulders creating a shadow over where I picked at my nails. "He's a dicknozzle." When I lifted my eyes to his, he grinned. "If you don't mind my saying."

I bit back a laugh and shook my head.

"And you're right, I should have asked you first. There is no excuse. I'm desperate for money and made a decision in the moment, hoping it would turn out all right. I didn't tell you last week because I didn't know if we'd make the first cut."

"That sounds suspiciously like you weren't confident you'd win, Mr. I-Don't-Lose."

"Look at you, little sassy pants. I just found out last night that we made it through."

We. The thought was laughable. We weren't a *we.*

"It's better to ask forgiveness than permission, right?" he said with an irritatingly cute smile, like a dog with its head out of the window.

I huffed.

"So, what do you say?"

"No."

"Come on." He folded his hand over mine, his thumb sweeping across my knuckles as his eyes roamed over me, more serious than I'd ever seen him. "Didn't you ever want something so bad, you'd do anything for it?"

My lips parted on a breath, and I blinked a few times, needing to clear my head. Between his stare and his soft voice, it was almost as if he was talking about me. I knew he wasn't, but it was easy to fall under his spell. And this was just another example of why he always got his way, why everyone loved him so much, because he was charming and had a good smile.

"Why do you want this house so bad?" I asked, backing away from him, needing more air and some understanding. Not that I was actually considering following through with this nonsense. I was only curious. "There are lots of other houses or apartments."

He hit me with a skeptical eyebrow. "In this market?" Then he dropped his chin toward his chest. "What did you mean before when you said people wouldn't believe we'd ever be together?"

I thought it rather obvious and rolled my eyes. "We're so different. You're all sunshiny, and I'm not."

"Sunshiny," he repeated sarcastically. With a slight shake

of his head, he rubbed his index finger over his upper lip, still not meeting my gaze. "That's it? That's the only reason?"

"And everyone knows you don't do relationships. You don't exactly hide it."

His knee bounced a few times. "I don't. Because I'm immature and never take anything seriously. At least, that's what Larisa told me. She was the one I was with from Christmas to Valentine's."

"Wait." I sat up in my chair. "*She* broke up with you?" I'd assumed it was the other way around.

He narrowed his gaze on me, all his good humor gone. "Yeah, though if she hadn't, I would've. Because that's what happens. I break up with girls before they can find out how immature and impulsive I am."

"You're not immature," I told him, but I didn't know for sure. "At least, I don't think you are."

He lifted a resigned shoulder. "That's why I want to buy this house. Because my whole life, I've been the idiot little brother in my family. I'm the guy girls call for a good time, but never when they want something real. I want to prove I'm not a joke, you know?"

I didn't know what to say. This visibly weighed on him, yet I barely knew him outside of school. Here, he was confident and quite the opposite of a joke. "But you're Teacher of the Year."

He broke out in a humorless chuckle. "Not yet."

"I don't understand." And this time, I was the one to hold his hand. "Why wouldn't people take you seriously?"

"I don't know if you know this," he hedged, "but I'm a lot to handle."

I blew out a breath and released my grasp of his hand. Full of drama, this one. "Yeah, I got that."

"I have ADHD, and when I was a kid, I was all over the

place. I couldn't ever sit down, made a mess of everything, constantly getting in trouble."

"I can't imagine," I deadpanned, and he flicked my knee. But he kept his hand close to me. If he or I moved one centimeter, he could've easily curved his palm around my leg. Not that he'd want to. Or I would want him to, for that matter.

He went on, despite how my mind wandered into dangerous territory. "I got used to being the class clown, and the older I got, the harder it was to break out of that role. Granted, I don't have a real long attention span for anything, including relationships, but I always break it off before they can see how little I have to offer them besides some fun." He met my gaze, unblinking as he said, "I'm going to be thirty. I want something to show for myself. I want this Teacher of the Year award, and I want this house."

Even though I absolutely was *not* going to take any part in his fake-dating scheme, this conversation was the realest one I'd ever had with him.

"So, what is it that you want?" he rasped as if his confession had taken everything out of him. "What is the thing you'd do anything to get?"

My mind blanked. I didn't have anything I really wanted, nothing I would do anything to get. And I didn't know if that was a good or bad thing. If that made me appreciative of my life or boring, like Eric accused me of being.

"I don't know," I said.

"You don't need money?"

I shook my head. I wasn't making bank working in a public elementary school, but I had a little in savings for an emergency. I was able to pay my bills on time and still support my hair-accessory habit.

"Career advancement?"

I shrugged. There weren't many more steps I could take as a librarian, but I loved my job. I was happy here.

"How about a car or a pet or a...boat?"

I refused to laugh. "A boat?"

"You seem like a girl who'd enjoy a boat ride with the wind in your hair."

"You going to get me a boat?"

He leaned back, crossing his arms over his chest, like he'd won. "If you do this with me, you can, maybe, get yourself a little boat. I won't take all the money. I'll split the winnings with you."

"Half?" I asked, playing devil's advocate.

He threw back his head and barked out one low, "Ha!" Then he smiled at me. "A quarter."

"A quarter? Not for faking it with you. I deserve half, minimum." This was all purely conjecture, of course.

"I'm not giving you more than half. This was my idea. I should get the majority of the winnings."

"That's if we win," I corrected.

He leaped up. "So, you're in?"

I shook my head. "No. This is all hypothetical. A thought experiment."

He dropped his head back, exhaling audibly before bending, a challenge in his eyes. "What if I told you your douchey ex-boyfriend was in this competition too?"

I felt my eyes bug out of my head. "He is?"

"No. It was another thought experiment to get your attention. Would you say yes if we were competing against dicknozzle?"

I glanced over to the clock on the wall. It was close to the time the buses would start arriving. "You better go."

"You're not answering because it's yes, isn't it? I see a fiery spirit in you. I'm not the only one who likes to win." He stood up. "So, we're doing this?"

"No."

"What can I say to make you change your mind? You want me to beg?" He dropped down to his knees right in front of me, my skirt swaying at his movement, his head near my hips. If anyone walked in here, they'd think something obscene was going on. "I'll beg, Miss Hart." He folded his hands together, and for one brief moment, my mind took a running leap toward his begging for something very different, and I had to forcibly shake my head to get rid of the image. Before he could utter any other syllable, I curled my hands around his elbows and lugged him up.

"Will you get off the floor? If someone comes in here, they're going to get the wrong idea."

"What idea would—" His face nearly split in half. "You naughty librarian, you." And in the space of one breath, his eyes darkened, his smile dropped, his gaze openly raked down the length of me, stalling around my waist. When he met my gaze again, it was like he was seeing me for the first time, and I felt my face flame. Even my ears when he teased, "I'm into it, though."

"Oh my god." I pushed him around the circulation desk and toward the door. "Go. You need to get out of here."

Before I could get rid of him, he clasped my wrist, towing me close to him, and I could smell his sugar with a side of coffee on his breath. It was messing with my head. "Please, think about it. Do me this solid, and I'll give you whatever you want. I'll even go fifty-fifty on the money."

I ignored how my skin tightened at the words *I'll give you whatever you want* and nudged him out of the library. He tossed me one last hopeful lilt then he unlocked his classroom door, ducking inside with a slap to the sign hanging on the cement wall, and I pivoted around, shaking off the feeling of his fingers around my wrist.

Working through the first half of the day, I tried to pretend my conversation with Jimmy hadn't happened, but his question kept circling through my mind. Would I have agreed to this no good, very bad plot if Eric were in the contest?

Jimmy was right that I would have, although not for the reason he assumed. I would do it to show my dicknozzle ex-boyfriend that I had moved on. To show the world I'd found someone who didn't think I was grumpy or boring. Or, better yet, they *did* think I was those things and didn't care. Because those twenty minutes with Jimmy this morning were honest and sincere. I'd learned more about him today than I had in the past four years I'd worked with him. And I was damn near close to telling him the truth.

That the one thing I wanted in life, what I would give anything for, couldn't be bought or won.

It was to find someone to love and who would love me for who I was. Someone to have my back and support me. Someone who wanted to get married and have kids and could be content with the little corner of the world we took up.

But Jimmy couldn't find me that person. Even if I agreed to help him, there was no IOU he could offer me.

At lunch, I filled Meredith in on everything, itching to get this outrageous idea off my chest and have her agree with me that it was pure nonsense.

Yet she didn't. She laughed, her fingers digging into a little bag of potato chips. "That's amazing."

"Amazing?" I squeaked.

"Yeah. He told you he'd give you half the money if you won. That's a pretty good chunk of change. Think of the shopping spree you could go on." She held up a chip. "Never mind, you and your responsibility will probably use it to pay off school loans or something."

She wasn't wrong. I wasn't able to apply for student loan forgiveness until after this school year, and the interest on my loans was killing me.

"So, do it. What's there to lose?"

I coasted my attention around my office, like I'd fallen down the rabbit hole and was at the Mad Hatter's tea party. Nothing made sense. "Mer, he wants me to fake a relationship with him. I can't do that."

"You mean ethically, intellectually, emotionally, physically...?"

I drew a checkmark in the air. "All of the above."

"It's only for a couple weeks. If you win, you get money, and if you lose, you spent some time with a fun guy. It's not like you're marrying him. You're doing a radio interview." She shrugged as if it was no big deal.

"And I would have to tell my family, and everyone here would know. It's not *only* a radio interview."

She considered that while chomping on a few chips. "So, you've got to sell it a little bit."

I dropped my head into my hand. "When did fake dating become a thing to do?"

"Um, since *How to Lose a Guy in 10 Days*, since *Pretty Woman*, since that one with Patrick Dempsey where he rides the lawn mower."

"*Can't Buy Me Love*."

She pointed a chip at me. "Yeah. That one. Besides, you're the one who loves romance novels. You know all about the fake-dating trope."

I stole her chip. "Those are books and movies, and it's the worst trope. So unrealistic."

Meredith waved her hand around, as if to demonstrate I was living the beginning of a terrible rom-com.

I wasn't.

This was no rom-com.

"Well, I'll totally do it if you don't," she said, and I jerked back.

"What?" I narrowed my eyes. "No."

My best friend's thin eyebrows arched like she'd caught me. "That reaction was interesting."

"That wasn't a reaction. It was me saying this idea is stupid, and you shouldn't do it either. Because it's so stupid."

"Uh-huh."

Avoiding her knowing gaze, I stared at my salad. It was the best thing I'd ever eaten.

"Could it be—now, this is all speculation—but could it be that you don't want to do this because you actually do?"

I shook my head, unable to answer with the small garden I'd forked into my mouth.

"I know you've always harbored a crush on him."

I widened my eyes, wildly waving my fork in the air.

"I think you're afraid if you do this with him, you'll actually admit you kinda like him."

"No, no, no, no, no," I mumbled around the lettuce.

"The lady doth protest too much."

I finally swallowed down my food and cleared my throat. "You have it totally wrong."

"Then tell me why you don't want to do it. It's just for fun."

"Because it's wrong. Some other people who are an actual couple should win. We would be defrauding them."

"This isn't some huge conspiracy. It's a game. And who's to say no one else is faking it? Or," she said, lifting her finger in the air like she was proving a point to a jury, "that no other couple will break up after they win? It's all a gimmick for the dying institution of a radio station to gain more listeners. It's not serious."

I lifted my arms in the air, needing to expand my ribs, anxiety building in my chest. "But *I'm* serious."

Meredith nodded, crumpling her potato chip bag in her hand. "Yeah, and you would take this contest very seriously, I know. Which is why you don't want to do it. Because you'd take it seriously, and he's only in it for the money."

I didn't have to verbalize it. She knew she was right, and I stood up, throwing my trash away, needing something to do with my hands, my brain. Something that wasn't thinking about how I wanted to give in to this terribly bad idea.

I was serious.

I was grumpy.

I was boring.

And I was okay with that. I liked who I was.

But.

It did feel nice to be *chosen* for once. I'd never been picked for teams in grade school gym class, I was never voted for anything in high school, didn't stand out in college, and I certainly blended into the background with my family. Yet, Jimmy chose me. He could have asked—or forced, depending on how you looked at it—anyone else, but he asked me. Serious, grumpy, boring old me.

Meredith stood up too, brushing off her hands, readying herself to leave.

"You don't think it's ridiculous?" I asked.

She snorted a laugh. "Oh, hell yeah, it is. But sometimes ridiculous can be really fun."

After she left, I stared at the wall, considering my best friend's parting words, and before I really knew what I was doing, I pulled out my cell phone and texted Jimmy.

I'm in.

Not even a minute later, Cher's "Believe" blared from across the hall. I imagined him fist-pumping to the techno beat.

JIMMY

Let's go get that money, baby.

CHAPTER SIX

Jimmy

Claire and I agreed to meet for dinner to hash out the details of our plan. To be honest, I had been 97% sure she wasn't going to go for it. She was smart. So smart, she certainly wouldn't say yes to my dumbass idea, but she did.

A miracle!

So, here I was, waiting for my "girlfriend" for half-price apps at Applebee's.

I played with the plastic menu, flipping it back and forth, then rearranged the condiments at the corner of the table before going back to the menu, flicking at the corner of it. I was probably going to order the boneless chicken wings, as per uzhe. I lifted the laminated drink card, checking out the specials, when Claire dropped down opposite me in the booth.

"Hey."

"Hi," I said, leaning my elbows on the table, unconsciously drawing closer to her.

She set her purse down in the corner and removed her jacket, revealing her short-sleeved sweater with pearl buttons that was both somehow 1950's housewife modest and unsuspectingly sexy with how it clung to her chest. Not to mention her flouncy skirt. "There's my little pop tart."

She froze mid-reach to the table. "Your little pop tart?"

I lifted a careless shoulder. "How was your day?"

"Well, seeing as how your playlist consisted mostly of Taylor Swift, it was pretty enjoyable."

"Good." I watched as she adjusted her headband and wound all her hair into a twist then dropped it over her shoulder. "You look really pretty today."

Her eyes met mine, wide and maybe a little offended. It was hard to tell with how her brows were narrowed in question.

"You look pretty every day. I didn't mean to insinuate—"

She held up her hand, stopping my rambling. I wouldn't ever describe myself as suave with women, but I did have a certain charm, frenetic as it was. I was always good to make them laugh, and if you could make them laugh, you basically made it to the promised land. But for some reason, I couldn't access that normally easy part of myself today.

"Thank you," she said after an eternity, saving me from myself as I started to spiral out about how my usual jokes wouldn't work. "But you don't have to do that."

"Do what?"

She flicked her hand by her head like she was overwhelmed. "Say things like that. This is...a business deal."

Well, fuck.

I didn't even know where to start with that.

"First of all, you're my friend, and, yeah, you're doing me a favor, but this isn't a business deal. Second of all—"

"Secondly," she corrected.

"I don't say things because I have to. I have no filter. You should know this." When she gave in with an inclination of her head, I went on. "So when I tell you you look pretty, it's because you do. Not because you're doing me a favor. Okay?"

She blinked a few times before finally nodding, her cheeks reddening slightly. "Okay."

"Good." I folded my arms on top of each other on the table as a waiter appeared next to us for our order. I told Claire to go first. She pointed to some kind of pink drink, but I stuck with water. When she raised her eyebrow in question, I explained, "I don't drink on school nights. But, please, go ahead."

"Would you like to put in any food right now?" the waiter asked, and I gestured to Claire.

"Um." Her tongue poked out, skimming over her bottom lip. "Do you want to share something?"

I blinked up to her eyes. She was waiting on me. "Yeah, sure."

I was about to offer up the suggestion of the boneless chicken wings, but she dragged her finger over the menu. "I'm not big on spicy stuff. How about spinach dip?"

"Oh yeah, sure. Whatever you want."

She turned, relaying our order of spinach dip—which, *gross* —to the waiter, before facing me once again. "So, can we wait until I have some alcohol in me to get to the specifics?"

"You that afraid?" I teased.

"Aren't you?"

I hated to sound flippant, but when you were used to jumping off a cliff without looking, there was no time to be afraid. Besides, I'd made worse decisions in my lifetime than asking Claire to partake in a fake relationship with me. In fact, this was one of my better ideas.

"Not at all," I said, earning a sigh.

"Aren't you worried about what our coworkers will think?"

I waved off the idea. "You know schools are like *Grey's Anatomy*, except with textbooks instead of surgery." That earned a tiny quirk of her lips, and my attention caught on the two freckles on her lower lip. "I thought you wanted to wait until your drink arrived to start planning."

"You're right. Let's talk about something else for a while. I guess we should...get to know each other, huh?"

"Yeah. Tell me about your dicknozzle ex-boyfriend."

"Whoa. Jumping right into the deep end, huh?" She sputtered a laugh, and I loved that I was the reason. She didn't do it often enough.

"If we were dating for real, these are the things we'd talk about."

Her eyes coasted around the restaurant as if searching for a rescue. It appeared thirty seconds later when the waiter arrived with my water and her pink drink. She downed about half of it. I was impressed.

"So, how long were you with di—"

"Eric, his name's Eric."

"But I like dicknozzle so much better."

She snorted, her lips wrapped around the straw of her drink.

"How long did you go out with him?" I asked.

"Um, about a year."

I huffed. "But he called you—"

She slapped her hands to her ears. "I know. I know. We don't need a recap, I was there."

"Why did you stay with him so long?"

She lifted one shoulder, burying her hands somewhere under the table, and I resisted the urge to find them, weave my fingers with hers. "He wasn't always like that. At first, we had a lot in common. We both have big families and—"

"Oh yeah? How big's your family?"

"I'm one of seven."

"Seven," I repeated in an awed whisper. "I thought being one of three boys was a lot."

She clucked her tongue. "My parents are a couple of hippie farmers, and they say they always wanted lots of kids, but I think it's really they needed bodies to work the farm." She started counting on her fingers. "Evan's the oldest and has a big hand in running the farm. Then there's—"

"What kind of farm?" I interrupted.

"Ever heard of Hart Family Farm?"

It rang a bell. "The place that grew the biggest pumpkin in the state a few years back?"

"One and the same."

"Oh, no shit," I said with a laugh. "Your parents own a pumpkin farm?"

"We grow other fruit too. It's a pick-your-own fruit farm, so we have strawberries, peaches, and cherries in the summer, apples and pumpkins in the fall."

"And you have a corn maze and stuff, right?"

She nodded, and I smiled, kind of excited. I'd chosen an excellent fake girlfriend.

"I'd love to go there. I've never been, but I see ads for it all the time. I never put two and two together with your last name."

She played with her napkin. "I'm one of the least interested in the farm. I always hated working as a kid. Evan's going to take it over once my parents retire."

"Right, sorry. I got off on a tangent." I gestured for her to continue. "You were telling me about your siblings. Evan's the oldest, and he'll take over. Then who?"

"Then Rosie. She's another one who never liked the farm, but mostly because she had to work the register all the time. She's got spina bifida and walks with crutches. She was married last summer and is living up toward Cleveland."

"What's that face for?" I asked when her brows crimped.

"She's kind of a humblebrag."

I covered my smile with my hand, really enjoying how animated she'd become since she started telling me about her family. I didn't know if she'd ever talked so much for so long with me, although that might've been more of an observation about my shit listening skills than her personality.

"She's really beautiful and is good at makeup and all that kind of stuff, and she'll be like, oh, I posted about my new book —she's a children's author, by the way—but all anyone wanted to comment about were my eyelashes." Claire rolled her eyes. "We get it. You're the prettiest in the family. She writes books about kids with disabilities, and I actually have a few in the library, but she started building her social media following from posting makeup videos. Then she parlayed that into becoming an author."

"That sounds like my brother," I said, when she paused to sip her drink. "He was injured while he was serving in the Marines and has a prosthesis. Now, he's an online personal trainer and sells protein shakes or some weird shit like that."

Her pink lips thinned into a line, noticeably trying not to laugh.

"What?" I asked her, not able to stop my own grin from crawling across my face.

"Weird shit like that." She giggled, and I snagged her drink, taking a whiff of it.

"What's in here? Loosened you up quick."

"I'm a cheap drunk. I don't drink very often." Then she stole it back from me and polished it off, the ice cubes rattling. "Liquid courage."

"And now how about some water?" I pushed my glass across the table to her, and she sipped from the same straw I was using. Like a real girlfriend would do. "So, there's Evan and Rosie. Who's next in line?"

"Julie. She lives in Texas and works for a local news station down there. Then me, stuck in the middle."

"Eye of the storm?"

She nodded. "Oh yeah. Especially with my younger brothers. Aiden's twenty-six and a CPA. Then came the twins, Ryan and Tristan. They were a surprise. They graduated college last year. Tristan's in grad school for creative writing, but Ryan plays for the Cleveland Rocks."

"No way. They're hilarious. I follow them on Instagram."

The Cleveland Rocks were an exhibition baseball team that were basically the equivalent of the Harlem Globetrotters. The Rocks were huge on social media for their midgame dances and antics.

"You go to a lot of their games?" I asked, and she shook her head.

"Not much interest."

"I thought my family was a lot, but you guys..." I blew out a rough breath.

"We were like a pack of wolves. Everyone was fighting for attention and running wild on the farm. I ran away a lot." She circled the straw in my water with a dainty hand, and I imagined her working on her big family farm and hating it. Pictured all those kids together, all so different, with Claire in the literal middle of it all, trying to find some peace and quiet.

"Yeah? Where'd you run to?"

"The library. It was always so loud at our house, especially once the twins came along. We had lots of pets too. Dogs, cats, a pig, even. It was too much for me, so I'd ride my bike down to the library. It was a couple miles away, but I'd go for hours. I made friends with all the librarians, and they didn't make me stick to the kids' section."

The thought of little Claire Hart in some frilly dress and

orange pigtails, riding her bike to get another stack of books, had me smiling. I was about to ask her what her favorite books were, but the waiter set our plate of wilted greens and cheese on the table. Not that I didn't like cheese, but the texture of the spinach gave me the heebie-jeebies. She pushed it over, in the exact middle between us, and offered the first bite to me. I took her up on it, dragging a chip through the weird-looking mixture, and popped it into my mouth. She followed, humming in appreciation.

I guess it wasn't *so* bad.

"What about you and your family? You said you're one of three boys?" she asked, stealing my focus from her mouth.

I didn't know when I'd become so obsessed with freckles. Or lips.

"Yeah, the youngest," I said, back to her question. "Mike, the one who used to be in the Marines, he's in the middle. Lives out in Chicago now with my best friend from when we were kids. Adam's the oldest. He's married with two girls. I'm the favorite uncle, obvs."

"Obvs." She covered her giggle with her hand. "What *was* in that drink? I'm going to need to Uber home."

"I'll take you home if you can't drive."

She stuffed another bite of dip into her mouth and shook her head, mumbling something I couldn't understand.

"Sorry, Cookie Monster, didn't catch that one."

"I said," she started once she swallowed, "you don't need to do that. Some water and food, and I'll sober up."

I nodded, because that was perfectly reasonable, and felt a needle in my gut.

When our server reappeared, I gestured to the menus still on our table, tucked away in the corner. "What else do you want?"

"Quesadillas?" she asked me, and when I shrugged, she

smiled up at him. "We'll have the quesadillas, and can we have another water, please? I stole his."

He was about to step away, but I stopped him. "No jalapeños. She doesn't like spice."

"Got it," he said, and Claire tossed me a funny look.

"What? Just reminding him. Don't want you drunk and sweaty, begging for milk because you're burning up."

She curled her lip in mock anger. "Such a gentleman."

"I do try. Didn't di—Eric do stuff like that?"

She intentionally stuffed a chip covered with dip into her mouth, but I waited patiently. She wasn't getting off that easy.

"I can't imagine you'd put up with someone like him," I told her, accepting the water from our waiter.

"How do you know what I would or wouldn't put up with?"

"I know you're one of seven kids and rode your bike to the library to get away from the family. I know you wear headbands every day and love Taylor Swift. I know you're best friends with Meredith and hate softball. I know your birthday is in January, so that makes you an Aquarius, which means you're loyal and creative, but you don't like to talk much until you get one half-priced Applebee's drink in you. Then you're Chatty Cathy."

She eyed me for a while. "You're into the zodiacs?"

"Yeah." I swiped my cell phone on, showing her my astrology app. "I get my horoscope every day. It's super interesting to think when we're born might influence the type of person we are. Like, me, I'm a total Gemini."

"Aren't Geminis the worst?"

"Ma'am." I laughed, pilfering the chip she held from between her fingers, and shoved it in my mouth. Okay, the spinach dip was growing on me. "We're known to be flighty and gossipy, but—"

"But that doesn't sound like you at all." She arched a sarcastic eyebrow my way.

I shook my head, because that was exactly me. "When is dicknozzle's birthday?"

"July 4th. He always thought it was funny. Said the fireworks were for him."

What a douche. "He's a Cancer. Of course it didn't work out. You need someone to complement you."

"And who is that?" she asked after our quesadillas were set down between us.

"You need someone who'll let you do your thing," I said, reaching for a piece at the same time she did, so our knuckles bumped. "You like your independence and don't have time for people's bullshit. Right?"

"So far, so good." Her eyes were suspicious slits. Even if I weren't into the zodiac, it wasn't as if she was that hard to read.

"You also probably like having your alone time, and that's where your wires got crossed."

She considered me as she chewed then slowly set her triangle of quesadilla down on her plate. "He said he couldn't understand why I never wanted to go out with him, and when we were home together, he couldn't just be with me. I wasn't enough to hold his attention."

She pitched her lip to the side, as if biting the inside, so her two freckles disappeared, and I hated he'd made her feel that way.

"You're more than enough, Claire."

A sad sort of smile crossed her features. "Thank you."

I cleared my throat, ignoring the thick tension sitting on the table between us, and dipped my quesadilla into the sour cream. "So, I figure to make this look real, we'll need to post stuff to our social media, maybe snap a few pics at softball games."

Our second game had been last week, and Claire had spent most of her time laughing in the outfield with Aggie and Lou. I really liked seeing her have fun at something she'd assumed she was going to hate.

And I especially liked how she'd worn my baseball cap again. She had tried to give it back to me, but it was hers now.

"What are we going to tell our families?" she asked.

I answered around a bite of food. "Nothing."

"Nothing? We have to tell them something. And I certainly can't tell them the truth, that it's all for show."

I shrugged. "What does it matter?"

"What does it— You haven't thought this through at all, have you?"

"I told you I'm impulsive."

She smacked her palm on the table, and I suddenly felt like a bad dog. "Jimmy, this is a public competition. Everyone will know, including our families."

"Ooh. Yeah."

"*Seriously*? You really didn't think about this? If we're going to be in a real relationship—" she crooked her fingers in air quotes over the word, and there was that needle again "— we're going to have to act like it. It's more than posting a few pictures online. My family is going to insist on meeting you. They're pissed over Eric, and they'll all want to vet you."

I offered her one of my best smiles. "I'm great with families."

"If you didn't think about what you'd tell yours, what *did* you think about?"

Easy. "Winning."

She rolled her eyes. "Of course."

I was a highly competitive person, and her reaction raised my defenses. As if it was a bad thing. "What's that tone for?"

"Is everything a game to you?"

"No," I snapped.

She only stared at me for a while, like she could see inside my head, and I tried not to shrink under her gaze.

"Why did you pick me?" she asked after a decade.

"Huh?"

"Why did you think you could win with me?"

My attention drifted around the restaurant, to all the other patrons eating and drinking and chatting, and I wondered if everyone's brain chugged along like a train, moving from thought to thought in orderly fashion, or if they were like me, a locomotive with creaky wheels and a drunk engineer at the helm switching off tracks at random moments.

Why did I think I could win with Claire?

I didn't think.

I saw the picture and said: yes, her.

Why?

Beats the hell out of me, but she was staring at me now like she wanted a five-paragraph essay with a clear opening, at least three pieces of evidence, and a cohesive conclusion.

In this thesis, I will...

I met her studious eyes. "I picked you because you're patient and smart, and I really do like your headbands. I like your whole thing." I circled the air with my quesadilla. "The headbands and skirts and the tops with the..." I fluttered my fingers by my throat, thinking of the dress she'd worn yesterday. It was green with a rounded collar and tiny bow in the middle. I didn't know why her girly fashion made me so giddy, but it did.

It wasn't much of an argument, and she sagged back against the booth.

"I don't know why, Claire. I didn't think about it. I just did it. I'm sorry," I said since that obviously wasn't the answer she wanted. But we had been friends for a while, and that part of the essay I'd written for the contest wasn't a lie. We'd been working together for four years, right across the hall from each other. I knew how she hunched her shoulders when she was having a bad day, and that she always crouched down to talk to students one-on-one so they could look each other in the eye. And even though she didn't smile a lot, when she did, it was almost always for the kids. She loved her job, and I really liked that about her. "Besides, you're really cute. Don't you know?"

Her cheeks went scarlet, and I realized her earlier reaction to me telling her she looked pretty was shock, not annoyance as I'd presumed. I wasn't lying; she was cute. Not in a traditional way, but she was pretty all the same. And it was as if no one had told her before.

Which was awful. I'd have to rectify that.

"Look at you blushing," I teased, having happily wormed my way back into her good graces even as my insides twisted.

She played with her hair, refusing to meet my gaze.

"Okay, well, how about we take a picture together now, and post it to our socials, then we can tell our families," I suggested. "Whatever you're comfortable with. I'll tell mine exactly what I wrote for the essay. That we were friends, and it was a slow road to realizing we were more."

She nodded then immediately shook her head. "This is absurd. I can't believe we're doing this. Is the money that important?"

Yeah, the money was important. I loved my house and didn't want to lose it.

But there was also a small part of me that liked hanging out with Claire. I needed money for a down payment, but being "forced" to spend time with her wasn't exactly a hardship.

"You can back out any time you want," I told her and then raised my phone, offering her time to throw in the towel. She did the side lip-chewing thing again, and I crossed every finger and toe that she'd jump off the cliff with me.

"Five thousand dollars would go a long way in paying down my student loans," she said finally.

I grinned and held up my phone, the camera screen toward us. "Smile, baby."

CHAPTER SEVEN

ROSIE

Did I see Claire tagged in a photo with a man tonight?

MOM

WHAT? WHEN?

RYAN

Stop yelling.

TRISTAN

So loud in here

DAD

I'll never understand how I can be sitting in the same room as my family and we will still text each other. That's the problem with this world. The breakdown of familial communications.

EVAN

Is it Eric? Tell me you're not back with him.

JULIE

Running to Insta.

AIDEN

Who's in the same room?

It's not Eric.

MOM

Who is it?!?!

ROSIE

He's cute.

JULIE

TheRealJ.Ewing

JULIE

I need to do a deep dive.

JULIE

Hold, please.

DAD

Ryan and Tristan came over for dinner.

AIDEN

Nobody told me. Why didn't anybody tell me?

MOM

It was a last minute thing.

AIDEN

I would've come over for dinner.

RYAN

It's cause no one likes you.

AIDEN

Fuck off, Ryan.

DAD

We love you, Aiden.

DAD

Fuck off, Ryan.

MOM

Claire! Stop avoiding!

ROSIE

Yeah, Claire.

ROSIE

Your boyfriend posts a lot of animal videos.

TRISTAN

I hate this thread. It's too chaotic for me. How
do I get out?

That's what I've been asking my whole life.

MOM

No one is going anywhere.

ROSIE

At least until Claire tells us who the guy is.

EVAN

I want to meet him.

ROSIE

Here. Look.

MOM

Oooh he's cute!

AIDEN

Do we even follow each other, Claire?

RYAN

See? No one likes you.

AIDEN

Are you still mad at me cause of Gia?

DAD

Who is Gia?

JULIE

We're getting off topic, people.

TRISTAN

WHOSE IDEA WAS IT TO PUT ALL
349334598 OF US ON ONE TEXT CHAIN?

EVAN

Dad's.

DAD

Because we need to stay in touch.

TRISTAN

We talk every day.

AIDEN

Who does? Why am I always being left out?

RYAN

Honest to god bro, next time I see you, I'm
gonna deck you.

DAD

What is going on with you two?

ROSIE

Aiden came up last weekend, and he went out
with the twins. Ryan was flirting with some
girl, but she went home with Aiden.

EVAN

Ro, you're such a shit stirrer.

Finally! Someone speaking the truth.

ROSIE

Rude.

AIDEN

Nothing happened with Gia.

MOM

Back to this cute guy with Claire.

TRISTAN

Everybody knows girls like the unassuming thing about Aiden. And glasses. Girls love glasses.

RYAN

What do you know? You're a virgin.

ROSIE

Who can't drive.

JULIE

HAHAHA. Nice.

EVAN

What?

ROSIE

Clueless.

JULIE

It's from Clueless when Tai is mad at Cher.

MOM

Oh, honey. You're a virgin?

TRISTAN

I hate everyone.

DAD

That's okay, son. Good for you.

ROSIE

Ry, maybe if you'd stop talking about yourself for five seconds and talk to a woman about herself, you'd know.

MOM

She's right. You could use a little more patience with women. It's not always about what you want.

RYAN

OMG

RYAN

You guys are the worst.

RYAN

Honestly.

JULIE

Moving on.

EVAN

I never liked Eric. There was something about him.

DAD

Smarmy.

MOM

He was kind of a know-it-all.

TRISTAN

Definitely a one-upper.

RYAN

And what was with his hair?

ROSIE

I don't know why you didn't break up with him earlier.

AIDEN

Because she's too nice.

> I'm not too nice.

RYAN

Right. You're grumpy and boring.

> Fuck off, Ryan.

RYAN

Sure, everyone take Aiden's side.

ROSIE

We've moved on from you and the girl you were never going to get anyway. If she went home with Aiden, clearly, she's interested in a different kind of person.

ROSIE

Get. Over. It.

RYAN

But she was so hot.

AIDEN

Did you even know she double majored in communications and economics?

RYAN

What does that have to do with anything?

TRISTAN

It proves he listened to her.

MOM

Claire, where did you meet him?

Work.

DAD

He's a librarian?

Second-grade teacher.

RYAN

He must be fun at parties.

MOM

Fuck off, Ryan.

AIDEN

I'm actually going to take her out this weekend.

RYAN

ARE YOU KIDDING ME?

RYAN

I thought you said nothing happened.

MOM

What's his name?

Jimmy

EVAN

Wouldn't it be better if we just waited to have these conversations in person?

DAD

I would love that.

TRISTAN

As if we don't talk enough.

ROSIE

So you and Jimmy are a thing now?

RYAN

Julie is the only one of you I trust.

JULIE

Thank you.

Yes.

EVAN

Yes to what?

Jimmy and I are dating.

MOM

I CANNOT BELIEVE YOU DIDN'T TELL ME ABOUT HIM BEFORE

RYAN

Stop yelling.

TRISTAN

So loud.

DAD

Are you happy?

MOM

When can we meet him?

It's really new.

JULIE

Now wait a goddamn minute.

JULIE

Look at what I just found.

RYAN

What does it say?

JULIE

You have to actually open the link and read it.
I'm not going to reiterate everything.

ROSIE

What the hell, Claire??!?!?!

EVAN

Claire, you little liar.

MOM

You're in a contest with him?

RYAN

For ten grand? Damn.

DAD

Why didn't you tell us about all this? This is
exciting.

EVAN

It's weird. Is there a reason you didn't tell us?

TRISTAN

I can't believe you want to do something like
this. Were you drunk when you agreed to this?

Almost.

DAD

But are you happy?

It's really new.

JULIE

Hate to state the obvious, but you already said that it's new. That has nothing to do with whether you're happy or not.

MOM

When can we meet him?

I doubt you'll meet him.

MOM

Why?

ROSIE

I'd like to meet him.

EVAN

Me too.

JULIE

I won't be meeting him anytime soon, but someone let him know that I have sources. I will find out the truth.

OMG

There is no truth to find out, and he won't be meeting anyone any time soon.

DAD

Why not?

MOM

It won't be a big deal.

ROSIE

Ha!

> Never in the history of ever has this family played it cool when introducing someone.

MOM

I am very cool.

DAD

The epitome of cool.

TRISTAN

Dad, you wear Van Halen T-shirts, and Mom, you hang all your dirty laundry out to dry. Literally. Your underwear is hanging on the line as we speak.

MOM

I will take it down before anyone comes over.

DAD

Van Halen is classic.

> That's what Jimmy says a lot.

DAD

That Van Halen is classic? Because he's correct. They are.

CLAIRE

No, just the word classic. He uses it a lot.

All of my siblings sent emojis ranging from the clown face to the skull and crossbones.

> Fuck off, all of you.

MOM

I'm sure he can't be any worse than Eric.

DAD

That's for sure.

> I don't trust any of you. Not even Joe.

DAD

Hey, don't drag the dog into this. He had nothing to do with it.

MOM

So we'll see you next weekend?

ROSIE

I'll be there.

TRISTAN

Me too.

AIDEN

Same.

RYAN

Yeah, I'm not missing this shitshow.

MOM

And you wonder why you can't get any girls.

EVAN

Boom.

CHAPTER EIGHT

Claire

It had only been a few days since Jimmy and I had gone "public," but in that time, the entire school staff found out, and I'd taken to hiding in the library. Meanwhile, Jimmy went about his day as usual, smiling at everyone, thanking them for their congratulations on us being together, as if he'd won some sort of prize.

I could barely look at him and attempted to stay away from the door, so as not to catch even a small sight of him. Which was why I noticed Anna lingering in the stacks. I might not have if I weren't actively avoiding "my boyfriend."

"Hey," I said, making my way over to her, and she startled. "Sorry. Didn't mean to scare you."

Anna was a quiet fifth grader with a pixie cut and a flair for printed button-downs, like the floral one she wore today. I appreciated good fashion sense, and even though she wore shorts every day, even in freezing weather, she always looked stylish. And she was almost always with her best friend, a boy named Carlos, and had a book in her hand. However, Carlos wasn't with her now, and she didn't have a book.

"Can I help you find something?" I asked, bending down to her level.

She swayed side to side, as if deciding whether she wanted to stay or go. "Just looking."

"For something in particular?" When she lifted one shoulder, I backed away. "Let me know if—"

"I found books online."

"Oh?" I bent back down.

Anna kept her eyes on the row of books geared toward kids at a higher reading level, like she was. "But I can't buy them for myself."

I nodded. I didn't know any kid who was given free rein to shop online. "Can you go to the bookstore? Maybe ask whoever your adult is at home."

She tugged at her shirt. "I don't...I don't know if my parents would do that."

"Okay. Well, do you remember what the titles were that you liked? Maybe I'll be able to get one here for you."

She rubbed at her nose, her feet unsettled as she swayed again. "It's, um..." She started away from me. "Never mind."

"Hey, wait, Anna. Let me help you."

She dropped her gaze to the floor. "I was..."

I gently nudged her shoulder, ushering her toward one of the tables, where we could sit and chat. Clearly, she needed it, but before we got down to it, I smiled at her. "How was your day today?"

"Okay."

"Yeah? How come you're not out at recess?"

She shrugged, her little body shaking because of her bouncing feet. "Wanted to check out some books, I guess."

"So," I started carefully, "I know I'm only the lady who lives in these stacks, but I think I'm also pretty good at listening. I'm always here if you need something."

Her shoulders rose on a breath like she was about to tell me something, but when her eyes met mine, she shrank back.

"You know, I was a lot like you as a kid," I told her. "I was always hiding out in the library, reading. I still am."

She scratched at a divot on the table. "What books do you read?"

My parents never talked down to me, and that was how I treated my students too. It was possible to engage them at their level without patronizing them. So I told her the truth. "Mostly books about falling in love."

"Like..." She slowly lifted her focus up to me. "Girls falling in love with boys?"

"Yeah, but not only boys with girls."

Her feet stilled under the table, her eyes widening ever so slightly, and suddenly I had a hunch what this was about.

"Sometimes I read about boys falling in love with other boys and sometimes about girls falling in love with other girls."

"Really?" she asked, quiet awareness in her voice.

"Yeah. Is that maybe a book you'd be interested in?"

She took another deep breath, but this time, she unleashed. "I just finished a book about a group of kids in space and they end up saving the station, but one of them was a girl and she dressed like me, not like..."

She started to point at me but dropped her finger, and I laughed. "It's okay. I like dresses and skirts and pink, but it's okay if you don't. So, the girl in your book dressed like you?"

She nodded and dropped her eyes. "And she liked another girl."

I folded my hands on top of the table, waiting until she looked up at me again. She had nothing to be ashamed of. "Yeah? It was a good book?"

"So good. I read the whole thing last weekend. Carlos was so mad at me 'cause I didn't want to play *Mario Kart*."

I shrugged. "That happens sometimes. A book is so good you can't put it down. I'm glad you found it."

"I borrowed it from Carlos's older sister."

"Oh, so it was more of a book for older kids?"

Anna nodded. Although she was a tween, her reading level was so high, it was often hard to find books that were suitable for her. But I thought she was mature enough to read some young adult books.

"And what about the books you were looking at online? They were similar ones?"

She nodded again.

"Well, I don't have anything like that in the library here, but I might be able to find something you'd like. I could put it in the Free Little Library."

Like lots of people around the country who put up Free Little Libraries in their yards or places of business, I'd asked Mrs. Kaplan if I could set one out in front of the school. Unlike the school library, this birdfeeder-like box contained books that were donated by anyone who wanted to drop a book they loved there for someone else to read.

It wasn't used all that often, mostly by the older kids who were readers. Or the occasional parent who stopped by the school for one reason or another and helped themselves to a book for their child. Last I'd checked, there were some evergreens like *Goosebumps* and American Girl books, a bunch graphic novels, a well-worn copy of Anne Frank's diary, a few Dr. Seuss books, and a really cool-looking book of fairy tales with gorgeous illustrations that I was tempted to take home myself.

Anna's whole face changed as she grinned. "Yeah?"

"Of course. That's my job." I playfully jostled her arm, happy she was smiling again, and stood up. "Give me a week."

"Yeah. Okay." She raced off with a wave.

I followed her to the door, calling after her, "Walk, please. Don't run!"

Jimmy was there, across the hall from me, his hands in his pockets. "Well, there you are. Seemed like you were hiding from me."

I forced a laugh. "Why would I do that?"

"I don't know." He glanced over his shoulder at his class. I could see behind him, where his kids were busy on their iPads, and he took two steps closer to me.

Like a magnet, I took two steps closer to him too.

"Why *would* you hide from me?" His voice was so low, I had to lean in. I honestly didn't know he was capable of whispering.

"I'm not hiding," I said.

"Feels like you're hiding."

I opened my mouth to argue, but he cut me off.

"You ready for the game tomorrow?"

In all the hiding I'd been doing, I'd nearly forgotten we had yet another softball game. Two games in and already the season seemed like it was dragging on forever.

"Ready is not the word I'd use."

"You're getting better."

"I never even touched the ball last week."

"Precisely." He grinned, backing away from me to shout into his room. "Thirty seconds, and then we're moving on to science." His students started murmuring, moving around, and he tipped his head to the side, his eyes roaming over me from head to toe and back. "You look pretty."

Before I could respond, he ducked back inside his room, clapping his hands a few times. I couldn't see him anymore, but I heard him loud and clear. "Are you ready, kids?"

His entire class shouted back, "Aye-aye, Captain!"

I rolled my eyes. The SpongeBob SquarePants theme song would be stuck in my head for the rest of the day.

When school finally ended, the kids racing out of the building, ready and raring to go for the weekend, it was almost as if you could hear all the teachers audibly sigh. Mrs. Kaplan stopped by, dropping off some supplies for Spring Fling week to be stored in the back room.

"TGIF, huh?" she said with a smile.

"Definitely."

"Big plans?" she asked, and I locked the closet door, the keys jingling in my hand.

"Um, I don't—"

"Yeah. I'm taking her out," Jimmy butted in from behind us, and Mrs. Kaplan practically lit up, her head swiveling back and forth between us.

"So, it's true?"

He nodded, strolling into the library like he owned the place with his backpack over his shoulder and the other hand reaching out toward me. I stood stock-still as he tugged at the end of a lock of my hair, the back of his hand brushing my bicep. "It is."

"That's so nice. So many good matches are made when teachers find each other." She circled her hand with her walkie-talkie in the air. "A lot of people don't have patience or understanding for what we do. They don't know this isn't a nine-to-five desk job. Our work comes home with us every day. If not literally then figuratively in our hearts. I'm so happy for you two." Then she sobered. "But I'm sure I don't have to tell you this is still a school and work environment. You two need to conduct yourselves as such."

My jaw flapped a few times. Not that she was scolding us, but I didn't do well with confrontation of any sort. I never got in trouble. I was a church mouse. Never seen nor heard. But Jimmy did his usual thing.

"Of course. Nothing will change here."

"I'd expect nothing less from you." She exited with a wave. "Have a great weekend!"

Between Mrs. Kaplan's warning and Jimmy's free rein over our apparent weekend plans, I was still frozen in shock as he leaned against the counter next to me. "So, you ready to get out of here?"

"I, uh...what?"

"Why do you look so scared?"

"You're acting like this—" I flailed my arms around "—is all normal. It's not normal."

His dark brows narrowed as he straightened up. "What's not?"

"You and me and this whole thing, and everyone thinking we're together when we're not, and my family wants you to come over, and I need to come up with an excuse because you can't, and I don't know if—"

With two fingers over my lips, he quieted me and my verbal vomit. "Hey. It's okay. It's okay."

I met his eyes, like melted toffee, and they crinkled in the corners. My rapidly heaving chest slowed down, even as he shifted closer to me. His smell, something sharp yet sweet like candied pine, enveloped me. "We don't have to do anything you don't want to, okay? If you don't want to go to your parents', tell them I'm sick. And I'm not taking you out this weekend."

My stomach dropped.

"Oh, okay," I said from under his fingers still resting on my lips. His gaze settled there, and I swear I felt his other hand brush over my waist, but it was gone before I could know for sure, and he dropped his hand from my face.

"I only told Kaplan that because it'd be something I'd do, if this were real. I'd take you out tonight, but..." He cleared his throat and backed away, and while I'd stopped rambling, my insides still didn't unknot. Sure, the idea of this fake relationship was ridiculous and I was scared of getting caught, yet the idea of going on a date with him sounded nice.

"I know you're freaking out," he went on, and I had to hold on to the cart next to me so I didn't sag back against the wall. "It's okay. We do what we have to, and that's it, all right?"

I nodded, but still, I needed... I didn't know what I needed.

Though he seemed to know and took hold of my hand. "This is supposed to be fun, Claire."

I really liked the way he said my name.

"It's only a game," he said, sending my heart back down to its rightful place after being stuck in my throat. I might have liked how he said my name all soft and sweet, but this was a game to him. Nothing more.

"A game you want to win," I added, and he licked his lips, his mouth hooking up to a half smile.

"Yeah, and I need you to start acting as if you actually like me, so we can win."

"Maybe we should go out, then," I suggested, with a whole lot more bravado than I felt.

"Yeah?" He grinned, once again close to me, his right foot between both of mine, my dress brushing along his pant leg. "You want to go out with me?"

"For practice. So I can pretend I like you."

His tongue ran along his bottom lip as he nodded with his usual swagger. "Well, all right, Miss Hart. I'll pick you up at your place tonight? Say, six o'clock?"

"Okay. I'll text you my address."

"Then I'll see you later, baby." He chucked my chin and backed away from me with a stupid grin on his face, as if he was really excited for tonight. I watched him pivot away as he reached his fist up in the air, singing the lyrics to "Breakfast at Tiffany's" at the top of his lungs.

"Not so loud, Mr. Ewing!"

He winked over his shoulder at me.

And damn.

I wanted to win too.

CHAPTER NINE

Jimmy

A little before six, I pulled up to the address Claire had messaged me. She lived on the upper floor of a house with metal steps outside leading to her door. I held on to the banister as I made my way up to knock on the door. A wreath made from a brass ring with some greenery and delicate-looking pink and white silk flowers on the bottom made me smile. It was so…Claire.

A moment later, her door swung open, and I was surprised to find her in only a robe.

"Uh, hi," I said, trying and failing to bite back a grin.

"I lost track of time," she explained as I stepped inside, closing the door behind me. "I didn't know what to wear, and then I had to do laundry, and—"

Since it worked earlier, I placed my index and middle fingers on her mouth, silencing her. "Even though I find your rambling adorable, there's no need for it. We're having fun, right?"

"Right." She nodded, her soft lips catching on my fingers, and the tiny hairs on the back of my neck stood on end.

"Wear whatever you want to. We're only going to grab something to eat."

And then, since I liked to torture myself, I smoothed my fingers down a few strands of her long hair. I tugged them straight before they sprang back up to the soft curl she must have made with a curling iron because she knocked my hand away, saying, "I just redid my hair."

"Sorry," I apologized, completely insincere.

Which, from her eye roll, she obviously knew.

"Give me a minute to get changed. I'll be right back."

She turned, striding down a short hall to where I presumed her bedroom was. I ignored my nosier instincts to check out her bathroom or even try for a peek into her bedroom and instead let my focus float over her small living room. It was cramped but tidy with a thousand pillows all over her sofa, including one glittery square. I picked it up, running my hand over it to reveal a picture of a brown rabbit with flowers on its head. I laughed and dragged my hand back down, flipping the sequins to their original gold. After tossing it back to the sofa, I moved on to her bookcase, each shelf overflowing with one kind of book. Romance.

I grabbed one that seemed a few decades old with a couple on the front. The woman's red dress was undone at the top, and the shirtless man had her bent backward toward a chaise lounge. With Claire still in her bedroom, I flopped down on her couch and flipped through it until I found a *good* part.

The duke had nearly gotten his hand up the lady's gown when Claire padded into the living room.

"What are you doing?"

I lifted my gaze to her. "Hm?"

"What are you doing?"

"Reading."

She huffed, gesturing down the length of my body, one hand behind my head on her glitter rabbit pillow, my feet crossed at the ankles at the other end of the couch. "You do this in everyone's house the first time you're there? Help yourself to a book and lie down?"

"I didn't think you'd mind." I stood up, taking in her dress with the ruffled skirt that for one moment had me imagining what it would be like to put my hand under it. What I would find there, durable cotton or soft silk or nothing at all.

Maybe it was all the talk of petticoats and corsets in her book.

Or maybe, I really wanted to know what she wore underneath her little skirts.

"This book is—"

"Don't say it." She cut me off with a flat hand through the air. "I don't want to hear your misogynist take on it."

"I was going to say it was good. Can I borrow it?"

She wrenched back. "Really?"

"Yeah. Don't be so surprised. I do read." Then I added as an afterthought, "More than the Junie B. and Ralph Mouse series."

"Yeah. You can borrow it." Her lips pitched to the side, and I could tell she was trying not to smile as she stepped into a pair of black shoes with no heel. She slid her arms into a denim jacket and crossed a purse over her body. "Ready."

"Yeah, you are," I said, but she only snorted, ushering me out of her door.

After she locked her door on the tiny platform, we made our way down the steps. "These must be a bitch in the winter. Do they freeze over?"

"Yeah, but the landlord does a pretty good job of keeping them salted," she told me once we were on the ground.

"A pretty good job or a good job?" I asked, not liking the idea of what could possibly happen to those steps in an ice storm.

"Good job."

I eyed her, but she evaded me, heading to my car. "It's fine."

"It's dangerous."

"It's fine," she said and settled in the passenger side. I dropped in behind the steering wheel, looking her over.

"Maybe you should find a different place."

"You want me to find another place to live after you gave me your whole speech two weeks ago about why we needed to even do this? Because the market is terrible, and you wouldn't be able to find another house to rent?"

I rubbed at my jaw. I did say that, didn't I? True, it was hard to find a good rental that wasn't astronomically priced. But also, in the moment, I'd sort of forgotten that was my motivation for doing *this*.

That we were even doing this whole fake-relationship thing.

For a few minutes there, it felt like we were two people going out.

I sidestepped her argument and started up Mariah before setting Claire's worn paperback in the back seat.

"You're really going to read it?" she asked me as I merged onto the road.

"Yeah." I handed her my phone, which was paired to the Bluetooth. "You can pick the music." She settled on some indie pop song I'd never heard before, and I glanced in her direction. "So, romance books, huh?"

"Yep."

"It looks like that's all you read," I said.

"Not all that I read, but for the most part. Historical romances are my jam."

"Why do you like them so much?" At a red light, I turned to find her eyes on me already.

"I love romances because I know there will always be a happy ending, and everyone deserves to have love, no matter what form."

I leaned my elbow onto the console between us so my shoulder brushed her arm. "I like that. Plus, the little bit I read was..."

When I whistled, she laughed. "That's the other thing I like too. I like that they're empowering for people, especially women. Some of the books can be problematic, like anything can be, but for the most part, they show women finding love and enjoying sex, which is really important. Teaches us not to settle and to ask for what we want in bed."

That caught me off guard, and I whipped my head around to her. "In bed?"

"Yeah, in bed and with our relationships."

My gaze immediately dropped to the few inches of her thighs peeking out under her skirt. All that creamy skin. And my mind went off the deep end.

But another thought, one that tugged at something buried in my chest, kept me floating above water. "Then why did you stay with dicknozzle for so long?"

She blew out a little puff of air between her lips. "I didn't say I was done learning yet."

Even though this was a *serious* conversation, I was desperate to know what she had learned about herself in bed. But I held back from asking. This was all fake after all. It wasn't my place to know.

"Seems like you were settling for him," I said after a while, and she didn't disagree.

"I'm sure you get this since we're about the same age, but it's really hard to date, right? At this stage in our lives. A lot of people find their partner in college, so the pool of available people is smaller. Your friends try to set you up with their, like, one single acquaintance, and when that doesn't work, you try apps. But that's a hellscape of dick pics and questions like *Does the carpet match the drapes?*"

I grimaced. "Guys really say that to you?"

"All the time."

"That's gross. I apologize on behalf of men." And I tried really hard not to imagine hair anywhere else on her body besides what was on her head.

"I guess I stayed with Eric so long because I didn't see it getting any better. With the other choices, I mean. Yeah, he could be condescending and made dumb jokes, but—"

"Calling you boring and grumpy is not a dumb joke. It's disrespectful." I didn't think when I placed my hand on her knee. "You don't deserve it."

"No, I know. I know. It's just..." She lifted her shoulder. "I guess sometimes it feels better to work with what you've got than keep waiting for something better. What if that something better never comes along?"

Stopped at another red light, I flattened my palm against her skin. It was smooth, and I could still make out the freckles dotting her kneecap in the hazy orange of the sunset outside the windshield. "But what if it does?"

She lifted her gaze from where she'd been watching my thumb stroke gentle circles to meet mine. "Then...I guess it's a lesson about self-worth."

I stared at her eyes, and I didn't know why I hadn't ever noticed they were like two shimmering drops of gray-blue diamonds. They were beautiful.

Before I could tell her, the light turned green, and I placed both of my hands back on the steering wheel and forced my attention to the road. We stayed quiet for the rest of the drive to the little Italian place. Once she had her chicken parm and I had my ravioli, she told me more about her family, her brothers who were constantly arguing, and her parents, who seemed supercool from her stories about how they both quit high-paying jobs to open their farm, and how they rocked out in their kitchen to eighties hair bands whenever possible. I was into it.

I told her about Sam and all the trouble we used to get into. Or, rather, the trouble I used to get her into. I showed her pictures of my nieces, Amelia and Emma, and before I knew it, two hours had flown by.

When I asked for the bill, Claire tried to pay, but I batted her hand away. "Put your wallet down."

She didn't listen. "We'll split it."

"No, Claire. It's my treat."

"But this isn't a date," she said, like a splash of cold water to my face, and I sat back in my chair, allowing her to slide her card in next to mine in the leather check holder.

This was the second time she'd reminded me tonight that this wasn't real, and I shouldn't have been so surprised. This wasn't a date.

It wasn't a date.

Not. A. Date.

Which was why I was even more surprised when she pointed down the street, to where the green-and-white sign of Barnes & Noble lit up the night sky. "You mind if we stop in there?"

"Nope. Let's go."

Inside the bookstore, I followed Claire around, my hands behind my back, my eyes staying resolutely above her waist and not on the sway of her hips or the shape of her legs. "Wait," I told her as she started off into the stacks. "I have a feeling this is going to take a while. I need refreshments." I tipped my chin toward the Starbucks café. "Want anything?"

She shook her head. "I'll be right here."

I bought a Frappuccino and met her back where I left her. But she was down on the floor, her legs crossed, her head tipped as she studied each book, and I fought valiantly not to check out her legs since her skirt had ridden up those glorious gams.

I crouched down next to her. "Whatcha lookin' for?"

"One of the kids is looking for more books to read, but I don't have them in the library, so I told her I'd see what I could find."

"You're really good at your job, you know that?"

She slanted her gaze to me, a ghost of a smile curving her lips. "Thanks. So are you."

I sat on the floor next to her. "What made you want to be a librarian?"

She took out one book, read the back, and replaced it on the shelf. Then she scooted closer to me, tilting her head to study the novels on the shelf above her head. "You know how much time I spent at the library as a kid. I eventually got a job there and loved it. I think everyone should read books. It builds empathy. Reading books keeps kids from growing up to be assholes."

I saluted her with my coffee. "Hear, hear."

"What about you?" she asked, standing up next to me, and her legs were *right there*. I curled my fingers more tightly around my plastic cup so I didn't loop them around her ankle. "Why did you want to be a teacher?"

"I made a bet with my friend that I couldn't last in an elementary education class for an entire semester."

"Evidently, you won that bet?"

"Evidently." I leaned away from her, so I wasn't staring up her skirt. Because I was a very good boy. "We had to do a couple of hours of observation in a class, and there was a kid in there who reminded me of myself at that age, and we connected. It's so skewed. There are disproportionally more men teaching upper grades and in higher ed, while there are more women in elementary. I mean, I don't have to tell you this. You know how it is. Sorry for mansplaining your own work environment to you."

She snickered. "No, you're right. It needs to be more evened out so kids have different role models."

I nodded in agreement. "I feel for students who are like me, who have trouble sitting still and concentrating. I love teaching for a lot of reasons, but being able to help kids like me, that's a big one."

Claire looked down at me with a pensive tilt to her brow as if assessing me, and I stayed perfectly still, hoping she didn't find me wanting. After a few moments, she reached her fingers out to me, so I placed my drink in them. "Give me your hand," she said, lips trembling in a valiant attempt not to laugh. "I want to go to the next aisle."

I curled my hand around hers, and she hauled me up. Once I was standing to my full height, she tipped her head back, pursing her lips around my straw, helping herself to a sip of my drink. I was mesmerized.

"Honestly. I don't know how you drink this stuff. It's so sweet."

I grinned. "Good, right?"

She passed it back to me, our fingers grazing on the exchange, but she didn't seem to notice. And I was back to following her and her swaying hips around the store. I thumbed my cell phone on to snap a picture of her.

I tapped her shoulder. "It okay with you if I post this?"

With her so close to me, I could smell her shampoo as she examined the photo. It was of her back to me, midstride. Her long hair hanging over her jacket, her skirt swishing around her thighs, her face in profile. Her cheekbone covered in freckles, a little gold stud in her ear. Underneath, I captioned it, *Just your average Friday night.*

Next to me, Claire inhaled deeply, the freckles at the corner of her lip disappearing in her now-familiar nervous tic.

"I don't have to. I thought it was cute. You looked so serious, and—"

"You can post it." She lifted her head, meeting my gaze, and I smiled.

"Okay. I will."

This was what we were supposed to be doing, making it look like we were together. But I didn't take the picture because I had to. I wanted to. I wanted to post it because I was having a really good time with her.

She watched me hit the button on my phone screen before turning away, back to the books.

"Hey."

She turned over her shoulder to me.

"Did anyone ever tell you you're really fun and interesting?"

She rolled her eyes, though she couldn't hide how her mouth quirked in a half smile, and I snapped another picture. This one for me.

For over an hour, we wandered around the store, and she didn't even mind when I dragged her off in random directions because a sign or toy or phallic-shaped display caught my attention. She only shook her head in faux impatience as her eyes sparkled with unbridled amusement.

We headed out of the bookstore with a few new books for Claire and a new weird obsession with ruffled skirts for me. And back at her place, I insisted on walking her to her door.

"You don't have to," she told me.

"What would happen if you slipped on those steps and I wasn't there to catch you? You'd break your neck, and then I wouldn't win the money."

She sighed and stepped out of my car. "Number one, I don't know why you're so worried about these steps. I've lived here for years and never had an accident. And if I did break my neck, you'd probably get a ton of sympathy votes and win anyway."

"I don't want to win that way," I mumbled, trudging up the steps after her. "I want to win fair and square."

She unlocked her door but didn't step inside. "Well, I think fair and square is already out of the question."

I ran my hand through my hair. Was it questionable that we weren't dating and entered a contest for couples? Sure. But tonight was a date, for all intents and purposes. Hell, even our happy hour at Applebee's was a date. The only thing preventing it from being categorized as such was our silent agreement not to call it a date.

So, *technically*, we were dating. And very much *not* cheating.

"Thanks for taking me out tonight," she said, her eyes somewhere over my shoulder.

"Of course. I love spending time with my little bookworm."

She sniffed a laugh as she shook her head. "You and your nicknames."

"What? You don't like them?"

"You don't call anyone else them."

"False. I call my brothers names all the time. I call Aggie my work wife. I call Sam—"

"I mean..." She lifted one shoulder, not finishing her sentence, and I inched closer to her, wishing she would. I wanted to know if she liked my silly names for her because I certainly did. "They're ridiculous," she said after a while. "Like you."

I blew out a disappointed breath.

"But I like them."

And then my heart rate sped up. "That means you like *me* too?"

"Yeah." She knocked her elbow into my arm. "You're all right."

"You're all right too," I said, bending my knees to cut the distance between us. Granted, she wasn't all that short, probably average for a woman, and I barely scratched 5'11", but there was something about her. Something I wanted to hold, protect, keep in my pocket, and carry around with me.

She licked her lips, her breath coming out in short bursts, as her eyes remained on mine, unblinking. An invitation if I ever saw one. Though, as I lowered my head to her, she ducked to the right and placed her hand on my jaw, kissing my cheek.

"This was fun," she whispered, a few wisps of hair catching on my stubble.

"Yeah," I whispered too, a little dazed.

I had told her this was supposed to be fun.

All fun and games.

Yet this slow-growing tingling sensation spreading out from my gut didn't feel fun. It felt a little terrifying, actually. Like this was a serious medical issue. Like maybe I had to see a doctor about why my heart was beating so fast and why my fingers were involuntarily curling into fists so my nails dug into my palms.

Even as she closed the door behind her, the lock snapping audibly into place, I had trouble regulating my breath. I made my way down the steps of death and gave my temples a massage, reminding myself that this was fake.

Fake.

Fake.

Fake.

And I'd definitely imagined how her eyes widened slightly.

And how the tips of her fingers lingered on my jaw for a second.

And how tonight didn't feel fake at all.

CHAPTER TEN

Claire

I found an open spot in the lot outside the softball field and grabbed my baseball hat. I mean, Jimmy's hat. Last week, when I had tried to give it back, he refused and told me he liked to see me wearing it. In the moment, I thought it was him being sweet, goofy, says whatever is on his brain Jimmy.

But after last night. I wasn't sure.

I wasn't sure of anything.

I'd agreed to this relationship, knowing it wasn't real and he was doing this for money. Nothing more.

And yet, as we wandered the bookstore, it felt like a date. It felt like a date when he took that candid photo, catching me unawares. It was like he was simply admiring me. And then when he would drift off, eventually calling out, "Hey Claire, check this out," only to inevitably show me something like *Softball for Dummies* or a historical romance, it was like we had our own inside jokes. At one point, he lined up a bunch of stuffed animals in the kids' section and sat down in front of them before handing me a book, saying, "Read to us?"

It was immature and silly.

And so goddamn charming, I had to force myself to roll my eyes while I ground my back molars together. He only grinned.

Then at my door, when he leaned down, his dark eyes roaming over my face as if he would have been perfectly content to stare at me forever, I could have sworn he was going to kiss me. And I freaked out. Because he couldn't have actually wanted to. We went out last night as part of this whole scheme, a few hours to get to know each other. At least, that was what I had convinced myself.

But now, I wasn't so sure.

My overactive romantic heart and I could have imagined it all. It was difficult not to get caught up in this, in *him*. And now, as I fitted his hat on my head, I wasn't sure what was fake and real anymore.

But as I made my way over to our team's bench, I saw Jimmy holding court with the team, and it was a reminder that everyone liked him for a reason. He was the sun, and all of us merely flowers bending to his warmth. It was easy for me to read into what happened last night, but I had to remember it was a game to him.

Like this softball league. He wanted to win.

I grabbed a seat on the bench, retying my laces. Aggie sat down next to me. "How are you today?"

I shrugged. "Fine."

"It's gonna be a tough game."

"Yeah. I heard they're a really good team."

"We have yet to beat them," she told me, her eyes on our opponents, their T-shirts blindingly yellow. "See that blond guy? Heavy hitter, that one, and the short woman next to him? She doesn't look like much, but she's got quite an arm on her. She's their pitcher. She and Jimmy Jam had a little thing a couple years ago. Ever since it went sour, it's like she's out for blood."

Inside my sneakers, I curled my toes, starting to sweat from nerves. After that first game, when Eric had humiliated me, I hadn't thought it could get worse. But learning Jimmy had something with this girl with a mean throw had me pondering the best way to fake an illness to get out of this game.

"Oh hey, I didn't mean anything by it," Aggie said almost immediately. "I don't want to upset you. I figured you might've known already since you two are together now. And I think you make a great couple. Balance each other out, ya know?" She bumped her shoulder into mine, smiling brightly. "I always knew he'd get snatched up by a girl smart enough to see how good he is."

I pasted on a semblance of a smile.

"I'm gonna go warm up," she said, leaving me and my knotted-up stomach alone. Maybe I wouldn't have to fake an illness. I could puke right there and then.

Before I could chicken out and run back to my car, Meredith appeared next to me, her blond hair piled up on the top of her head in a messy bun doing nothing to disguise how much time she must have put into getting ready today. With her fake eyelashes and matching pink athleisure set, I knew she meant business.

"What are you planning?" I asked in a hushed tone.

"To get Hassan naked by the end of the day."

"And you think trying hard to look like you're not trying hard will work?"

She waved me off. "Men always say they want girls who don't wear makeup and love sweats, but when it comes down to it, they don't actually want to see the real us. They want the illusion." She gestured down the length of her tall and slender frame then plopped into a folding chair. "And I'll give it to them."

"What are you giving?" Jimmy asked out of nowhere.

"Sass and attitude," Meredith answered without taking her eyes off Hassan.

"I'd expect nothing less." Jimmy folded his arms, his eyes crinkling in amusement, as he moved to stand in front of me. "What's up? You look anxious."

I was absolutely anxious. About being here, out in the open, with people thinking we were together. About what last night meant to him and how it felt different to me. And about how I'd have to face down some girl who knew how he kissed while she struck me out.

"Everybody keeps talking about how good they are. And, you know...I'm not."

"Here. Come here," he said, wiggling his fingers in my direction so I'd take his hand. It didn't help my stupid imagination at all. "Let me show you a few things." Snagging a bat, he led me a few yards away from the team gathering at the bench. The ground was slightly uneven, the grass patchy, and he situated me in front of him so my back was to the fence and the opposing team.

"Okay, first things first. Let's work on your stance. You want to keep your feet hip-width apart and your knees bent, hips slightly hinged." Like I was his doll, he poked and prodded me until I was in a satisfactory position. "Good. Now let's work on the grip."

He lifted the bat, placing it in my hands, and then covered them with his own. I could smell his soap again. It was so familiar to me, it didn't even surprise me. Though the closeness of his mouth to my ear did. "Keep your elbows up and a loose grip. Move your fingers up a little higher. Up here. Like this. Good."

"You'd get along well with my brother," I said because apparently my brain was turning to mush the longer he was so close to me.

"Ryan? Yeah, I can't wait to meet him."

"You won't."

"But you did say they wanted to meet me, right?"

"Yeah, but I wouldn't actually put you through that," I said, trying to shake the fog away from my brain to focus on his words and not the heat coming off his chest, my butt literal centimeters from his groin. "You're not really my boyfriend."

"Uh-huh." He tore his gaze away from mine and cleared his throat. "Now, when the pitch comes, you need to keep your eye on the ball." His fingers tightened on mine. "Step toward it with your left foot." He demonstrated and waited for me to repeat the action. "And follow through with your swing." With his arms around mine, we swung the bat at air.

"Feel good?" he asked, and I swallowed down the dust in my throat, though it didn't help me speak. I nodded instead, and he let go of me, his hands drifting down to my waist, giving me a pat before letting go. "It's weird to bat from the other side for me. I hope I explained it all right."

When I found my voice, I turned to him. "Is it hard for you? Being left-handed in a right-handed world."

He shrugged, his hands on his hips. "One more thing to make school more difficult for me." Though that was a serious observation, he said it with a half smile, like it didn't bother him. And I supposed it didn't. Not if he'd figured out how to harness those frustrations into making him an excellent teacher. "But I can be pretty ambidextrous when I put my mind to it."

And that half smile grew to a full-on lewd grin.

My cheeks heated, and he jostled the bill of his—now my—hat. "I stayed up last night to read some of that book. I normally lose interest in most books, but I was glued to that one."

Leaning my weight on the bat, I tried to appear cooler than I felt. "Yeah? What did you like about it?"

He inched closer to me, his voice low. "It was funnier than I expected, but the sex was, obviously, the best part. I like that they didn't get right down to it, you know? He really had to work hard to get her, and then when they finally ended up in his room, the anticipation of it, with him unlacing her dress and getting the corset off, then the shift. There were so many layers, he was dying by the time he was finally able to touch her." He stroked his index finger over my wrist. "I was too."

I briefly closed my eyes, blowing out a slow breath, attempting to stabilize my pulse. I knew I didn't imagine the drag of his fingertip over my skin. Or the way his hand curved around my arm now.

My eyes flew open to find him staring down at me. "If I finish this book, can I come over to look through your library more? Borrow another one?"

I nodded, drawn into him like a moth to a flame, and he ventured his hand up to my shoulder, where he wound a few strands of my ponytail about his fingers.

"But does your library have late fees? I can't promise I'll return my book on time."

"I think..." I licked my dry lips. And I definitely didn't imagine the way his eyes followed the movement. "I think I could make an exception for you."

He tipped his head, a slow-growing smile crossing his features as he looked me up and down. "You look cute today."

As usual, the simple compliment sent me into a tailspin. "It's only leggings and a T-shirt."

"Yeah. But I really like dinosaurs." He tugged the hem of my navy shirt, a brontosaurus resting its head on an enormous pile of books. "What's your favorite?"

"Book?" I asked.

"No, dinosaur."

I doubled over as I laughed.

He chuckled too. "What? I'm serious."

"I know. That's why it's so funny," I said once my giggles subsided.

"Mine is velociraptor. Did you know they had feathers? Scientists only found evidence of that a few years ago. Amazing, right?"

I massaged the heels of my palms into my cheeks, sore from smiling. "Amazing."

He slung his arm around my shoulder, turning around to walk back to the bench, but that was when I noticed her. The woman with the torpedo arm, Jimmy's ex.

"I heard you used to date her," I said, subtly tipping my head in her direction.

He glanced in her way. "Dating is a term to be used loosely."

Right. Because he didn't date. He didn't do relationships.

And this was all a game.

I crossed my arms. "Is that why she hates you now?"

"Hate's a strong word."

"She's glaring over here," I said, leaning away from him, but he only pulled me closer.

"Elle and me had a...fling a couple summers ago. It wasn't that big of a deal."

"Clearly, it was to her."

He narrowed his eyes at me in question.

"If she's *still* that upset. What did you do?"

"Nothing." He held up his free hand. "On purpose."

"That sounds ominous."

His mouth bent in chagrin. "We hooked up for the summer. That was it. Then she wanted to introduce me to her parents, and I told her that felt like it was making what we had into something else. And then I may or may not have accidentally made out with her roommate that night."

I elbowed him. "Oh my god. Jimmy!"

"I didn't know they were roommates! I swear. I was out at a bar, met this girl, and we kissed a little, and then she invited me back to her place. Lo and behold, it was also Elle's place."

"You are the absolute worst," I said, covering my face with my hand.

"I didn't know. I swear to god. I may be an idiot, but I wouldn't do something like that on purpose."

"No. She only looks like she wants to kill you."

"Yeah." He towed me in front of him, and with an arm around my shoulders, he yanked my back to his chest. "That's why you're my shield."

"I'm not getting in between you two."

"I did it for you," he said against my ear. "When Eric was on the other team. Your turn now."

He had me there, and I wrapped both of my hands around his forearm like it was the most natural thing in the world. "I guess having a fake girlfriend is good for one thing at least. Even if we don't win the money."

It took him a while to answer a muttered, "Guess so," as he slipped away from me, and though I meant it as a joke, I could tell I upset him. I just didn't know what part of what I said tripped him up. Mentioning the money or Elle.

He dropped down onto the bench as the other team took the field. We were up to bat first, and he folded his arms as Hassan walked out to the plate. Normally, he'd cheer and clap and shout encouragements or outrageous digs at the other team. I'd assumed he'd yell something about their highlighter shirts, but he sat silent.

He looked pissed.

But what did I know?

I was only his fake girlfriend.

CHAPTER ELEVEN

Jimmy

We were getting beaten. Not that I didn't expect it, but I was extra annoyed about it. It was the bottom of the last inning, and we needed a grand slam miracle to win.

When Kim, a fifth-grade teacher from Roosevelt Elementary, struck out, I kicked at a loose stone on the ground. I wouldn't say I was a sore loser. I just...really liked to win.

To make matters worse, it was mostly my fault we were losing. My pitches had been wild and all over the place or so slow my nieces could have hit them. And it was because I couldn't stop thinking about Claire. My eyes kept reflexively finding her ass.

It was a real problem.

Not her ass.

That was great. Big and soft-looking. A perfect pillow for my head. A place to rest my dinner plate.

The problem was how I couldn't stop staring.

But she'd made it perfectly clear; there was nothing going on between us. I knew she'd meant it as a joke, mentioning how her being my fake girlfriend was useful for not only the contest but also shielding me from Elle. Yet her words were like getting hit with a sock full of nickels.

With the weird in-between space last night and the literal space between us now, I didn't know what to do. Claire spent most of the game chatting on the sideline with Meredith and Aggie, who seemed to have given up on this game since she'd taken out her lemon bars, passing them among our team.

I waved off the treat as it was Claire's turn to bat. She chose a random bat, which was her first mistake since it was too big for her, but I let that go and stood up as she passed me.

"You got this," I told her, and she snorted.

"Thanks."

"Hey." I caught her arm before she could step out onto the dirt infield. "Keep your elbows up." I held said elbow up in a straight line parallel to the ground. "You keep dropping them."

"I'm sure that'll help," she mumbled, and I let her go.

"And remember to bend your knees. Step into your swing and follow through. Show me that power."

Then—I swear I didn't do it on purpose. I didn't even think about it—I smacked her ass as she walked away.

Like, *good game!*

She whipped her head around, her brows narrowed at me under the shadow of my hat, and I could only smile. "Lookin' good, slugger."

She rolled her eyes and turned back, striding to the plate. And she really did have a great ass.

I didn't have a type, but I liked big butts. I could not lie.

Claire was bottom heavy with a waist that flared out into wide hips and thick thighs, and her usual uniform of skirts covered up all that goodness. But the skintight leggings she wore for these games were a spotlight on my favorite thing.

As she took her place at the plate, I could see her shoulders rise on a deep breath as she stared out at Elle on the mound. Claire had yet to get a hit during any of the games we'd played so far. She didn't seem to mind, but something about the way she kept her gaze out on Elle seemed different.

Like she had something to prove.

She didn't.

What Elle and I had was long over. It was a funny, embarrassing story I told. Unlike Eric. I *did* have something to prove with that dicknozzle.

I had to throw down the proverbial gauntlet on behalf of my little rain cloud.

If I'd had a leather glove, I would've smacked him with it and challenged him to a duel.

But Claire didn't have to do that with Elle.

There was no need.

And yet.

I liked seeing the fight in her. She was normally so passive, never one to say more than necessary or ever raise her voice in excitement, but this little bit of fire might as well have been a blaze.

In our league, every player went to bat with one ball, one strike, so there were fewer opportunities for a hit. It was nice because the games were quick, but it was unfortunate for players like Claire, who needed all the chances they could get.

"Come on, Claire Bear!" Meredith shouted, and some of our teammates joined in cheering her on, but I called out a few more reminders.

"Eye on the ball and follow through!"

At the mound, Elle wound up and pitched the ball straight down the middle. Claire, with her elbows down, swung and missed.

I stepped around the fence, mimicking how she needed to fix her stance. "Elbows up."

I swore I heard her sigh even from where I stood yards

away with cars speeding by in the background and some dog barking as a couple walked it.

"You can do it."

She shook her head at me, and I shook mine right back as Elle curved her hand around her mouth, shouting to her team, "Last out! Let's get the W!"

She was trying to get into Claire's head. Not that she needed to try all that hard with how bad Claire was at softball, but I took two steps out toward Claire anyway. I was way louder than Elle.

"You got it, baby! Come on!"

On Elle's next pitch, the ball was high, and Claire rightly didn't swing.

"Yes!" Another two steps closer to her. "That's what I'm talkin' about! Good eye, baby. Good eye!"

The corner of Claire's mouth ticked up as she raised her bat again. This time, she appeared a little more confident. With her knees bent and elbows up, Claire's stance was good, and I clapped a few times.

Elle's next pitch was fast and down the middle. Claire did exactly as I said, kept her elbows up, stepped into the pitch, and followed through with all her weight.

"Yes!" I jumped up as Claire stood frozen, staring at the third basemen who ran to snatch her grounder. "Run, Claire, run!"

She snapped into reality and tossed her bat, streaking up the first base line. I ran next to her, both of us laughing as our team cheered. She stepped onto first base beautifully flushed and out of breath. I threw my arms around her, lifting her clear off the ground. "You did it!"

"I did it!"

"I'm so proud of you," I said, spinning her around, not caring that the other team was yelling at me to get off the field.

I set her back down with an unthinking kiss to her cheek and another smack to her ass.

She beamed at me, and I shuffled off the field, still clapping and cheering for her even as Lou took his place at home plate. On Elle's first pitch, he got a piece of it, popping it up in the air so it was easily caught by the shortstop. Our third out.

While the other team celebrated their win, I celebrated Claire's hit, meeting her halfway as she trotted off the field. She jumped into my waiting arms, and I think I fell halfway in love with my fake girlfriend.

Meredith ran out, making it a group hug. "Claire! You looked like a real baseball player!"

"Thanks." She laughed.

And suddenly, the rest of the team was there. Meredith let go of us to hug Hassan, although he stood stock-still, arms at his sides, as she wrapped herself around him like a human vine. I released Claire so everyone else could congratulate her with back pats and high fives.

"Time for a drink?" someone asked, and agreements went up all around.

I hooked my arm around Claire's shoulders. "You're coming, right?" She'd had a drink with us the first week, but last week, she'd ducked out. "I'm buying," I told her, hoping to sway her. "We have to celebrate your first hit."

Her lips twitched.

"Your first of many."

"Getting ahead of yourself there."

"Nope." I threw a wave to the stragglers of the team behind us, and we made our way toward the parking lot, my arm around her the whole time.

I leaned against her car as she opened her door and tossed her bag in. She faced me with her hands on her hips.

And I wanted to put my hands there too.

Instead, I folded my arms across my chest. "You should come out with us. You didn't last week."

"I need to go home and shower."

"We all do. We just played a softball game. But before you do that, come out with us."

She removed my—her—hat and combed her fingers through her ponytail, her eyes off somewhere in the distance, and I bent my head, impeding her line of vision. With her mouth quirked to the side, those two freckles on her bottom lip disappeared under her teeth, and I realized I was pressuring her, probably the same way dicknozzle used to.

"I'd like you to come, but don't feel like you have to."

She flicked her eyes to me. "You want me to?"

"Of course. I like spending time with you." And curiously enough, that was the god's honest truth. I didn't feel forced or like we needed to under the guise of making it appear as if we were together. "One drink?"

"One drink," she agreed.

Callaghan's was small and family owned, frequented by an older crowd, and almost always nearly empty in the afternoons. There was one lone pool table in the corner, a few dart boards on the wall among the tin beer signs, and a digital jukebox by the door. The bar ran along the back wall, wooden tables and chairs were sporadically set around the length of the room, and as usual, we'd all crowded in. Without a place for Claire to sit, I towed her into my lap.

At first, she fought me, muttering something about being in public, but when I banded my arm around her waist, she gave in and accepted the beer I poured her.

Now, she was delightfully loose in my arms.

"My family won't stop texting me," she said, wrapping her arm around my neck, sitting horizontal across my legs.

"About what?" I let my hand drift down to her butt, gently cupping it. So she didn't fall off me, of course.

"You. They want to know when they can meet you."

"My calendar is wide open."

After a sip of beer, she gestured with the pint glass toward the windows. "You did tell me earlier that you didn't want to meet Elle's family because it was making too much of what you were. I know I didn't imagine that."

I nodded once. "Correct."

"But you want to meet mine?"

I nodded again. "Correct."

"But we aren't together. Why would you want to meet them?"

I didn't know why. Normally, I had the attention span of a squirrel, but for some reason, I kept coming back to Claire. I sighed and scrubbed my hand over my hair, and when it flopped down on my forehead, she brushed it aside with a crooked smile.

And *that* was why. I liked putting that smile on her face. The one that was a little impatient but also amused. I don't know why I wanted to meet her parents or even why I'd thought of her to enter the contest. I couldn't explain it.

Or maybe, I simply wanted her.

Maybe I always had.

Yet, instead of saying any of that, I took the easy way out.

"It'll look better for us to win. I can learn more about you, they can vet me, and we'll get some more votes out of it, right?"

She stared into my eyes for a moment in which I thought she might catch me lying. I sort of *hoped* she might catch me lying, and I could admit all the stuff I'd been thinking, but she only accepted my answer with a nod and swig of her beer. "I guess I'll let them know we're coming next Sunday."

"Perfect," I mumbled, my stomach slightly nauseated.

What started out as a good idea, hanging out with our team, sitting Claire on my lap like we were really together, had me feeling like shit.

This whole pretending thing was torturous. Because I didn't have to act. I didn't have to pretend I liked her. It took no effort at all, but every chance she got, she reminded me we were pretending. Or, at least, she was.

She didn't like me. This wasn't real for her.

It was fake.

Fake.

Fake.

With an aggravated sigh, I tapped her hip, nudging her to move. "You ready to get out of here?"

She nodded and stood. Across from us, Hassan was in an intense conversation about state testing with Stacey, a fourth-grade teacher who'd been on the team since we'd first formed it. Meredith sat next to him, her chin in her hand, listening intently. For all her bluster, she was great at her job. Despite trying to bag Hassan every chance she got.

"We're outta here," I said to the team. Most of them booed, but Aggie waved at me from her spot by the dart board. She had told me, on multiple occasions, how happy she was that I was with Claire. Thought we made a great couple.

As if I needed to feel worse about this.

On our way out the door, I caught the look exchanged between Claire and Meredith, and as soon as we were in the parking lot, I asked her about it. "What was the—" I imitated her narrowed gaze "—to Meredith about?"

"Nothing."

"Mm-hmm." I stuck my hand in my pocket for my car keys. "What was it?"

"You're like a dog with a bone," she grumbled.

"Woof-woof."

She rolled her eyes. "She knew that I..." She stopped, sighed, and crossed her arms before starting again. "She was the one to convince me to do this...whole thing. I told her about your ridiculous plan to win the contest—which is *still* ridiculous, by the way—and she told me to do it. Best-case scenario, I won some money. Worst-case, I got to hang out with you."

I tossed my keys in the air and caught them in my fist. "I knew I always liked her."

At Claire's car, I set my elbow against the roof. "What are you up to the rest of the weekend?"

"I have some stuff to finish up for next week," she said. "Gotta get a few last-minute supplies. But right now, I'm going to go home, shower, relax, maybe do a facial treatment."

I nodded, knowing she had a lot to do for Spring Fling activities since she was always somehow roped into coordinating things like that. "You have your crazy socks or accessory picked out for Monday?"

"Of course."

"What is it?"

"I'm not telling," she said with a hint of a smile.

"Come on," I whined.

"What are you wearing?"

"Lederhosen," I said, and she burst out in laughter for the second time today. I puffed up my chest a bit over the fact that I was able to make her laugh. Multiple times.

She shook her head, unable to wipe the smile from her face as she met my eyes. "You told me straight-faced you're wearing lederhosen to school on Monday. That's why I like you."

"Aha!" I pointed my car key at her. "You do like me."

She sent me a bland look. "I told you before I did."

"Yeah, but I like hearing it."

She heaved out an impatient breath like I was her needy puppy.

I was.

The end.

Take me home.

Pet me.

Let me sleep at your feet.

"I'll most likely spend the rest of the day reading your book," I told her. "Gotta find out how it ends."

"Spoiler alert," she said, getting into her car, "they will always end up together."

"Good."

After throwing me a little finger wave, she drove away, and I stared after her car for a while.

Until I was hit with an idea.

Enjoy your shower.

LIL GRUMPMUFFIN

I will.

I'm gonna need you to send a picture of yourself when you get out.

For ethical purposes.

To make this relationship more real.

LIL GRUMPMUFFIN

You're cute but not that cute.

But you think I'm cute soo

A win is a win.

CHAPTER TWELVE

Jimmy

SAMMY THE BULL

Who's the girl?

?

SAMMY THE BULL

Don't play coy with me.

I know not to whom you refer.

SAMMY THE BULL

The one you keep posting. Red hair, freckles,
THE GIRL.

SAMMY THE BULL

Who is she?

My girlfriend.

SAMMY THE BULL

And

And...?

SAMMY THE BULL

And who is she, where is she from, how did
you meet her, why didn't you tell me
about her?

Believe it or not, my fine, feathered friend, I don't tell you everything.

SAMMY THE BULL

False.

SAMMY THE BULL

You tell me everything. Even shit I don't want to know about.

SAMMY THE BULL

And I find it suspect you haven't mentioned her at all.

SAMMY THE BULL

And yet you told me about the raccoon you saw.

CAUSE IT WAS HUGE AND OUT IN THE MIDDLE OF THE SIDEWALK LIKE SOME TRASH MONSTER WAITING TO POUNCE AT ME

SAMMY THE BULL

Anyway

SAMMY THE BULL

You're the opposite of Mike.

Please don't tell me about your sex lives.

SAMMY THE BULL

Oh.

SAMMY THE BULL

The.

SAMMY THE BULL

Irony.

SAMMY THE BULL

I mean that you never shut up unless it's important to you. He never talks unless it's important to him.

All right, all right, all right

Enough of you psychobabble.

*your

Though maybe that was actually correct.

Like

Enough of you, psychobabble.

SAMMY THE BULL

Who is she?

Her name is Claire.

I work with her. She's the librarian.

SAMMY THE BULL

So she's smart.

Really smart. Has her master's.

SAMMY THE BULL

You like her?

I really like her.

SAMMY THE BULL

I thought so.

Don't be so smug about it.

CHAPTER THIRTEEN

Claire

"Good morning, Miss Hart."

At Jimmy's droning voice, I spun around from where I'd been setting up some books for a new display and found him in full German getup. He sauntered inside the library, his eyes roaming over me. "Don't you look cute."

My wacky socks were black polka dot knee-highs, and my accessory was an antennae headband. Paired with my black skirt and red polka dot shirt, I was a ladybug. "Morning."

He offered me his drink, and I took a sip of the sweet mixture. It was really starting to grow on me.

"How was the rest of your weekend?" I asked, handing him the drink back.

We'd texted a bit, but like he'd said, he was hyperfocused and read the entirety of my book, so his messages were sporadic at best. Now, he sat on the edge of the table next to me as I finished up with the display. "I fell down a YouTube rabbit hole about raccoon videos." When I tossed him a look over my shoulder, he flapped his hand in the air. "It's a whole thing between me and Sam. Did you get everything done that you needed to?" When I nodded, he huffed. "Never did send me that picture."

"Never did say I would."

He grumbled playfully behind me before I felt him move away. "What's this?"

I glanced at the box he pawed through.

"Extra socks and stuff for the kids who forgot or didn't have any." I wasn't asked to have them, but ever since my first year working here, when one of the kids was downright heartbroken that her friends all had funny hats and she didn't, I made sure to always be prepared.

Jimmy set a tall wizard hat back into the box and closed the space between us. "You really do think of everything."

"I try."

He held up his fist between us for a bump, which I reluctantly met with my own. He blew his up.

"You're such a dork," I said, biting back a smile.

"A cute dork, though, eh?"

"Get out of here. The kids will be arriving soon."

He tweaked my ear. "Whatever my little ladybug wants. Have a nice day, Miss Hart."

"Hey."

He stopped expectantly at the door.

"Try to keep it down over there."

He dropped his head back and let out one single "Ha!" then walked across the hall to his room, where he smacked the sign, as always, and opened his door, already singing a song. It sounded like Harry Styles, but I couldn't be sure.

Until a few minutes later, as I took my place behind the circulation desk, when Harry blasted from across the hall.

I didn't know if it was a coincidence or not that Harry was one of my favorites.

Either way, I sang along until Anna popped her head around the door of the library.

"Hey, good morning," I said, smiling.

She waved shyly, and I gestured for her to come behind the counter.

"I got a book I thought you might like. I put it in the Little Library this morning."

She bounced on her toes. "What's it about?"

"It doesn't take place in space, but it's about a twelve-year-old girl who is having really weird dreams, and one day she wakes up inside the dream. To get out, she makes friends with another girl from the dreamland, but she also kinda has a crush on her too."

Anna's answering grin was the reason I was a librarian. "Thanks, Miss Hart."

"Of course. That's what I'm here for."

She scooted out of the room, waving to Jimmy where he stood at his door, greeting each of his students as they entered his room with a semi-complicated handshake. Every kid had their own with him, and I had no idea how he remembered them all.

When his kids were all inside, he winked at me before spinning around, hollering, "Guten morgan!"

A chorus of confused *huhs* and *whats* rang out.

"It means good morning in German."

"What are you wearing?" one of the kids asked.

He stuck his foot out to the side, his hands fisted on his hips. "Lederhosen. Rad, right?"

Another kid yelled, "Classic!"

And Jimmy pointed to them. "Gosh darn right, they're classic." Then he clapped a few times to a beat, a familiar callback. "Wake me up!"

His entire class yelled back, "Before you go-go!"

Then they quieted down, and he said, "Everybody say good morning to Miss Hart."

His class droned good morning to me, and I waved.

How he even knew I was still standing behind him watching this all take place, I didn't know. He was endlessly surprising. And I was sure it wouldn't stop any time soon.

The rest of the week followed in similar fashion. Jimmy showing up every morning to greet me in the library, maxed out in whatever the theme was. Tuesday was school colors day, and he arrived with purple hair. Wednesday was 1980s day, and he dressed up like the missing fourth white member of Run-D.M.C. and carried around an actual boom box on his shoulder any time he left his room. Thursday was the ice cream social at lunch, which I was pulled in to help with, and even though it wasn't a dress-up day, Jimmy strutted into school wearing the uniform of an old-school 1950s soda shop guy, tiny hat included.

"My least favorite thing today was you playing 'Candy Man' on repeat," I told him as we left school together.

"If you had a least favorite, that means you had a favorite. Which is…"

I tipped my head side to side as I reviewed the day. I'd spent half of it cleaning up melted ice cream. "The push-up contest you had in the hall."

"I smashed them all," he said, nodding proudly.

I refused to laugh. "They're eight. You're bragging about beating eight-year-olds in a push-up contest."

"Hey. Tasha's a tough cookie. For a bit there, I was worried she'd actually get to twenty."

"You're ridiculous."

"That's why you like me."

"Only certain times of the day."

His honey-brown eyes lit up so my insides knotted all up. "How about right now?"

"Everyone loves you. I don't know why you're so concerned about me liking you."

He pursed his lips in silence as he followed me to my car. I never quite knew what to do with him when he was quiet, like the calm before the storm. The best thing to do was run away.

"You don't have any food allergies, do you?" I asked as I slung my stuff into my car.

He shook his head. "Why?"

"My mom is planning on a banquet for you." I shot my hand out. "But don't let it go to your head. She does this for everyone. You're not special."

He slapped his hand over his heart. "You know how to wound a man, Claire."

"Sorry," I said flatly. "You're very special. The only man who could pull this off." I waved a hand down the length of him, referring to his get-up, and he flexed his bicep.

I shook my head at him, earning a grin.

He was so annoying.

"See you tomorrow, Miss Hart."

———

The next morning, I was running late after getting stuck in traffic and needing to stop for gas. I was usually one of the first people in the building, but today, I jogged inside only minutes before the first bus pulled up. I hightailed it to the library, the laces of my sneakers whipping against my ankle, but I didn't bother to stop to retie them.

Jimmy was waiting outside his room, his usual smile greeting me. Today was field day, when every grade would partake in outdoor activities and games. Kindergarten through second grade in the morning and third through fifth grade in the afternoon. I was expected to help out all day, so I'd put on black leggings with a matching zip-up and braided my hair in two pigtails.

"There's my little heartbreaker," he said, his eyes dragging over me from top to bottom. When he noticed my laces, he kneeled down and retied them, but stayed on the floor for a heart-stopping minute when he tipped his head back, his dark eyes flaring with heat.

"What are you doing?" I rasped, trying not to think about how this wasn't the first time he'd been on his knees in front of me, and how much I would love to be anywhere else but at school when he was in this position again.

"Admiring the view."

I swallowed down the watermelon in my throat, rolled my eyes, and tugged the big lug up. "You're—"

"Ridiculous, I know." He stuffed his hands in his pockets, looming over me with an arrogant smile. Like he knew he had my pulse rioting.

Always a game with him.

"I'm late," I said, unlocking the library door. "I told Aggie I'd help her set up."

I tossed my purse and lunch on my desk and hustled back out into the hall as I heard the first pitter-patter of little feet. "I gotta run. I'll see you later."

If he responded, I didn't hear it as I took off toward the back doors. Aggie was already outside setting up different games. She instructed me to finish filling up balloons for the water balloon toss, and after twenty minutes and two laundry baskets' worth of balloons, I carried them over to the lines she'd drawn for the game. Then we constructed the small obstacle course.

After a few minutes, the volunteer parents showed up. Three women and two men, including one named Austin, the dad of Shandi in Jimmy's class.

"She's really sweet," I told him as we finished spray-painting lines in the grass for the three-legged race.

"Yeah, she is. So much like her mother."

I took the canister back from him, and we turned, heading back toward the group.

"I only wish Shandi had had more time with her."

I slanted my gaze to him in question.

"Tessa passed when Shandi was only three."

"Oh my god." I pressed my hand to my heart. "I'm so sorry."

He accepted my condolences with a nod. "It took a while for me to find my footing being a single dad, but..." He shrugged. "We're doing it, me and Shan."

I offered him a smile. "Like I said, Shandi is a great kid, so I know you're doing a wonderful job at home."

"Thank you. I appreciate that." He smiled back at me. And though I'd never ever date a parent of a student, I couldn't help but admire him. With dark skin, close-cropped hair, and light eyes, he was really good-looking. Plus, he earned bonus points for helping out. "Thanks for coming in today. It's usually like pulling teeth to get parent volunteers in."

He propped his hands on his hips once we stopped by Aggie. Mrs. Kaplan was making her way outside, leading the first classes out of the back doors. "I recently transferred jobs, which has allowed me a more flexible schedule. I'm planning on coming in more often."

"Really? That would be so helpful to us here."

Before we could continue our conversation, we were assigned to different games while the kindergarteners ran buck wild. Every so often, I'd catch Austin's gaze, and we'd smile good-naturedly at the kid who cried because he lost the race or the one who fell and scraped her knee. When the hour was up, the wee ones were scooted back inside to make room for the first graders. They weren't much better than the kindergarteners. There was less arguing over who won, but no less screaming.

"Are all school events wild like this?" Austin asked once the first graders filed back into the school.

"Not all of them but a good many of them."

He blew out an amused breath, his muscular arms crossed over his chest. "Might have to rethink this whole volunteering thing."

"No, don't," I said with a laugh. Out of the corner of my eye, I noted the second graders race out to the field with Jimmy pulling up the rear. "If you don't like this kind of thing, we always need people to help out in the workroom or even in the library with me."

"Oh yeah?"

I nodded as Jimmy cupped his hands around his mouth and yelled, "Listening ears on! Don't make me sit you down and force you to listen to disco music on repeat."

Austin directed his thumb in Jimmy's direction. "That guy's a trip. Shandi loves him."

"Yeah. He's everyone's favorite."

Just then, a head full of curly dark hair raced over, slamming into Austin. "Daddy!"

"Hey, honey girl," he said, sinking down to hug her. He ran his big hands over her head. "What happened to your hair?"

"My hair tie broke."

He stood and fished into his pocket for an elastic band. My mouth hung open as Austin proceeded to pull her hair back and make quick work of her hair, braiding it.

"Look at you."

He spared me a grin. Then he kissed his daughter's cheek and sent her off. She ran toward Jimmy and his class.

"It's a shame more dads don't learn how to do their daughter's hair," he said with a shrug. "It's a lot of quality time for us, me watching YouTube videos for an Elsa braid or whatever else she wants me to learn to do with her hair. Gives us a chance to talk a lot as I practice."

"That's so sweet," I said, noticing Jimmy watching me. I lifted my hand in acknowledgment, but he didn't smile or even nod in return.

"Hey, can you two run the water balloon toss this time?" Aggie asked. "I think Mr. and Mrs. Hightower are losing their patience with it."

I peeked around Austin to find the parents of Brandan Hightower arguing quietly off to the side, and I sucked air through my teeth. "Yep. We're on it."

"Great. I'm going to put him on the obstacle course, and her on the races." Then she clapped her hands once and trotted off like we were playing in the big state final game. Austin and I exchanged a smile and headed off toward the balloon toss.

We spent time explaining how each pair of kids had to throw the balloon back and forth and then take one step back away from each other. The last team to still have their balloon won, although most of the teams burst their balloons within a few steps. At one point, Austin and I decided to join in on the fun and lobbed a balloon back and forth. The kids laughed and squealed around us as we stepped farther and farther away from each other. Eventually, he launched the yellow balloon at me with so much force, it burst when I caught it. He ran to me in apology, even though we were both laughing. Thank god I was wearing black.

Again, I noticed Jimmy staring at me. Or rather, glaring.

I waved, but he only turned away from me, his arms stiff at his sides. But I didn't get to talk to him about it because the second graders were dismissed, and so we were. Time for lunch.

I ate in the library, all the while wondering what Jimmy

was upset about. His door was closed, though I heard his class through it. He almost never closed his door.

Especially on a day like today, when the school was in an uproar of fun.

I finished my salad and yogurt then made my way back outside for round two of field day. The afternoon passed more slowly, with the older kids needing less direction and wrangling.

Anna stopped me toward the end of the fifth-grade hour. "I finished the book."

"Already?"

She nodded proudly.

"Good for you. I put another book in the Little Library you might like. This one is about a girl that's a little bit older than you are, but it's a space opera so I thought you'd like it."

"Awesome! Thanks, Miss Hart!"

"No problem!" I waved as she scooted off, her best friend, Carlos, in tow.

Once all the kids were back inside, we cleaned up the debris of broken balloons, loose balls, and Hula-Hoops. Austin shuffled into the school with me, explaining that he was taking Shandi home with him.

"I'm right across from her room."

"Perfect. You can tell me more about what you need from volunteers in the library."

As we walked, I told him parents usually came in to read, but the more adventurous ones learned the computer system and helped me organize books if they had a few hours to spare.

"Well, you can count me in to help whenever you need it," he said outside of the library door.

"You're a lifesaver. The end of the year is a mess for me, and I'm always begging the PTO for more volunteers."

"So, I should sign up through them?"

I nodded. "They'll be sending out a form soon."

He bowed his head. "Well, it was really nice talking with you today, Miss Hart."

"Call me Claire."

"Claire." He smiled.

That was when Jimmy opened his door.

"Hey, Mr. Ewing. I'm here to take Shandi home," Austin said.

Jimmy's eyes zipped between the two of us before landing back on him. "Yeah, sure. Shandi, up and at 'em. Time to go."

Shandi appeared at the door a few seconds later, her glittery pink backpack on her shoulders. She and Jimmy performed their handshake, all the while Austin grinned happily at his daughter. Then he took her hand in his and offered a wave to Jimmy and then to me. "Have a nice weekend."

"You too," I said. "Bye, Shandi."

When I turned back to Jimmy, his eyes were narrowed, mouth in a thin line.

"What's wrong? You look like Starbucks burned down."

He huffed and spun toward his classroom. "All my car pickup kids, line up."

I shrugged and pivoted around, dropping down into my chair exhausted while the sounds of all the kids exiting the school faded into white noise. Scrolling on my phone, I hadn't realized how much time had passed until Jimmy stormed his way into the library and slammed the door.

"What the hell, Claire?"

I startled. "What?"

"*What?*" he repeated, throwing his hands up. "What was that?"

I looked around the library, unsure what was happening. "With what?"

He flung his hand out to the closed door. "With Shandi's dad."

"Austin?" I sat up, still shaking my head in confusion. "What about him?"

"You were flirting with him."

"I was not flirting with him."

"Oh, come on, Claire. You were smiling and laughing," he said in the most accusatory tone I'd ever heard. As if smiling and laughing were a crime.

"I do that sometimes." I jerked up from my seat to grab my stuff. "No reason to be so affronted."

He followed me to the door. "I am affronted. On all fronts!"

I swung around on him. "You're ridiculous is what you are. And lower your voice. There is no reason for you to be yelling here, especially at me, over nothing."

"Over nothing?" When I turned, he slapped his hand on the door so I couldn't open it, his mouth next to my ear. "You're my girlfriend, and the two of you were looking awfully chummy all goddamn day."

I angled my head, fury pricking over my skin. There were so many words to pick apart, I didn't know where to start, so I plucked out what seemed the most obvious. "I am not your girlfriend."

"The hell you aren't."

I ducked under his arm, needing to get away from his now-familiar smell and the heat of his chest against my back that made this argument feel all too real. Keeping my voice low and even, I held out my hand. "Despite what you think you saw today, I wasn't flirting. I was having fun with the father of one of our students, who is going to be coming in to volunteer at the library."

He shot his arms out at his sides, his eyes wide, his brow raised as if to say *See?* "Volunteering." To make matters worse, he added air quotes to the word.

In the short time Jimmy and I had gotten to know each other, I hadn't realized he had the capability for being such an asshole. "Why are you acting like this right now?"

"Because you're supposed to be with *me*, Claire." For the first time since he'd thundered in here, I saw a flicker of the truth. He was hurt. Although with how he was hollering and condescendingly air quoting words, I had a hard time finding any sympathy for him.

"I don't understand where all this anger is coming from. Even if I were flirting with Austin, which I was not, it wouldn't be a problem to begin with because we're not actually together." I pointed my index finger at him. "You have no reason or *right* to be jealous."

He batted my hand out of the way, stepping closer. "I have every right when you're mine, for all intents and purposes."

I closed my eyes, my heart stumbling over that statement. *You're mine.* Only to be pushed down and run over by that second phrase. *For all intents and purposes.*

We weren't together. What we had between us wasn't real. It was for show. For a contest. And he was pissed that I had given the game away.

I held my bag a little tighter, determined to get away from him. There was no winning this argument if he was going to act like he had some claim on me, when this was all a competition to him. I shoved him away from the door and stomped out into the hall. "I am not some pawn. This might all be fun and games for you, but I'm a person with real feelings, Jimmy." I locked the door, meeting his eyes one last time. "I'm doing exactly what is expected of me. If you have a problem with that, you can find someone else to play your game with."

Then I spun on my heel and marched out of the school and away from my fake boyfriend.

CHAPTER FOURTEEN

Jimmy

Claire didn't answer any of my texts Friday night, so I shouldn't have been surprised when she messaged the softball group thread to inform us she wouldn't be at the game. The players looked at me for explanation, and I made some excuse about her not feeling well, when really it was me who wasn't.

I was sick to my stomach. Losing my goddamn mind.

After we lost the game, I didn't feel like going to Callaghan's and instead headed home to once again try to get a hold of Claire. I didn't bother showering out of my sweaty clothes and instead plopped myself down at the dining room table and called her.

She didn't pick up the first time. So I tried again.

And again.

And one last time until she answered. "What do you want?"

"To talk. I'm sorry."

She responded with silence, and I dragged my hand through my hair.

"I'm really sorry. I barely slept last night, thinking about how I acted. You're right. I was an asshole."

"Yep."

I sighed. "You're not going to make this easy on me, are you?"

"Nope."

"I don't have an excuse. I saw you with him, and I...I don't know. I felt... Shit, Claire..."

"What?" she prompted curtly. "I want to hear it. You felt what...?"

I dropped my head into my hand, holding my phone closer to my ear. "I'm not great at expressing my feelings. You want me to entertain a crowd of ten-year-olds? Sure. Tell a story at a party? Of course. But I can't do feelings."

"Why not?"

I rubbed the heel of my hand into my eye. "I don't know. Because I'm a Gemini. Because letting anyone know how I really feel makes me uncomfortable. Because I'm shit with words when it's important. Take your pick."

"So," she said, dragging out that one syllable. "Gemini men really are the worst."

I huffed out a laugh. "Yeah."

And when she didn't say anything else, I thunked my head down on my table. "Want to come over?"

"Not really."

"Stone-cold."

Silence. Yet again.

"Yeah. Good idea. I have to clean anyway. I want the house to look nice the first time you see it. Best foot forward and all."

"Jimmy," she huffed, and I slumped back against the chair, my head feeling like it weighed a thousand pounds.

"I hate when you say my name like that."

"You exasperate me."

"I exasperate myself." It was the absolute truth. It was hard to go through life like an unwieldy cart, running downhill and careening out of control. Sometimes, I didn't even know which direction I was going in next. "Can I still take you to your parents' tomorrow?"

She didn't answer for a long time, and maybe this time, my cart would crash and burn with the one good thing I had going for me.

"Yeah. We better see this thing through, right?"

See this thing through, she said. Like I was a difficult task she had to endure. Not even the fun-loving class clown. But the detention she had to sit through because I got her in trouble.

Here I was, the idiot who thought I could win a stupid contest with her. I was falling all over myself for her, while she was doing me a favor, clearly not having any fun anymore.

"I'm sorry," I said, curling my fingers into a fist on my thigh. "I don't know what I was thinking yesterday. Well, I mean, obviously, I wasn't thinking, which you know is a problem for me. I was immature and a dick. I understand if you're done with me."

"Done with you?" Her voice was almost a whisper. "Why would you say that?"

"Because...I'm using you. This whole thing, I knew you'd say yes to me because you're a good person. I took advantage. I was selfish. I am selfish. And I'm sorry."

She let out what sounded like an annoyed sniff. "You didn't push me into anything. You didn't take advantage of me. I jumped off the cliff with my eyes wide open."

For the first time in what felt like years, a smile lifted the corner of my mouth. She had no idea what that meant, for her to jump off the cliff *with* me.

"Aside from that breakdown or whatever it was you had yesterday, it's been really fun spending time with you. And quite frankly, it's freaking me out a little bit that you're ready to give in so easily. That's not like you at all."

"Yeah, well..." I scrubbed my hand over my face. I both

hated and loved how she saw the worst parts of me and still wanted to pick me up and dust me off. Like *I* was the one who needed comforting. She didn't realize how utterly wonderful she was. "You know I'm no good at relationships. Fake or not."

"You're no good because you don't try," she corrected with a gentle voice. The same one she used with our students. "You said you break up with people before they can find out what you're lacking, but did you ever think you have more to offer than you know?"

I stood up from the chair, needing to walk, to relieve some of this sudden energy buzzing through my veins.

"You can't be that oblivious to the way people fall in love with you," she went on. "You know everyone loves you. You underestimate yourself."

And I couldn't help the hope that bloomed in my chest. If everyone fell in love with me, did that mean her too?

"I bet you'd be really good at relationships if you put your mind to it," she said, and that sounded oddly like a challenge.

"You know what?" I grinned to myself. "I bet I could."

CHAPTER FIFTEEN

Jimmy

I showed up to Claire's apartment with a bouquet of pink tulips.

"What are these for?"

"A tulip for my little tulip."

With her face buried in them, I couldn't see her mouth, but I could tell she was smiling by the way her eyes crinkled. "Let me put these in a vase, and then we can go."

I followed her into the kitchen. "Is there anything pressing I should know about your family? Topics to avoid?"

"Yeah. Don't ask the boys about who they're dating."

I wouldn't anyway, but now I was curious. "Why?"

Stretching up onto her toes, she reached for a tall, slender glass from a top cabinet, and when she had trouble, I assisted her. Real hero move.

"Thanks," she murmured, moving to the side, which only brought her ass into direct contact with my groin. Today, she wore a pretty sundress, not very far off from the color of the tulips. It was loose and long, and it obscured all her best bits, but I felt them. I only hoped she couldn't feel what it did to me.

At least not *yet*.

But I was determined to get there.

I leaned against the counter as she filled up the vase with water at the sink. "Aiden went to visit the Cleveland trio."

"Ryan, Tristan, and Rosie?" I asked, making sure I had the Hart family tree correct, and she nodded.

"They all went to the bar for a bit, and Ryan was hitting on some girl, but she ultimately went home with Aiden, and they went out on a date last week, so Ryan's pissed at Aiden, but then Ryan, in his fit of rage, also revealed in the family chat that Tristan's a virgin."

My brow rose.

"So Tristan's pissed that he somehow got dragged into it. He's supposedly in love with his critique partner."

"Saving himself. Very cool."

She set the tulips on the windowsill before turning to me. "Yeah, but she doesn't know he's in love with her. So, that's a whole thing."

I nodded. I understood that more than she knew.

"Okay, don't ask about girlfriends. Got it."

"And don't ask about Evan's wife."

"What's going on there?" I lagged behind her as she picked up her cell phone from the counter, absently checking it before tossing it into her purse.

She shrugged, the movement causing a few strands of her sunshine hair to fall in front of her shoulder. I pushed them back, allowing my fingertips to trail over the skin of her collarbone. She froze, her hand in the middle of the space between us, so I stepped closer, forcing those fingers, with nails painted pastel purple, to touch my chest.

"You look really pretty," I told her. "No headband today, though. Half a point deduction."

She fought a smile, her mouth thinning into a wiggling line. "From whom?"

"The Russian judge. Harsh, that one."

She pushed her palm into the center of my chest, her eyes rolling playfully as she scooted past me. Once we were back down by my car, I opened the passenger side door for her.

"What's with all the chivalry today?" she asked when we were both settled inside. "If this is still about Friday, you apologized, I accepted. I'm not holding it against you."

I slanted my gaze to her, my hand on my key in the ignition. "Maybe you should. Maybe you shouldn't forgive so easily."

Her orange brows narrowed. "If I held a grudge against every guy who did me wrong, I'd be single for the rest of my life."

I aimed for an indifference I didn't feel as I started up Mariah. "You shouldn't settle. You deserve the best. Only the best."

As I pulled out onto the street, I could feel her steady gaze on the side of my face. She stayed quiet while I filled her in on the game yesterday and flipped through my Spotify, asking her opinion on what we should listen to, only for her to snatch my phone out of my hand, mumbling something about "No more 'Breakfast at Tiffany's.'"

Which was offensive. Deep Blue Something was classic.

"I don't get you," she said after a while, once she finally settled on another one of her indie pop songs. I had to check out her playlists.

"You don't get me? What's that supposed to mean?" At a red light, I faced her. "I think I'm pretty uncomplicated."

"You're uncomplicated..." She circled her hands in the air. "In a complicated way."

I motioned for her to continue as I drove through the green light.

"We started this to win a contest, and..." She let out a rough exhale. "I know it's not real, but sometimes you say things to me, and I have a hard time knowing what's real and what's not."

I sent her a wry glance. "I always say whatever's on my mind. No filter, remember?"

"Except for when it's big emotions, and that's why you're confusing. Because you say these really sweet things that I know don't mean anything to you, but…" She licked her lips, her fingers knotted in her lap. "They mean something to me."

I covered her nervous hands with mine, grazing my thumb over her knuckles. "I say whatever's on my mind, but that doesn't mean it's not real. I'd never lie, especially to you."

"See? That's exactly what I'm talking about. This is fake. You can't say stuff like that to me with that voice and not expect me to get ideas."

"Ideas?" I spared a second to smile over at her. "Sounds ominous."

She breathed out what sounded like an annoyed exhale, but before we could continue the conversation, she pointed to a dirt road. "That's it."

"There's no road sign."

"I know. The GPS always gets confused."

I followed Claire's direction, ignoring the voice coming from my phone, informing me not to turn for another three-quarters of a mile. Mariah's tires crunched over gravel and dirt, large rocks and trees eventually giving way to neatly trimmed grass and, in the distance beyond the house, fields.

I parked next to a slew of other cars all lined up outside the unattached garage. The house itself was not as big as I'd pictured, with gray siding and a wraparound porch filled with rocking chairs and potted plants, a few hanging wind chimes that all clinged and clanged at different times. There was a dilapidated barn, a shed that was half the size of the house, another garage of sorts, and…an outhouse?

I pointed to it. "What's that?"

"My mom's She-Shed. Used to be the outhouse."

I thrust my fist in the air, having guessed right. "Huge property."

"Evan lives over that hill." She pointed in the direction of his house, hidden from view, as she led me to the front door. "We have a few golf carts to drive up to the farm if the weather's nice. Otherwise, it's in one of the trucks."

I nodded because it made sense, but I'd never hung out with any actual farmers before. I didn't know what to expect.

Although it certainly wasn't someone yelling, "Oh, fuck off, Ryan!" as a little girl chased a cat toward us.

Claire sidestepped them. "Hey, Riley."

The little one barely paused to wave. "Hi! Bye! Come here, Felix."

"Felix almost never comes out of hiding," Claire told me, taking my hand in hers to tow me further into absolute chaos.

Bon Jovi blared from some unknown place as a body strolled across the small hall, a door clicking shut behind them.

"Bathroom," Claire informed me, stepping into the kitchen, which was the source of the music. Her mother, I presumed, had her back to us, facing the counter as she put together a kick-ass charcuterie board. Her dad was dancing with a golden retriever, holding its paws in his hands. On a spin, he spotted us.

"Oh hey, Pikachu!"

"Pikachu?" I repeated with a laugh.

"Evan was big into Pokémon when I was born," Claire explained.

Her father pulled her in for a hug while the dog hopped around on his hind legs, begging for a rub. I gave it to him.

"Dad, this is Jimmy. Jimmy, this is my dad."

I'd barely gripped his hand for a shake, hadn't even gotten out a greeting, before her mother was barreling at us.

"Sweetie pie! So glad you're here, and who is this?"

"Don't act like you didn't Facebook-stalk him, Mom."

I grinned. "Nice to meet you, Mrs. Hart, Mr. Hart."

"Please, call me Toni. And this is Scott."

Toni was short and bottom heavy like her daughter, but almost completely gray, though her eyes were similar in their diamond shine. Scott, on the other hand, was tall, well-built, and covered in tattoos. His T-shirt was one of those ones found in thrift stores or at fairs with a wolf howling at the moon. I was pretty sure he wore it unironically. And I loved him instantly.

"Thanks for having me."

Scott slapped my shoulder. "Had to meet the new guy. We didn't like the last one."

I nodded. "Me either."

"You know him?" Toni asked, shoving a bowl of fruit salad into my hands.

"I know *of* him. Ran into him at one of our softball games. He was on the other team."

"That's right." Scott snapped. "You got Claire into sports now."

"That's a stretch," Claire said, dutifully taking the platter of tomato and mozzarella her mom handed to her.

"She had a good hit two weeks ago," I said. "We're working on it."

She only snorted in my direction.

"Well, you have to understand we're very protective of our kids," Toni said, and I nodded.

"Of course. I'm happy to withstand any interrogation you might have for me."

"Attaboy." Scott scooped up the plate of shrimp and veggie skewers. "Come on outside. Meet everybody."

I followed him out through the sliding door, which had to have been a new addition since the wood paneling on the walls appeared to be from two centuries ago. Or at least, what I could see of it. I'd never seen more knickknacks, wall hangings, and decorative tin flowers in my entire life.

I couldn't be sure, but I swore I heard Toni say behind me, "He's cute," before being shushed by Claire. I bit back a grin as I walked out into the backyard, laden with tables and umbrellas, coolers of drinks, and random kids' toys spread out. An excellent tree house stood about fifty yards away, next to a swing set that appeared ready to crumble, and a volleyball net set up.

"This is great," I told Scott, setting down the fruit on the table Toni pointed to.

"I know, right? Been here over thirty years now."

I attempted to do the mental math in my head, guessing how old the Harts were. Mid to late sixties, maybe. "Claire told me you guys both used to be higher-ups in Big Pharma and left it all behind."

He inhaled deeply like a man who enjoyed fresh air. "Yep. Best decision we ever made. We were both unhappy, running ourselves ragged, and quite frankly, it was wearing on our hearts, you know? There's only so much bad shit you can put out into the world without expecting it to come back and bite you in the ass."

I liked that Scott didn't have any compunction about telling the truth. "So, what made you decide to buy a farm?"

"That was my wife's idea. Her grandparents lived on a farm in Indiana, and she spent all her summers out there with them. Loved it. We knew we wanted to do something we loved, that was fun, and that would leave a positive impact on the world."

"Well," I started, watching Claire talking with her mom, "you did have Claire. Right there's your positive impact on the world."

Scott barked out a laugh and slapped my back. "You're goddamn right. Come on, come meet my other impacts. Not all so positive." He ushered me toward a guy by the grill as he said, "We never meant to have so many kids, but after the first two, we moved here and thought, *might as well keep going*. Plus, as babies, they're so goddamn cute. But then they get older and... This is Evan."

"Hey, nice to meet you," I said, and Evan looked me up and down before acknowledging me with a nod then returning to his job at the grill. Like his father, he was tall and muscular, presumably from all the manual labor, but not nearly as friendly.

"I hope you like your burgers bloody."

"I, uh..."

"Knock it off, Evan," Claire said, suddenly next to me.

"If he can't take the heat, he should stay out of the kitchen, Pikachu."

I toggled my eyes between the siblings, uncertain what to say. Her parents were cool, and I didn't know what to do with this first test.

"I'm just messing with you," Evan said after a while, and I blew out a breath, relieved I wasn't about to insult the chef.

Claire punched her brother in the arm and hauled me to a table, where her sister Rosie sat. I only knew from the crutches that rested next to her. Like Claire had said, her sister was beautiful, blue-eyed and dark-haired with pouty lips and thick eyelashes, but I assumed it wasn't all natural since she was the makeup influencer. I noticed Claire watching me intently, and I tipped my head, not sure what she was so curious about. A moment passed before she settled down at the table and introduced me to Rosie and her husband, Mark. Both lovely people.

"What was that face for?" I asked quietly once I had her attention again.

With Rosie occupied on her cell phone, Claire dropped her voice so only I could hear. "Whenever I bring a guy home and they meet Ro, they usually fawn over her."

"Oh...kay." I frowned. "Was I supposed to?"

"No, but that's why I was surprised."

Yes, Rosie was objectively pretty, like a commercial for lotion pretty, but she wasn't Claire. "Man, every single guy you've ever brought home must've been a real loser."

"That include you?"

"Ma'am," I intoned, and she laughed.

After searching the yard, she asked no one in particular. "Where's Aiden?"

"Late, as usual," someone said, another one of Claire's siblings.

"Like you aren't late all the time too," Rosie snipped with an eye roll. Not one of amusement like Claire gave me all the time.

"That's Ryan and Tristan." Claire tipped her chin to the one with a baseball cap on first then the other who looked exactly like him except he was missing a hat and a beard but had the addition of a small child on his shoulders.

Ryan strode right over to me, his hands casually in his shorts pockets. "Heard you play ball."

"In a summer league, yeah."

"We should play sometime," he said with a challenge in his voice.

"I'd love that. I'm a big fan of your team."

He eyed me from under the shade of his cap then nodded

once and headed off in the direction of the open yard, where he chased the dog, calling. "Come 'ere, Joe!"

Tristan was slower to greet me, busy playing with the little girl, who was apparently Evan's other daughter, Ari, but once he sat down at the table next to ours, I learned he was working on a book of short stories for his thesis and that he shared an apartment with Ryan.

Once Aiden showed up, the entire family welcomed him with an assortment of claps, shouts, and a boo coming from Ryan. Aiden shot his middle finger up at his brother, uncaring that his two nieces were watching it all.

The Hart family sang, danced, cursed, and made fun of one another in equal measure.

"I'm staying here forever," I informed Claire after we each had a plate of food from the banquet Toni had indeed spread out for us. Then again, she was feeding an army.

"You can. I'm not."

"Cool. I'll sleep on the floor. I'll be good with a pillow and sleeping bag."

"You're ridiculous."

I threw my arm around her shoulders, tucking my nose against her hair. "But that's why you love me."

"Aw, look how cute you two are," Toni said from somewhere I couldn't see because I was too busy counting the freckles on Claire's eyelids as she slowly blinked at me.

Her lips parted, but no words left her tongue, and I jumped without thinking.

Thankfully, her mouth was a soft place to land.

CHAPTER SIXTEEN

Claire

The fork I'd been holding dropped to my plate when Jimmy's mouth touched mine. My eyes widened in surprise, but the hand he had on my shoulder moved to the back of my head, his lips pulling softly at mine, and I gave in. Figured I might as well enjoy this wild ride while I could.

The kiss was chaste and soft yet lit a fire inside me that spread from my belly to the tips of my fingers that found their way to his neck of their own volition. Like they didn't want to let him go either. His own fingers curled into my hair, tugging ever so slightly, changing the angle, and if this was how he kissed me, his fake girlfriend, I wondered how he kissed his real girlfriends.

His mouth curved into a smile against mine, an amused sound leaving the back of his throat, and it echoed in my ears.

Or it was Evan grumping, "Not around the kids, huh?"

Jimmy backed away a centimeter, allowing me to gulp down fresh air, smell the grass, as opposed to that spicy-woodsy scent I'd become used to. Even before he laid that earth-shattering hint of a kiss on me.

I blinked away from him and into the sunshine, clearing

my throat as Rosie raised her brow. "My god, you look like you never kissed him before."

The laugh that I forced out was downright manic.

Next to me, Jimmy pressed a kiss to my temple and hair, offering the back of my neck one last squeeze. "Nah, I just tend to take her breath away is all."

I dug into my food, stuffing my mouth full so I didn't have a chance to give myself away while Mom held up her phone, my sister on FaceTime.

"Everybody's here," Mom squealed, arcing her phone around the yard so Julie could see.

"Hey, hey," Julie said then Mom shoved the screen right up in Jimmy's face.

"And look, Claire's new boyfriend."

"Mom," I whined around a bite of watermelon, cucumber, and feta salad.

"Hey, Julie. I'm Jimmy. Nice to meet you."

"I heard you two have your radio interview this week," Julie said, and I had no idea how she knew that.

"Yep. Wednesday."

"I don't know if you know this, but my sister gets stage fright. I'm almost positive that fear will translate to microphones and sound waves."

"Oh my god," I moaned, searching out Ryan. "You're right. Joe is the only one to be trusted."

Joe trounced up to me when he heard his name, begging for food. I slid him a piece of chicken.

Ryan saluted me with a shrimp skewer. "Told ya."

"Well," Jimmy started, "I'm sure it'll be fine. My girl's never had a problem talking to me, and that's all it'll be, right?" He smiled over at me. "Like we're talking to each other."

"With the world listening," Rosie added, and I eyed her.

Evan shook his head. "It's a local station. It'll be a few thousand at best."

I rubbed at my forehead, and Jimmy chuckled. "Hey, all right, let's cool it on the audience talk. The point is, it's supposed to be fun."

I nodded to myself. That was right. The whole point of this was fun. Not serious.

Not at all real.

No matter how much I liked seeing him with my family, joking around and chatting about nothing in particular, fitting right in.

Kissing me.

After a few minutes, Mom and Julie hung up, and Dad plopped down in a chair after getting seconds. "So, Jim, tell me what it is you like about my daughter."

"Oh, come on, Dad," I moaned.

Jimmy toyed with the ends of my hair. "Let me count the ways."

Tristan settled his back against his folding chair, raising his face up to the sky. "'To the depth and breadth and height. My soul can reach, when feeling out of sight for the ends of being ideal and grace.'"

Jimmy lit up next to me. "That's beautiful, man. Did you write that?"

"No." Tristan dropped his chin, his brow crimped as he met Jimmy's gaze. "Elizabeth Barrett Browning. A pretty famous poet of the Romantic movement."

Jimmy nodded. "No wonder why 'let me count the ways' sounded so familiar. And, damn, that's really romantic."

That had everybody chuckling.

Mom held her chin in her hand. "You've worked together for a few years, so what took so long?"

Jimmy slanted his gaze to me for a moment, his tongue

skirting his lower lip, his eyes on my own mouth, and my pulse raced. That kiss had been for show.

Hadn't it?

It was impossible to tell.

Especially when he turned to my mother. "I don't know how much Claire has told you about me or how much you've found out from your stalking of my social media…"

"Only that you're a really good teacher and that you have a lot of pictures of different pints of beer."

"Oh, that's for an app I have. I input all the different beers I've drunk and—"

"Untappd?" Ryan asked, and when Jimmy nodded, my brother took out his phone. "I'm on there too. I'm gonna follow you."

Rosie waved her hand. "So, anyway, you were saying…"

"Oh." Jimmy wiped his palm over his mouth, his gaze drifting down for a long while, and I wondered if he was stuck because he didn't know what his lie would be. Or if, like my stupid, arrogant heart wished, he was struggling because he had trouble expressing important emotions.

I held my breath, my hand reflexively finding his, hoping there was a reason he picked me. That he wanted *me*.

He lifted his head and laced his fingers with mine, answering without looking at me. "I'm loud and obnoxious and have ten thousand thoughts going through my head at one time, so sometimes it's hard for me to sort through everything. It's hard for me to notice what's right in front of me. And Claire is so…" He gave a hard shake of his head, his curls bouncing. "She's a precious stone. If you don't dig down deep, you'll miss how bright she shines, so it took me a while until I realized that she'd been there all along, waiting for me to find her. Plus, you know, I have a thing for headbands and skirts."

Tears pricked at the corners of my eyes, and I dipped my

chin down, blinking rapidly, while Mom crowed about how perfect Jimmy was. Tristan clapped him on the shoulder. Aiden saluted him with his drink, and Dad actually gave him a standing ovation.

Everyone in my family—even Ryan—was smitten with him. And it was a problem.

Because I had no idea what was true or false anymore.

"All right. Let's go. Who's up for a game?" Ryan grabbed a volleyball and tossed it in the air. Riley and Ari sprinted toward the net, followed by most everyone else. Evan clapped once and put his hands up, silently asking for the ball.

While the entire Hart clan ambled over toward the net, I kept Jimmy from following with my hand like a claw on his thigh.

"What?" he asked, sitting back down from his half-crouched position.

"What was that?"

"What?" He shrugged. "Your family wanted to know what drew me to you so—"

Well, yeah, that too. But more importantly. "The kiss."

His brow knit. "You didn't like it?"

"No, I..." I closed my eyes to rid myself of the fantasies that had sprung to life with that kiss. Because I couldn't take hearing the words from him. That he didn't feel the same way I felt about him.

He wound his hand into my hair, urging me to open my eyes to him and his smile that sent my heart cartwheeling out of my chest. "It was an impulse."

"You didn't have to do it."

He bent closer to me so his breath that smelled of soda and fruit wafted over my cheeks. "But I wanted to."

I attempted to swallow past my stomach that was currently lodged in my throat. "You...wanted to?"

"I know this…" He moved his hand down to my jaw, brushing the pad of his thumb over my cheek. "I know it wasn't real when it started, but I can't stop thinking about you."

It took a few seconds for his words to sink in, and I clutched his forearm. "Really?"

"You that shocked?"

"Kinda." I lifted one shoulder. "Yeah."

He dropped his hands to my chair, yanking it right into his. With his legs outside of my knees, he ghosted his hand over the top of my thigh. "Why?"

"For the same reasons I thought people would never believe we were together."

"People…or you?"

I felt my skin flush, and he slowly lifted his other hand to trace the collar of my dress, settling at the hollow of my throat. Then, without any more warning, he leaned in and kissed me.

This one not at all chaste.

He combed his fingers into my hair, cradling my head as he slid his tongue between my lips, another one of those gruff sounds emanating from the back of his throat when I met him stroke for stroke. This didn't feel like a kiss of someone pretending. This didn't taste like someone who wasn't as hungry as I was.

And without having to verbalize it, I knew the truth.

It wasn't fake anymore.

What we had was real.

He nipped at my bottom lip, and I squeaked out a gasp, pulling away from him, my chest rapidly rising and falling. His was too.

He drifted his palms over my arms and down to my waist, his fingers pressing into me like he was barely containing himself from towing me into his lap. "Tell me again, who thought we wouldn't ever make sense together?"

"I don't know. Some moron," I said, leaning in for another kiss. I dug my fingers into his hair as I sipped and sucked at his lips, wanting to savor it, but I was too impatient to wait, needing more.

"Get a room!"

Jimmy and I immediately split apart once again, this time at arm's length, and I lifted my attention to find my family all staring at us.

I ducked my head, covering my heated cheeks with my hands.

I felt more than saw Jimmy wave his hand. "Sorry, not sorry. I really like her." When I tried to elbow him, he dodged out of the way, throwing his arm around me. "Come on. Let's go play volleyball. I'm feeling extra lucky today."

CHAPTER SEVENTEEN

Jimmy

We'd spent all afternoon at the Hart farm. It was amazing. Claire's family was cool and funny, and thank the good baby Jesus, it gave me an excuse to finally kiss her. A fun fact I learned, Miss Hart tasted like lemon. I knew she liked lemon in her water. I'd seen her carry her fancy water bottle around with the yellow slices in it on multiple occasions, but kissing her was a small slice of summer. Fresh and delicious and just a little tart.

But more than that, being honest about how I felt about her was like a deep breath after being submerged in the ocean. Now, I was practically buoyant. I could walk on water. Which was good because by the time I pulled up to her place, it had started to rain. Not heavy, but enough to wet those damn metal steps leading to her door.

"Careful," I warned, keeping one hand on the railing and the other on her lower back as I followed behind her up the staircase.

"It's fine."

"It's a deathtrap."

She snorted as she reached the landing, sliding her key into the lock. Once I was inside, she closed the door, and I didn't hesitate to pull her into me. "Maybe we should talk to your landlord about putting some kind of slip grip on those stairs."

"You're making a big deal out of nothing."

Then it was my turn to snort. Though it wasn't as cute as when she did it. "You're right, keeping you safe is a very big deal."

She curled her fingers into my shirt, easing herself against the wall, and my attention dropped to her lush mouth, the swipe of the tongue over her lips, the disappearing freckles. I trailed my thumb over her chin, tugging the corner of her lip free.

"What we *should* talk about is what happened earlier," she said, and I dropped my forehead to hers.

"You mean that part where you mauled me in front of your family?"

Her fists tightened their grip on my shirt, towing me to her, and she growled into a kiss like the perfect little animal she was.

How I wished she'd maul me for real.

I curled her hair around my hand, tugging her head back, and I found all the sweet corners of her mouth, obsessed with the needy way she clawed at me, as if she liked the slightly hard touches.

Noted.

And when she looped her arms around my neck, bringing her body flush against mine, I sighed in relief. She was soft and supple under my marauding hands. I couldn't stop touching her, couldn't stop sliding my hand up and down her back, over her waist and hips. Now that I was allowed, I was addicted.

Nothing could stop me.

Nothing except, "Jimmy, we have to talk."

I froze with my fingers groping her ass and my lips on her throat.

"Do we have to? I feel like this is working pretty well for us."

She tossed me one of her adorably annoyed and amused headshakes before taking hold of my hand and dragging me to her couch.

She kicked off her shoes and settled into the corner, her legs crossed under her, while I grabbed her glittery rabbit pillow, keeping my hands busy by brushing the sequins back and forth.

"I hope today wasn't so bad for you," she said after a while.

"No, it was great. I'm seriously going to take your brother up on the offer to go to one of his games. And I'm pretty much in love with your dad."

She smiled. "I think he likes you too."

"Likes or loves?"

"Is the distinction important?"

I tossed the pillow down to set my arm along the back of the couch, dropping my fingers near her head, catching a few tendrils, winding them around my finger. "Yes. But I'm sure you aren't surprised to know I thrive on people's admiration of me."

Her mouth flattened into a line, her brows narrowed at me. "I know you're joking, but this is why we need to talk, because *I'm* the one who needs reassurance."

I shifted closer to her, resting my other hand on her thigh, toying with the hem of her dress. Seriously. I couldn't stop touching her. "About what?"

"You. Me. Us."

"Okay..."

"Jimmy." My name was a flustered sigh, and I forced myself to remove all points of contact between us.

I crossed my arms, ready. "What do you want to talk about?"

"I need..." She squeezed her eyes shut as if she needed a second to gather her thoughts then flicked those gemstone irises up at me. "I need to know this isn't a game to you. That whatever happens with this contest, what we have is real. I don't think..." Her throat bobbed on a delicate swallow. "It would hurt...a lot...if this all fell apart next week."

I understood. I'd never hid my history, from her most of all, and she was worried I'd float on to the next one. I wished I could go back, rewind everything, and redo every dumb decision I'd ever made, every flippant comment I'd ever made about women, every position I'd put myself in to make it look like I was a careless asshole with people's emotions.

Unfortunately, I couldn't. But if she let me, I could show her I was able to be focused and patient and steady. If she gave me the chance, I could be all those things for her.

"The last thing I want to do is hurt you," I told her, and she nodded, her teeth sawing into her lip. "You aren't a game to me, Claire. What I feel for you is real, and I know..." I plowed my hand through my hair and slumped my head to the cushion, my eyes on the ceiling. "I know what you think of me. I know what everyone thinks of me, that I can't be serious. But I can, and it sucks because I don't know how to convince you."

She stayed quiet for a minute, and I slanted my gaze to find her staring at me in that unnerving way of hers. Like she could see into the cobwebs of my brain. "You could start by telling me why you picked me to do this in the first place. I like my ego stroked sometimes too."

I huffed a laugh and cupped my palm around her leg, silently urging her to lay them across my lap. It was always easier for me to talk to her when I was touching her.

Being physically close helped me spill my secrets. She was my blanket fort, keeping the world out.

"I honestly don't know why. I saw that picture of us and

clicked on the link to send it in. There wasn't much thought involved." I circled my index finger around a cluster of freckles by her knee, drawing out goose bumps along her skin, but she didn't stop me as I continued, my circles growing bigger with every pass. "All I know is that every morning I come into school, and I can't officially start my day until I see you. Until I see what headband you're wearing, if it matches your shirt, and how long your skirt is. And why do you always wear skirts?" I glided my hand up and down her shin. "Pants are nice too, you know? Not that I don't like the skirts. I *love* the skirts. I'm just saying pants that show off your legs would be a nice change every once in a while."

When she shook her head in amusement, her eyes glittering, I waved my hand in the air. "What I'm trying to say is, I like you. A lot. And I don't know why. I can't articulate it, but if you wanted someone who could make sense of their feelings and life, you probably wouldn't have said yes to me in the first place."

"I'm sorry." She curled her hand around her ear. "It sounded like you said you liked me a lot."

"It's true."

"That's good." Her cheeks flamed, and when I brushed my fingers over the color, she nuzzled into my touch, her voice barely above a whisper, although in the quiet of her apartment, she might as well have screamed her words. "Because I like you a lot too. I have for a long time."

Like a pistol at the start of a race, my heart took off at a sprint, and I lunged at her, trapping the echo of her perfect, sweet words between our lips. She laughed, I assumed at my very ungentlemanly and ungainly handling of her, but I used the opportunity to get another taste of her tongue.

I leveled myself over her while at the same time attempting to roll to the side, allowing me some room to explore the expanse of her body, but her small couch was quite the cockblock.

Thinking on my feet, I tossed her plush blanket and menagerie of pillows to the floor. Maybe I should have asked about moving this tryst to her bedroom, but I was too impatient.

"Come here, baby," I murmured, towing her down to the floor with me. The blanket and pillows created a cozy little cove, and I didn't hesitate to pick up where we left off. On my side, I wove one hand into her hair and traced the other down the length of her side, from her shoulder to her thigh and back up to her breast, her nipple a hard point against my palm.

Her dress was soft with a ruffled skirt and puffy sleeves at her shoulders, but the great part of the design was all the wrinkled material over her chest. All I had to do was tug it down a bit to reveal her sheer lace bra. I should've known I'd find something girly and wonderful underneath.

The tips of her breasts were large and almost the same color pale pink as the bra, and I dragged the flat of my tongue over one and then the other, leaving a trail of slightly darker lace in my wake. I gripped the bottom of her dress and hiked it up to her waist to glide my fingers up the length of her inner thigh. "I feel like I've waited so long for this."

She breathed out a moan, her fingers sliding into my hair as I dragged my teeth across the swell of her breast, and I was treated to nails scraping over my scalp. My cock lengthened behind the zipper of my jeans, and I ground against her hip, needing some relief, but it was then Claire whispered her next request. "Can we go slow? I'm still trying to get used to the idea that we're...a we."

"Yeah," I breathed out against her throat. "Yeah, okay. We'll go slow."

"I mean, I normally do that anyway," she said, her mouth

next to my ear as I sucked on her neck. "There has to be emotional attachment there, you know?"

No, I didn't know, but I nodded anyway. I was basically a primate. If I liked something and my dick got hard, I did what I had to do to make it better. No feelings had to be involved. All the better if they were, although not a necessity.

But I wanted—needed—to make sure Claire got what she needed and wanted. She wanted to wait. So, I'd wait.

There were plenty of other things we could do besides sex.

"Can I go down on you?" I asked, taking in the flush of her skin, the way her breasts rose and fell with each breath. My own chest heaved, my heart beating in my ears. Only a few minutes kissing her, and already I felt like I could crawl out of my skin, needing release.

When I hooked up with girls, the only thing that calmed me, helped me to last longer, was going down on them. I could concentrate on what they liked and needed to get off, to forget about the throbbing in my dick. But more than anything with Claire, I wanted to see her let loose. Have the reserved woman go absolutely wild.

Her eyes shifted between mine as she reached for me, raking her fingers into my hair, kissing me in a way that let me know what her answer would be. "Not this time."

I swallowed my disappointed whine, but I did push back a little. "Are you sure? I could make you feel so good." I dragged my fingers along the crease of her thigh and the lace of her underwear so she knew where I was headed, giving her time to say no. When she didn't, I palmed her shape over the thin material. She was warm and soft, and I traced my middle finger down the seam of her pussy. "Please." I licked the tip of my tongue along her jaw before nipping at her earlobe, showing her what I would do. "It's my favorite thing."

Her throat bobbed, and I sucked on her pulse point,

gently nudging her thighs apart. "I want to taste you, fuck you with my tongue, suck on your clit until you're screaming."

"Oh my god," she half laughed and half moaned. "You have a dirty mouth."

I grinned against her collarbone, instinctively rolling my hips, rubbing my cock against her thigh. "You surprised?"

"A little, yeah," she whispered, her fingers finding their way under my T-shirt. Her hands were small yet searing, both holding me to her and keeping me away from what I really wanted.

"Let me show you what else I can do with my mouth." I slipped my tongue over her bottom lip. "I can be slow." Then I thrust my tongue into her mouth, finding hers, plying it with my own until she chased me, but I broke the kiss. "Or I can be fast. How do you want it?"

She stared up at me, eyes lazy and lust-filled. She was so beautiful.

"I bet if I slipped my fingers inside you right now, you'd be wet."

A slow smile unfurled across her lips. "You'd be right."

I took that as an invitation and shifted up toward the pillows to slide my hand into her panties. She inhaled a sharp breath when I cupped my hand over her pussy, but she surprised me too. She was completely bare. "You shave?"

She tightened her grip on my hair, and I was never cutting it again. So long as she kept pulling on it like that. "Don't you know you're not supposed to ask a lady about her hygiene process?"

"Don't you know I'm like a dog with a bone when I'm curious?" I skimmed my fingers over her soft skin. "You do this for me?"

She rolled her eyes. "Believe it or not, not everything is

about you. I wax because it's better for my skin. I get my eyebrows done too."

I inspected her amber brows, arched in the middle and in tidy points at the ends, then dropped my gaze to where my hand had conformed to her. "I have to get a closer look," I told her, earning a laugh. "Lemme see."

She shook her head, but her smile dropped when her jaw shot open on a moan as I slipped my middle finger into her. "Jesus, you're so tight and wet," I murmured, taking my time stroking my finger in and out of her, coating it with her arousal before circling her clit. I kissed the corner of her mouth. "Imagine my mouth doing this. I'm so good at it."

She licked her lips, her breaths coming out faster. "You think so?"

"I know so."

"I don't want to know how much practice you've had."

And I didn't want to tell her. "I know what my strengths and weaknesses are, and I know I'll need to eat you out every chance I get, so I'm not some two-pump chump."

She grinned into a kiss. "You're so..."

"Persistent? I know."

"No, you're—"

Her words cut off when I pushed my index and middle fingers back into her. Her neck arched, and I licked a line under her jaw. "Thorough? Yes, when it comes to making you feel good, I will always be thorough. That's why I think you should let me use my mouth."

I didn't have the best angle on the floor like this, but I'd rather chew off my own arm than stop now, not when I felt her inner walls starting to clench around my fingers.

"No," she whimpered, "you're so..."

I swiped my thumb over her clit, her nipples hard points

under her bra, and I hungrily hooked a finger over one side, baring her breast to me, and I sucked the tip into my mouth.

"Oh my god," she moaned.

I lifted my head, pushing up enough that I could take in what I was doing to her. The way her legs were open and trembling, the curve of her thigh and the grip of her hand on my forearm, just above where it disappeared under her dress, the red marks I'd left on her cleavage from my scruff. "Look at you. These tits are—"

Squeezing her eyes shut, she let out an impatient growl. "Ugh. God! That's your problem. You never shut up. All you do is talk, talk, talk. Just shut up and kiss me."

I loved the snap in her voice, and I did exactly as she said. But not before a, "Yes, Miss Hart."

Then I curved my hand around her neck, holding her steady as I invaded her mouth with my tongue, quieting her needy sounds while my fingers worked over her swollen clit. She was wet and warm and ready to go off, and I plunged my fingers back into her, needing to feel it when she came. When she finally orgasmed, she let out the tiniest, squeakiest sound I'd ever heard. Like a delicious little hiccup from her chest.

I pecked kisses along her throat and collarbone before backing away from her. I moved to my knees to give her some space to readjust her dress.

"You're so pretty," I told her. "Especially when you come."

She shook her head at me, in the perfect amused way she did, and with my fingers still wet from her orgasm, I stuck them into my mouth.

And sweet baby Jesus, she tasted so good. As I was literally on my knees, thanking the good Lord for this woman's pussy, I was sure I'd go to hell, but I prayed at the House of Claire Hart now. Cue the angels.

Amen and hallelujah.

I couldn't wait until she let me go down on her. I knew I wouldn't be able to get enough. I'd feast on her until she yelled at me to stop. As it was now, though, I was the one telling her to stop when she reached for my zipper.

"No, baby, it's okay."

"But don't you want...?"

I shook my head and stood up before leaning down to help her do the same. She looked wonderfully dazed and sort of thoroughly fucked. "I do. God, do I want you to touch me. I want your hands and your mouth and your pussy. I want it all," I said with a half smile, half wince because my dick was painfully hard. "But not tonight."

I curled my hand around her jaw, kissing her softly. "I want to prove that you're not a passing fancy for me. I'm not here because of the contest. I like you and want to be with you, and I don't want you to think this relationship is transactional even though it started that way."

She blinked once then twice, taking in my words, and I saw the moment she realized the truth. That no matter how much of a clown I could be, I wasn't playing here. I wouldn't let her down. She threw her arms around me, knocking me back a step, but I found my footing and banded my arms around her waist. We stayed like that for a long time, simply hugging and breathing into each other, fingers curled into clothes and hair, lips sometimes skating along skin.

Until my phone alarm blared. "That's my reminder to get all my stuff ready for school tomorrow."

"You have an alarm for that?" She stepped back from me, and I instantly felt colder even though she didn't go very far. Only a few inches, her fingers lacing with mine.

"I've got an alarm for everything. Sometimes I don't even remember why I set some."

She laughed as she walked me to her door, setting me on

my way with a kiss to my cheek and a promise to see me tomorrow morning.

I didn't know when or why or how it happened, but Claire Hart had snuck up on me, twisting my heart until it beat in a funny rhythm, like I'd run a few miles.

There wasn't much I was certain about in my life, but if there was one thing I was damn sure about, it was asking Claire to be my fake girlfriend so she could become my real girlfriend. It was the smartest decision I'd ever made.

Then again... I took my phone out of my pocket and texted her.

> Just to clarify

> You are my real girlfriend now, right?

LIL GRUMPMUFFIN

Yes.

> Does that mean I finally get a naked photo of you?

LIL GRUMPMUFFIN

You're still not that cute.

CHAPTER EIGHTEEN

Claire

The mornings weren't all that different now that Jimmy and I were *real*, except when he greeted me in the morning it was with a kiss and a coffee. Instead of his pound of sugar, he brought me my favorite, a flat white. He still played his music as loud as always, but when we left the building at the end of the day, it was hand in hand.

"You ready for this?" he asked as we made our way to my car.

"Not really."

"Ah, come on. It'll be fun." He jostled my arm. "They said they'll ask us some get-to-know-you questions, and then we'll play a sort of Newlywed Game, and that'll be that. Simple."

"Right. Simple."

"Don't give me that adorable frowny-face," he said, imitating my supposed adorable frowny-face. When I pouted, he kissed my lips. "I'll meet you there."

He waited until I was in my car to walk to his own. Even though he had offered to drive me to work, I had turned him down. He thought it was silly we had two cars here. It was a nice offer, though I suspected he was hoping a ride to and from work was another chance to get his hand up my skirt. Not that

I minded. Sunday had been explosive. I'd never been with a guy who had been so...desperate for me.

Intimate moments with men had always been...fine. But being with Jimmy was like being shoved in a rocket and sent to outer space. Stars and comets and super light speed.

I felt better about taking part in this contest since we were together now, but I still didn't know much about him. The insignificant details people learned about each other in a relationship, like what side of the bed they slept on or what color toothbrush they used or what they put in the drawers in their refrigerator. I didn't know any of that about Jimmy.

But I did know the important things. That he loved his job, he loved his family, he loved *my* family, and when he loved something, he loved it with his whole heart. There were no half measures with him. He was all or nothing.

Which was why it was still so incredible to me that he was here, next to *me*, holding *my* hand.

He chose me.

I couldn't wipe the grin off my face as I pulled into the parking lot situated almost right off the highway, the sign for the station in big blue letters on the top of the building.

"That's what I like to see," Jimmy told me as he looped his arm around my shoulders. "My little grouchy girl smiling."

I jabbed his side, and he laughed into a kiss at my temple.

"You ever hear of the Muppet Theory?"

"I...what?"

"Muppet Theory," he repeated, opening the door for me. "It's this theory that everyone is either a chaos or an order Muppet. You know, like Kermit is an order Muppet. Animal and Gonzo are chaos Muppets."

"I've never in my life heard of this," I said as we stepped up to the young man, who I assumed was some college intern, at the desk. Jimmy gave him our names, and he handed us badges before pointing to the elevators and telling us to see Jenny on the third floor.

"I was thinking about it on the drive here. Which Muppet you'd be."

"Obviously not a chaos Muppet," I said.

"Right." He took my hand once he had the button for the third floor pressed. "You're order and I'm chaos. That's why we work so well. I'm a Gemini, Enneagram seven, and—"

"A what?"

"You've never heard of the Enneagram personality test either?"

I leaned into his side. "Never."

"I'm a seven, so that's, like, basically the guy who jumps off roofs at parties."

I nodded. "Makes total sense."

"And I think I'm Miss Piggy."

Refusing to laugh, I met his serious gaze. "You do love to put on a show."

The elevator dinged when we arrived on our floor, and he gestured for me to step out ahead of him. "You're an Aquarius, and I don't know what Enneagram you are, but we'll find out later. Whatever it is, it's probably a one or two, and you're an order Muppet."

"I'm not Kermit, though."

"No, not all." He waved to a woman as she made her way toward us. "Maybe Bert."

"Is he the one with the unibrow?"

"I can never remember," he said with a shrug, "except that Ernie is the chaos one of that relationship."

"Hello!" Any more talk of the Muppet Theory was put on hold as the woman greeted us. "You must be Jim and Claire. I'm Jenny, the producer for Stef and Matt's show." She shook our hands. "It's so wonderful to meet you. If you'll follow me, I'll get you set up."

Jenny's long ponytail swished behind her as she power walked down the hall, but Jimmy was in no rush, keeping us lingering a few paces behind. "I was thinking," he explained, "that I'm so drawn to you because you're nothing like me. You're patient and sweet and understatedly hilarious." He pointed at my face. "Like right now. You must practice these expressions at home. Because I'm such a sucker for them. When you stare blankly at me like I'm some idiot puppy, so funny." He bent down, his mouth close to my ear. "But when you roll your eyes at me, like you don't know whether to strangle me or sit on my face, that's my favorite."

I choked on a breath and shot my gaze to Jenny's back, making sure she didn't hear. "We're in public. You can't say stuff like that."

"Why? Because it makes you want to sit on my face, huh? I can't wait. Let's do it tonight."

I really did roll my eyes then, pushing away from his side. He laughed behind me.

Jenny opened the door to the sound booth, escorting us into a room with one window, looking out onto the highway, old music posters on the walls and a series of microphones and cables set up along the table. "This is Stef and Matt," she said, waving her hand out to the tall Black woman seated behind a laptop with headphones around her neck and a short white guy with chubby cheeks next to her. They both grinned. "Like I said in my email, this will be really easy. Stef and Matt will lead you through some questions. You'll play a matching game, and before you know it, the thirty minutes will be up. My co-producer is Bowen." She pointed to the guy with his back turned to us, through the glass wall. "We'll be in the booth. Before we start, do you need anything? Coffee or water?"

I shook my head, already too nervous to accept any liquids. I was sweating buckets. I didn't want to have to pee too.

"We're good," Jimmy said, and she helped us get situated at the desk with the headphones and mics, testing the volume with Bowen. Then she handed us Expo markers and small dry-erase boards for the game.

"All the interviews will be completed by the end of the week, so your profiles will be up on the website on Friday, and listeners can start voting for their choice. Remember, the more charming you are during this interview, the more they'll want you to win."

"Our very own *American Idol*," Matt said cheerfully.

"Except completely talentless," I joked, and both of the radio hosts stared at me.

Jimmy immediately stepped in, smoothing over my waves. "Aw, come on, baby. Your singing isn't that bad." Then he turned to Stef and Matt. "I'm the one with the voice. Right, Claire Bear?"

"Right," I huffed.

"She gets so annoyed with me all the time because I play my music too loud."

I shot him a faux look of irritation. "Who wants to listen to Hootie and the Blowfish on repeat all the time?"

He leaned toward Stef and Matt, smirking. "I do it to get her attention." Then he shrugged, all charm and ease. "But it works."

"Oh my god," I mumbled under my breath, and Stef laughed.

"I can see you two are going to be fun."

Under the table, Jimmy yanked my rolling chair as close to his as possible and squeezed my thigh. I relaxed with his reassurance and let him do the talking for the most part once we were live on air.

Stef and Matt asked us softball questions about where we were from, how we met, and why we wanted to enter the contest. We answered truthfully—and somewhat haltingly on my part. Honest to god, it was like I was being asked questions in front of a firing squad, but I couldn't help it. It took me time to warm up to people, for them to warm up to me, and I couldn't bat my eyelashes and sweep people off their feet like Jimmy. I wasn't good at this, and I wrung my hands together, knowing I was blowing his chance of buying his house.

"Okay," Stef said, "we're going to see which one of you knows the other best. Grab those markers and boards, and just to make sure there's no cheating, we're going to have you turn back-to-back."

Following direction, Jimmy and I rolled our chairs so we couldn't see each other.

"I can already see you peeking over there, Jim." Matt chuckled. "And you're supposed to be the role model for our future generations."

"Hey, man, if there was going to be one person I'd cheat off, it'd be her."

"But you shouldn't need to cheat," Stef pointed out. "Unless you don't actually know each other very well."

I forced a laugh, swallowing past the guilty lump in my throat.

And, Jesus, I'd have to go home and immediately change out of these sweaty clothes. Also, research a new antiperspirant.

"All right. Let's get started. Claire and Jim, how deep is your love?" Matt flicked his thumb toward the booth, and Jenny pressed a button that began the chorus to "How Deep is Your Love" by the BeeGees. Behind me, I could feel Jimmy bopping around in his seat. I stifled a laugh.

"First question," Stef declared. "What did your partner wear on your first date?"

"Oh god," I said out loud, earning some laughs.

"I know. It's burned in my memory." Jimmy scribbled on his board. I knew because his marker squeaked as he wrote.

"Can I pass?" I asked hopefully, and Stef started to hum the *Jeopardy* countdown music. I wrote down "Jeans."

"Okay, boards up. What do we have?" Matt read the answers out loud for the benefit of the listeners. "Jim wrote down short-sleeve pink sweater with fake buttons, puffy animal skirt, and black headband. That's quite detailed."

"Well, if you'd have seen her in that outfit, you'd remember the details too."

"And in my defense," I said, sticking my marker in the air. "It sounds ridiculous with that description, like I got dressed with my eyes closed, but it's actually really cute together. It's a maxi skirt and—"

"And it's really hot," Jimmy butted in. "Like 1950s house-wife but also jungle. Know what I'm saying?"

"Perfectly," Matt deadpanned as he shook his head, and Stef burst out in laughter.

"And Claire wrote down jeans for her answer."

"I didn't wear jeans on our first date," Jimmy said.

"Yes, you did. What else would you have worn?" I argued.

"My work clothes." He gestured down the length of his body.

"What? No, you didn't."

"When do you think our first date was?" he asked, and Stef and Matt both made teasing noises into their mics.

"When we went out to eat and then to the bookstore," I said, but he shook his head.

"It was Applebee's."

"You took her to Applebee's?" Matt asked incredulously. "*Dude.*"

"Hey. Half-price apps," Jimmy said in defense then turned back to me. "That was our first date."

"We weren't even..." My sentence trailed off as my gaze moved to the radio hosts, watching us with interest. They probably thought we were a cute, argumentative couple, when really, I was trying to discern if the first few times we went out even counted as dates.

"Weren't what?" Stef asked.

"I was still trying to woo her," Jimmy explained easily.

Matt snorted. "With half-price apps?"

Jimmy gestured to me. "It worked, didn't it?"

Stef held up her arm like she was refereeing this game. "All right, next question, which Muppet would your partner be?"

"You're kidding," I sputtered at the same time Jimmy raised his arms.

"See! Muppet Theory."

Then we both looked at each other over our shoulders and cracked up.

"I think we've lost them, folks," Matt said after a few moments.

"I feel like we're in *When Harry Met Sally*," Stef added, obviously referencing our giggle fest. "I'll have what they're having."

Matt agreed with a laugh. "I don't know what they had, but, listeners, if you could see this couple now, you'd be smiling too."

CHAPTER NINETEEN
Claire

Once we finished up and thanked the staff, Jimmy and I headed out of the radio station the same way we entered.

"That wasn't bad, right?" he asked.

"No."

He linked his fingers with mine. "I think they liked us."

"Yeah? Why?"

"The fact that Stef said 'I really like you two.'"

"Oh yeah, okay." I laughed. "That's nice."

"It's in the bag," he murmured, tugging me into him, his mouth against the top of my head. "Do you want to come to my house?"

"When?"

"Right now. I haven't seen you since last weekend."

"I'm standing right in front of you now. You've literally seen me every day this week."

"Yeah, but I mean *see* you." He walked me to my car, gently pushing my back against it. "I need one-on-one time."

"You need more attention is what you mean." I combed my fingers through his hair, and he nuzzled into my hand.

"Yeah. Same thing." He grinned into a kiss. "I want to show you my house. I cleaned yesterday."

"Yeah," I said, giving in with a playful sigh. "I guess I should see it since it is the reason we're doing this after all."

"Best worst decision of my life." He kissed my cheek and texted me the address to his place, keeping one hand on my waist, his fingers pulling at the band of my skirt. I didn't think he even realized he was doing it, but I liked knowing that even when he wasn't consciously thinking about it, he still wanted me. "We can order something for dinner."

"Sounds good."

With one last kiss, he waited until I was seated in the driver's seat to head back to his car, a few spaces down. And I guess he was starting to rub off on me, because I rolled down my windows and blasted the classic Taylor Swift song "You Belong with Me" as I pulled out of the lot and followed my phone's directions to his house.

It was about fifteen minutes to his neighborhood, set back about a mile from a shopping center with a grocery store, dry cleaners, and nail place. With the trees in full bloom and the lawns full of green grass, it looked like summer had arrived early. Jimmy's house was a split level with brick and beige siding and green shutters on either side of the windows. I parked in the driveway, behind where he pulled into the attached garage. He waved me in to follow him, and I wasn't the least bit surprised to find a multitude of sports equipment hanging on the walls.

"How many sports do you play?" I asked.

"I don't know. A lot. I'm in a bunch of leagues throughout the year. Gotta burn off all my excess energy." He took my hand, leading me into the house. Directly inside the door from the garage was a small room that I supposed was a dining room of sorts with a square wooden table and four chairs, although the table had a few piles of papers, envelopes, a tiny cactus, and a pair of socks. Other than that, it was super clean.

The bay window was spotless, the early evening sunset lighting the whole place in orange hues, including the sitting area in front of the kitchen. Even the wooden floors gleamed and smelled faintly of polish.

He snatched the socks from the table, clucking his tongue. "I did clean, but sometimes, and by that I mean all the time, I forget where I leave things."

I waved him off and stepped into the kitchen, painted a cheery light green. Along the back of the counter was a drying rack with clean dishes and utensils, a few containers of spices on a plate, a coin jar, and random tchotchkes, including a little wooden reindeer.

When I picked it up, he let loose a chagrined whistle. "I keep forgetting to put that away with the other Christmas stuff."

I snickered, seeing as how we were more than five months into the year, then turned to the refrigerator, which was covered in dry-erase paint and lots of scribbled lists. Magnetic markers were all over, and a few pictures clung to it, including one with a group of people I assumed was his family. When I pointed to it, he stood with his chest against my back, extending his arm around me to point out each person. "That's my dad, my brother Mike and Sam, my best friend, my sister-in-law Lauren with my niece Emma, and that's Amelia on my shoulders, my brother Adam, and my mom."

The women were all in dresses and men in suits, though Jimmy's tie was missing, the top buttons of his shirt undone. "When was this taken?"

"February at Sam and Mike's wedding. They got married on Valentine's Day."

"That's sweet." I leaned in, studying the bride. She wore an ombre dress that was pale pink at the bust and faded into a deep purple at the bottom. "She's pretty. Her dress is incredible."

"Sammy's not one for tradition. They got married on a Wednesday, which was...cool, I guess. We all went up for the day, my family, her family, and some friends. They did the ceremony right at this restaurant and had lunch. We hung out for a few hours, and then we walked down the street and found a bar where they were doing trivia."

"Did you win?"

He huffed. "No. I was third-wheelin' it with the newly-weds, who were completely useless to me since they weren't even paying attention, making out the whole time."

"On their wedding day. How dare they."

"I know, right? And Sammy's best friends are all paired off, and the six of them wiped the floor with us. A bloodbath."

"You could've used another teammate."

He tilted his head down to me as he curled his arm around my waist. "You offering?"

"Maybe."

He kissed my temple, and I was truly amazed at how often his lips found parts of me. The top of my head, the corner of my mouth, he gave me absent kisses to my cheek or hand or fore-head. Like earlier, with his fingers tugging at my clothes, it seemed as if he didn't even think about it. And for me coming out of a relationship where the only time he touched me was when he wanted to have sex, it was extraordinary to feel like I was enough. Simply standing next to him, asking him ques-tions about his family, it was worth earning affectionate touches and brushes of his lips. It was almost as if he really enjoyed being around me.

What a revelation that was.

"Check out the backyard." He tugged me around the kitchen to the sliding doors in the sitting room, which led out to a deck, up a few feet off the ground and big enough to fit a long table with eight chairs and a big umbrella. A set of steps led down to a stone patio and another set of doors that I assumed opened to the living room.

"Wow. It's big."

"That's what she said."

I sent him a reproachful glare, and Jimmy sniffed a laugh, resting his forearms on the railing. "If I ever get to buy it, I want to put in a fire pit and fence. I'd eventually like to get a dog."

I smiled out at the rolling green before me, imagining him out here running around with some floppy-eared thing. "I can see it."

"Yeah? What do you see?"

"Knowing you, a volleyball net, corn hole. You'll need a shed for all your games."

"Obviously."

I squinted, fluttering my fingers to the side where I pictured the future. "I can see you with some kind of Slip 'N Slide or sprinkler in the summer."

"A baby pool," he corrected.

"*Obviously*." I continued with a grin. "And in the fall, you'd probably put up tons of huge Halloween decorations. Those skeletons that are as tall at the house."

He straightened. "How do you know me so well?"

"You don't hide what you like and dislike."

"You know what I'd really like right now?" he asked, slipping his arms around my waist.

With his hips pressing into mine, I had a pretty good guess. "What?"

He bent, drawing his nose along my cheekbone, whispering in my ear, "A nap."

I dropped my head to his shoulder. "I totally thought you were going to say something else."

"What did you think I was going to say?" he asked once I tipped my chin up to meet his gaze.

"Sex."

"Oh yeah, that too, but I'm so exhausted. I get up early on Mondays, Wednesdays, and Fridays to take my brother's online workout class, and then I lost track of time last night and didn't get to bed until after eleven. I didn't fall asleep for a while." His hands tracked up my back, pressing me into his chest. "Will you sleep with me for a bit?"

"Really? That's what you want?"

I felt him nod above me.

"Okay, let's go sleep."

He hustled me back inside and up the few steps to the second floor with a full bath and three rooms. His bedroom was at the end and, like the rest of his house, it was clean and structured to his personality, with multiple laundry baskets along the far wall, a bunch of Post-its with reminders on the mirror, approximately one thousand wires connected to a charging station for a phone, iPad, laptop, and Apple watch. There was also a Swiffer tucked into the corner, evidence of his cleaning.

But he did have a headboard. Which I thought was a win for a single guy.

He turned to me, his hands working on the buttons of his checkered shirt. "I like that dress."

I idly tugged at the hem of the denim shirtdress. It was soft, and with the belt around my waist, I liked the shape it gave me. "Thanks."

"You gonna leave it on to take a nap?"

"Is this your way of getting me naked?"

"No," he said, and when I rolled my eyes, he laughed, stripping off his shirt, revealing a white undershirt that clung so tightly to him I could see his smattering of dark chest hair underneath. "Honestly, I'm not. I just want you to be comfortable. I can give you shorts and a T-shirt if you want."

Before I even answered, he opened up a drawer and yanked out a dark shirt and a pair of athletic shorts and tossed them on the bed. I froze midstride when he used one arm to strip off his undershirt. He reached behind his neck and shucked it right off. I didn't know why I found that so hot. He wasn't even paying attention to me, too busy stepping out of his shoes, removing his socks, all the while not noticing how I stood like a deer in the headlights.

Next were his pants, leaving him in only his boxer briefs, and it wasn't my fault that my focus dropped down below his waist. I was oddly disappointed. I expected his underwear to be printed with donuts or French fries or some other design. Instead, they were plain gray.

He tossed all of his clothes into one of the laundry baskets then pivoted to me, totally cool with me ogling him in the open. He was on the paler side, but he'd already gotten some sun, evidenced by the slight tan of his biceps and forearms. He was fit but not overly muscular, merely a guy who worked out yet also enjoyed daily Starbucks drinks that were 15,000 calories. And though his chest hair was dark and narrowed down his stomach, sinking below the waistband of his underwear, I could tell he trimmed it. Which didn't help with my task of keeping my attention above his waist.

He picked up the clothes he'd thrown onto the bed and offered them to me. "Hurry up. I wanna cuddle the shit out of you."

CHAPTER TWENTY

Jimmy

With a wry curl to her lips, Claire accepted my clothes and headed down the hall. In the meantime, I hopped into bed, turning on my sound machine before asking Alexa to set an alarm for twenty minutes. Not that I'd get a good nap in, but I really just wanted some quiet time with Claire in close quarters.

I tucked one arm behind my head, smiling to myself about how she had remained unmoving while I changed. She watched me as if stunned I wasn't going to sleep in my work clothes. Or perhaps *more* clothes. But I ran hot, and when I was home, I almost never wore a shirt. It didn't occur to me to keep one on.

This whole thing with Claire was new.

This whole big-feelings thing was new.

I didn't get attached to women. Whether it was conscious or unconscious, I didn't feel the need to open myself up and be honest with the women I'd been with. There was the shallow shell of smiles and jokes and good times, but I never let it get any further. And I honestly didn't know why it was different with Claire.

Maybe because she'd known me for years.

Or maybe because I had to convince her to say yes to me.

And I didn't know if *that* was the real reason I'd pulled the trigger on the contest before I'd talked to her about it. Because it gave her a reason to give me a chance. Otherwise, what else did I have to offer her?

I still didn't know what I had to offer, but when Claire reappeared in my doorway, her fingers plucking at the cotton material of my T-shirt that was snug around her middle, my shorts tight on her legs, my mouth went dry. She seemed apprehensive, and I was desperate to give her something.

Something I'd never given anyone else before—the truth.

"I've never had a girl sleep in my bed before." When she remained silent, I sat up, sweeping my hand around my room. "I don't know if you've noticed, but I have a hard time staying organized, so I set, like, a million alarms and reminders. I have Alexa set up in every room in this house, and all my lights are on timers, and I still forget stuff. I can't remember to take my laundry out and always have to rerun the wash. I'm forever misplacing things. The other day, I couldn't find my deodorant, and it was because I'd put it in the refrigerator. I'm constantly doing three things at once and I almost never finish anything and I've never wanted anyone to come over and see all these quirks, and I always thought if I could get my life in order, if I could show someone how neat and tidy I could be, then they'd want to stay."

I finished my garbled thoughts in one long breath, but Claire still didn't react, and I tensed. "So...I guess..." I rubbed the back of my neck. "I guess what I'm trying to say is I...I don't even know. I like you, and I don't want to freak you out, and it never occurred to me to put on clothes because—" I motioned to my bare chest "—this might weird you out. But I basically walk around in my underwear when I'm home, and I didn't think about it, even with you here. And that should freak *me* out. That I even want you here to begin with because you're seeing my...mess, but I'm not freaking out, so I hope you aren't either."

She stalked toward me, a soft smile playing on her lips. "I'm not freaking out." She set her shoes and folded-up dress in the corner of the room before padding over to the bed, sitting next to me. "Thank you for inviting me in. It makes me feel special."

I dragged my hand from her shoulder, down her arm, sprayed with freckles. "Because you are special."

She twisted her mouth to the side, and I lifted my hand to trace over her bottom lip until it relaxed, releasing from her teeth. "Did you know you have two freckles right here?"

She nodded, the movement brushing her lips over my finger.

"They're my favorite."

"Your favorite?" she repeated, all smoke and pebbles.

"I know." I shrugged. "It's like picking a favorite star in the sky, but they are."

"Shut up," she said with a cynical laugh.

"I will not."

She shook her head at me, her *you silly rabbit* look on her face, but I ignored it and towed her down to the mattress, curling so we were on our sides, her back to my chest, my knees tucked up behind hers.

"Is this okay?" I asked into her neck. She'd taken off her headband and piled all her hair up on the top of her head in the way that was totally complicated but took girls five seconds to do. I'd always loved that. Didn't know why.

I didn't know why I liked a lot of things, but somehow it seemed they all converged into this one girl, here in my bed, warm and soft in my arms, and smelling like dewdrops on grass in the summer.

It didn't make sense to me, but that was what her scent reminded me of...morning time. My favorite.

She let out a quiet hum and wiggled a little bit, and I yawned into her shoulder. "I like you wearing my clothes."

"They barely fit. My butt's too big."

"Your butt's perfect." To prove it, I snuggled even closer, nestling her ass right in my lap and recited a few lines of Sir Mix-a-Lot. She snorted, and I adjusted my head on the pillow, closing my eyes. "Comfortable?"

"Mm-hmm."

"Next time, you can be the big spoon."

She breathed out a laugh. "Next time, I'll bring my pajamas."

"I like that idea."

And before I knew it, Claire was jostling me awake as she turned under my arm while Alexa beeped in the corner. "You fell asleep. I didn't think you would."

I stopped the alarm and yawned up at the ceiling. "Me either, actually."

"Expected you to lean over at some point at say, 'Hey, are you asleep?'"

"You were waiting for it?"

She gave in to a smile. "Kinda, yeah."

I scrubbed my hand over my face then repositioned myself to my back, urging her head to my shoulder. "When I was a kid, I was always the last one to fall asleep at sleepovers. Sometimes I didn't sleep at all."

"I was usually the first one to fall asleep," she said. "Not like I went to all the many, but..."

"What were you like in school?" I asked, combing loose hair behind her ear.

"Not much different from now, I suppose. I didn't have a

whole lot of friends, only two best friends and that was pretty much it."

I thought back to my childhood, all the dumb shit I did. Nothing illegal, but not particularly smart. Like the time I tried to rescue the squirrel caught in our broken gutter and ended up pulling the whole thing down from the side of the house. That other time I accidentally started a small fire in chem class in high school. Of course, there was that incident in eighth grade when I very publicly and not very kindly dumped my girlfriend Emery. But she had been mean to Sam, and I wasn't cool with that.

"So, you didn't get into much trouble?" I asked after a while.

"No, but Lexi's parents were divorced and her dad had HBO, so she'd record all the late-night sex stuff, and then we'd dissect it at our sleepovers." I blew out a big laugh as she continued, "We were fascinated."

"I bet you were, you dirty bird."

She lifted one shoulder, her hand finding its way to my ribs and eventually to the middle of my stomach. "I'm sure you were hot-wiring porn."

"I did convince my parents it was Adam, not me, when I accidentally purchased a subscription online. Who would think innocent thirteen-year-old me would do that, as opposed to the twenty-year-old home from college?"

"Who, indeed?" she said against my pec, and I chuckled into her hair, gliding my hands along her back to her neck, tilting her head so she'd meet my eyes.

"How hungry are you on a scale of one to ten?"

"Mmm. Five, maybe."

I nodded, thankful, then bent to take her lips between mine. Without any hesitation, she climbed on top of me, her hands flat to the mattress on either side of me with her legs bracketing my hips.

God, she was a delight.

Like a decadent dessert to be nibbled and enjoyed slowly. I kept one hand on her neck and allowed the other to journey over her hills and valleys, along the side of her breast to the dip of her waist and farther to her hip and ass, where I pressed her down, urging her to sink her weight onto me. When she finally did, the heat between her legs was so perfectly torturous against my swiftly hardening cock, I moaned into her mouth.

That was when she began to move, rocking back and forth along my length, finding the speed that felt good to her, and I dug my fingertips into the swell of her ass, so soft and sweet and delectable. I dragged my mouth away from hers to place an openmouthed kiss on her throat, and her breath caught, a slight hitch in her rhythm. I took advantage, rolling her to her back, so I could lick and nibble down to the slope of her shoulder, tugging at the collar of my shirt around her neck, roaming my other hand up her stomach to her chest.

With her mouth near my ear, I couldn't miss her tiny exhale that sounded almost painful when I dragged my thumb over her nipple. I did it again and again, until those exhales grew louder and harsher, her hips writhing beneath me. With my hands on the bottom of my shirt, poised to take it off her, I paused, silently asking—begging—if I could remove it. She raised her arms, and I slipped the cotton over her head before resuming my kisses over her throat and collarbone, licking a line between her breasts. I flicked her bra away with the handy snap in the front.

"Why aren't all bras made like this?" I asked absently, reveling in how her tits perfectly fit in the palms of my hands. "So easy to get off." Then I smirked. "Like you."

She didn't find my joke funny and pulled me down for a kiss with a muttered, "Shut up."

"Come on. That was a little bit funny," I said then sucked on each of her pale pink nipples in turn, earning lust-filled sighs that turned my cock to granite. I moved my mouth lower, down her stomach, connecting the dots of her freckles with my tongue until her hips were thrusting up into the air, then attempted to venture even farther south, but she stopped me. "You don't have to."

With her hands on either side of my face, I couldn't move. I furrowed my brow. "I don't have to? I *want* to."

"Yeah, but..." Her focus shifted somewhere over me.

"But what?" I prodded, unable to keep my finger from exploring the skin underneath the elastic of my shorts, finding the edge of her panties.

She licked her lips and took a deep breath, meeting my eyes with a careful gaze. "I don't... I have a bad gag reflex, so I'm not good at reciprocating, and I'd rather you not go down on me. Before, if I didn't return the favor—"

I flew back up her body, kissing away her explanation while my hand slid into her underwear. She moaned into my mouth, and I nipped at the corner of her lips, where my favorite freckles resided.

"Please don't finish that statement, I'm begging you." I sucked on the spot below her ear. "I will literally die right here if you tell me about other guys you've been with, especially ones who were assholes because you wouldn't give them a blow job."

She breathed out a laugh, her round belly rippling beneath me with a movement. Holding myself up over her with my forearm, I curled the index finger of my other hand into her, finding the spot that had her arching her lower back off the mattress. "It would be awfully difficult to explain to the police why I'm half naked and dead in bed on top of you."

She silently nodded, her hot inner walls contracting around my finger as I stroked her.

"I want to go down on you because I love it. Because I want to make you feel good. Because if I had my way, I'd live between your legs."

Her breath was hot against my cheek, her chest heaving with each inhale and exhale. I leisurely circled her clit a few times, and I was desperate to suck on that sweet little pearl. "And as far as I'm concerned, I'm the first guy to ever eat you out."

I drove two fingers back inside her, and her grip on my forearm tightened, her fingernails creating divots in my skin. "Yes," she groaned, her face screwed up in pleasure. "Yes, please."

"I don't care that you don't like to go down on me. In fact, I don't want you to."

When I swept my thumb over her clit in time with a thrust of my fingers, her legs tensed.

"This is not a reciprocal relationship. This is an I make you come so many times you can't see straight relationship."

Her eyes squeezed shut, her head shaking back and forth incoherently.

"And I don't want to hear any shit about it. I own this pussy. You understand?"

When she didn't answer, I ground my palm down hard on her clit, nudging her legs open wider with my knee. "Claire, look at me."

She did as I said, and I rewarded her with fast, even strokes of my fingers until she was panting and trembling. "All of your orgasms are mine." I rubbed her clit. "This sweet little thing is mine." I added a third finger inside her, and she cried out.

"Give me number one, and then I'll give you numbers two and three with my mouth, and after that, maybe I'll let you rest."

"Oh god," she moaned.

"That's more like it."

She managed an eye roll a moment before her trembling transformed into her body tensing from head to toe, every bit of her immobile as she rode out her orgasm, her eyes glazing over. Then little by little, she came back to me.

I stared down at her, desperate. "Please, *please* let me go down on you. You'll like it, I promise."

She drew her tongue along her lower lip like the minx she was. "Be gentle."

"Now that I *can't* promise," I said, not wasting any time in yanking my mesh shorts and her underwear off her, revealing her naked and glistening pussy. I groaned as I dragged my index finger down the center, parting her flesh. "Jesus, you're so pretty."

I dropped down between her legs and wrapped my right arm around her thigh, holding her open with my thumb and forefinger, so I could see how perfectly pink she was inside. And then I gave in to the thing that I'd wanted to do for days. Though it felt more like weeks, months...years, even.

I sucked on her sweet center. Sucked so hard, she jerked in my hold.

She sighed, her fingers tightening in my hair, and I ground my erection into my mattress. Between her flavor and sounds and heat, it was possible I'd die of a pleasure-induced heart attack before I got her off.

Sinking a second finger inside her, I licked her clit until she was shaking.

"I'm so close," she told me even though I already knew.

I hummed against her, keeping steady. If there was one thing I'd learned, it was if a girl was almost there, you didn't change a goddamn thing you were doing, no matter how bad you wanted to.

And sure enough, a minute later, Claire went off like a beautiful bomb.

That was number two.

I gave her only a moment to recover, let my fingers drag out of her to trace the length of her opening. She shifted, assuming I was done.

The hell I was.

"Don't move," I told her gruffly. "Put your head back down on the pillow."

"Huh?"

"That was only two. I want at least one more."

"Jimmy," she started, but I just raised my eyebrow, pushing my fingers back into her. A lot less gentle this time around.

"I'm not done with you yet." And I shoved my shoulders up under her thighs, banding my arm across her hips, keeping her from moving too much. Because orgasm number three came much faster than the two before. I didn't even get a chance to do my trademark move, humming while pulsating back and forth like a motorboating son of bitch.

"Up here," Claire breathed. "Come up here."

"I'd really rather not," I said, but she yanked on my arm, pulling me up over her. She didn't care that my lips were swollen and covered in her arousal. She kissed me anyway, sloppy and sucking on my tongue, and my dick jumped in my underwear when my body came in contact with hers. I ground it against her hip, needing to fuck now that I wasn't between her legs anymore, and right when I couldn't take it any longer, she slid her palm over me.

Not a moment too soon. I moaned into her mouth as her fingers found their way into my underwear, wrapping around my shaft. The relief of her touch overwhelmed me enough that

I could focus and double down on my efforts to make her come one last time on my fingers. I concentrated on her clit, circling it over and over until her nails bit into the skin at my shoulder, her hand on my dick constricting so hard, I could tell she was losing it.

Again.

Oh, my little sex maniac.

I loved it.

I loved her.

I think.

I was sex-crazed and maybe drugged by her pussy.

I couldn't be sure.

But it didn't matter, not when she was groaning sweetly against my mouth, another orgasm overcoming her so she went stock-still in my arms.

Once her grasp on my shoulder relaxed, she nestled her head back into the pillow, her eyes opening up to me, sleepy and gorgeous. I placed chaste kisses up and down her throat until she pushed me away. "My turn now."

"I thought you didn't…"

She directed me back to my knees and towed my underwear down enough that she could grip my cock with both of her hands, and given how the tip was leaking, it wouldn't take more than a few tugs to finish me off.

Dead, maybe.

Who knew with how she swept her thumb over me, her other hand drifting to my balls.

"Fuck yes," I muttered, and she repositioned herself on the bed, lowering her mouth. "No, baby, you don't have to do—"

My words cut off with one wet glide of her tongue along the sensitive underside of the head.

"A few licks are okay," she rasped, and to demonstrate, she repeated the motion.

"Shit," I hissed, my hips thrusting reflexively. But as I predicted, I was a two-pump chump. "Claire, let me go. I'm gonna come." I moved to grab a tissue, but she put one hand on my ass, holding me in place as she stroked along my length from root to tip, her eyes peering up at me from under heavy lids.

"I want you to come on me."

I nearly swallowed my tongue. My skin prickled, my mouth watered, my dick twitched. "That's what you want?"

She nodded, and I bent down, not so gently shoving her hands aside to take over as I laid her back down on the bed. Her bright hair was splayed over my pillow, her pale skin flushed. "I like that you're this sunny, effervescent guy, but here, you're different," she said quietly, her cheeks blushing so sweetly as she continued her confession. "You're a little rough and dirty, and I like that. I like that I'm the one who sees this other side of you."

That was all I needed to hear. No, I needed to hear less than that. She had me at *I want you to come on me.*

Because what I heard was, *I want to be yours.*

I want you to make me yours.

Mark me as yours.

Heat scorched up my spine, raising the hairs on the back of my neck, and I held myself up above her with one hand, using the other to finish myself off, spurting my orgasm all over her chest and stomach. She stared down at it for a moment then met my eyes, and the self-satisfied smile she gave me was the hottest thing I'd ever seen.

I swiped my index finger over the line next to her belly button and lifted it to her mouth. She sucked it off, her tongue swirling around the tip, her cheeks hollowing slightly, and *that* was the hottest thing I'd ever seen.

Pulling my finger out of her mouth with a pop, I grinned down at her. "You're mine now."

"Good."

"Good," I repeated then patted her hip and hopped off the bed before offering her my hand.

We cleaned up, dressed, and made our way to the living room, where I tugged her down next to me on the sofa, deciding what we wanted to order for dinner. We DoorDashed Chipotle, and we watched an episode of some K-Drama she liked, but I didn't have the attention span to read the translations and ended up scrolling through my phone, although she didn't seem to mind. In fact, she seemed downright comfortable with my head in her lap and her fingers absently playing with my hair.

But when Alexa sounded with an alarm, I checked my calendar, a reminder to take the garbage out.

"I should get going anyway," Claire said, standing up.

"You sure? You could stay over, if you wanted."

It wasn't that late, not even nine yet.

"Another time," she said with a kiss, and I snuck in an ass-grab before she trotted away from me. As I shuffled to the kitchen to start the task of collecting all the garbage, she changed in my room and reappeared a few minutes later, her hair still up and even messier in its knot, but her dress back on. "Thanks for having me."

"Thanks for coming. Over, I mean. But also, for coming."

The corner of her mouth twitched. "If you're expecting me to thank you for making me come, you're going to be waiting a long time."

"Undoubtedly." I kissed her forehead and led her to the front door. "See you tomorrow, Miss Hart."

"See you, Mr. Ewing."

I waited until she backed out of the drive and into the

street before turning around and plopping on the sofa. I was halfway through my fourth episode of a *Seinfeld* rerun when I remembered I had to take the garbage out.

After I finished the task, I headed back to my room and threw myself on the bed, finding my pillow still smelled like Claire. I texted her to tell her.

Jimmy: My sheets smell like you.

Lil GrumpMuffin: Is that a good or bad thing?

Jimmy: Very good thing.

Jimmy: When can you come over again?

Jimmy: Tomorrow?

Lil GrumpMuffin: You're not sick of me yet?

Screw that. I called her. When she picked up, I immediately said, "I don't know if I'll ever get sick of you."

"But we see each other at work, and then you really want to see me after? It's a lot."

"It's not."

"I feel like you answered too quickly."

I groaned. "You want me to answer more slowly for you to believe me?" I repeated myself, stretching the words "It is not" into as many syllables as possible.

"Okay, okay," she said with a laugh. "I'll come over tomorrow after work."

"To sleep over?"

She hummed in thought. "Yeah. I'll stay over."

"Great. Now, what are you wearing?"

"Good night."

CHAPTER TWENTY-ONE

Claire

"How's my little lollipop this morning?"

I lifted my attention from where it was on my computer screen to Jimmy, strolling in through the library doors.

I refused to give in to a snicker. I wasn't short, maybe on the lower side of average. My plus-size ass that he was so fond of certainly wasn't small either, and it wasn't like he was so much bigger than me to refer to me as "little." Yet, I loved that he called me those silly nicknames. Not that I'd ever admit it.

Although with how he grinned down at me, I was sure he already knew.

"I'm tired," I told him as he rounded the counter.

"Yeah?" The wheels of my chair squeaked when he pulled it away from my desk, swiveling me to face him. "Any particular reason?"

I let my gaze drift down to his lips for a moment, remembering all the wicked things he'd done to me. "I don't think so."

"No? So, you weren't thinking about me?" He bent his mouth to my ear, his words barely above a whisper, his stubble catching on my flyaways. "You weren't thinking about how you looked with my come on your chest?"

My gaze flew to the doors, making sure no one heard him.

"You can't say stuff like that here."

"Because I couldn't stop thinking about it."

"Jimmy," I warned, but he only curled his hands around the arms of the chair, boxing me in.

"What?" he asked, all innocence and charm as he laid one heck of a greeting on my lips.

"You're bad," I said once he extracted his mouth from mine.

"I'm just saying good morning. What's wrong with that?"

I pointedly stared down to where his hand had curved around my breast, and he became the living embodiment of the oops emoji face.

"How'd that get there?" He shrugged and ghosted his thumb over my nipple, hardening it to a point.

"You are an absolute menace." I pushed him away and stood up to open the blinds of the windows at the far end of the library. When I faced him again, he had his hands folded in front of himself like a choir boy.

He grinned. "So, listen, I think we need to talk strategy for getting votes."

"If you're about to tell me we should canvass neighborhoods, you have definitely picked the wrong girl." I gave him a wide berth as I skirted around him so he couldn't put me under his spell again with those wandering hands, then sat back down, opening up my email. I kept my eyes on my screen but my ears open to Jimmy.

"No, but I don't think it would hurt if we posted about it every day. We only have a week to garner as many votes as we can. And did you listen to any of the other interviews? The one from Tuesday was a couple in their seventies, who lost touch after he went to Vietnam. He suffered amnesia, and it took them decades to find each other again. I mean, how do we compete with that?" He flicked his hand between us, sounding unusually worried. "We're cute, but not *that* cute."

My smile faded as I found an email from early this morning with the subject line in all caps: MEETING REQUESTED. I clicked it open, and my stomach immediately dropped when my brain picked up a few key words like *distressing, disgusting, pornography, demand.* I blinked rapidly and shook my head once, trying to clear it so I could understand the message through the fog of anxiety.

"Claire, what's wrong?" Jimmy asked, leaning against my desk.

I didn't answer him, reading the email from the top. It was addressed to me, and Mrs. Kaplan was also cc'd.

Miss Hart,

I am writing this morning as I had a very distressing conversation with my daughter. I was informed that you have been giving your students, including my daughter, books that contain completely inappropriate material, for anyone, not the least of which for impressionable children. These books are disgusting, only a few steps away from pornography. I cannot imagine what other content is in the books you are choosing to have in your library. I demand to have a meeting to discuss what actions will be taken to rid the school of these books.

I hope to hear a response from you very soon, or I will be taking other action.

Vanessa Brooks

Tilting his head so he could view my screen, Jimmy asked again, "What is it?"

"I, uh, Anna's mom emailed me. She's pissed and wants a meeting." My heart, which had already been beating out of control, threatened to pump right out of my chest at the thought. Never in my life had I ever been in trouble. Not even as a kid. I wasn't a goody-two-shoes, but I didn't do much of anything to warrant attention. I always kept to myself. I still did as an adult.

And I would certainly never do anything to put my students in harm's way.

"What the hell is she talking about?" Jimmy snapped, his hand flying to my computer, obviously having read Mrs. Brooks's message.

"I...I'm not sure."

"Pornography!" Jimmy shouted, and I held my hand up to quiet him as the familiar clack of Mrs. Kaplan's heels echoed down the hall at a fast clip. I assumed she'd read the email too.

"Claire," she said, her voice and face grim. "We need to have a conversation."

Jimmy straightened next to me.

"In private," Mrs. Kaplan added, and Jimmy glanced down at me, where I was cemented to my seat, unable to do much but open and close my mouth like a dying fish. I nodded at him, and he offered my shoulder a squeeze before he shuffled out of the library with a subdued "Good morning" to the principal.

"Mrs. Kaplan, I'm not—"

She held her hand up to me, and I immediately silenced. My boss's shoulders rose and fell on a deep breath while she folded her hands around her walkie-talkie. The buses would be arriving soon. There wasn't much time for whatever this conversation was.

"From Mr. Ewing's agitated yelling, I am guessing you have read the email from Mrs. Brooks."

I nodded.

"What books is she referring to?"

"I don't..." I swallowed, hating to even say the word out loud. "We don't have any pornography. I have no idea what she's talking about."

"I know that, Miss Hart. I know *you* would never have any books like that here. *I* would never allow any books like that here, but I need to understand the full picture." Mrs. Kaplan was strict but fair and always kind. She stood up for her staff and supported us however she could, even when red tape with the district or problematic parents made the task difficult. She held up her cell phone, reading from the email. "'Books that contain completely inappropriate material,' what is she referring to there? Books in this library?"

"You know what books are here, most of them are decades old. I don't even—" Then it struck me. "The Free Little Library."

"What about it?"

I started to sweat, and I stood, flapping my hands as guilt clawed up my throat. "Anna had come in here looking for some books, which we didn't have."

Mrs. Kaplan nodded for me to continue, and I tried to swallow but my throat was like sandpaper, my voice even worse. It was barely a whisper. "I just wanted to help her."

Mrs. Kaplan's face dropped, her eyes softening, and she took a few steps toward me, extending her hand out so I'd sit back down. She followed suit, moving another chair close to mine, then she handed me a tissue and waited patiently while I blotted my eyes and blew my nose.

"I need you to start at the beginning and explain everything in as much detail as possible."

I sucked in a weary breath and started at the beginning. I explained how Anna had been interested in books with characters who were, in not so many words, exploring their sexuality. I told my principal exactly what I told Anna, that we didn't have any books like that here, but I'd be able to find some she might like. Then I purchased two books and put them in the Free Little Library out front. They were both at the appropriate reading level, upper elementary and lower middle grade, and there was nothing close to pornographic in the books. One was a fantasy about a girl stuck in another world. She realized she liked her best friend, who was also a girl. The second book was about a girl from another planet, fighting with a group of rebels, against a military trying to take over. Again, this girl realized she wasn't like "other girls." She liked fighting and wearing "boy" clothes, and she thought the girl who snuck her out of space jail was cute.

"I read both of the books," I told Mrs. Kaplan. "I would never recommend a book to any student without reading it first and knowing what was in it. These books are nowhere close to being inappropriate for her grade level or maturity, and there was absolutely no physical contact of any kind between the characters in the books. In fact, both of these books had secondary characters being killed. If anything was inappropriate, it was that."

Mrs. Kaplan nodded, her hands in her lap, her walkie-talkie forgotten on the counter for the time being, even as it crackled at a low volume. "I understand everything you've told me, and I trust your assessment of these books to be correct. I also believe you thought you were acting in Anna's best interest."

Every word of Mrs. Kaplan's reassurance sounded good until that small caveat, "I believe you thought..."

Because then she went on to say, "As teachers, we can offer suggestions and opinions for our students' academic careers and well-being, but we cannot make the decisions for them. By putting those books in the Little Library, you essentially were putting books in Anna's hands that her mother has deemed inappropriate."

"But Anna shouldn't be prohibited from reading the books she wants to," I tried to argue through watery eyes, knowing I wasn't arguing only on the behalf of Anna, but every kid who wanted to read more, including me.

"That isn't your decision to make," Mrs. Kaplan said. "I appreciate what you were trying to do, and maybe, if it were another student with a different parent, they would be rejoicing you spent your time and effort trying to help out their child, but we have to deal with the situation in front of us now."

I cleared my throat. "I'm so sorry. I didn't mean to cause trouble. I only wanted to help Anna."

"I know. I know you did." She patted my shoulder and stood up, her walkie-talkie back in hand as the sounds of the first bus pulling up in the lot rang through the small machine. "I will email Mrs. Brooks back and cc you. I do not want you responding to it. I will set up the meeting for tomorrow afternoon, and hopefully, after you apologize and promise to take those books out of the Little Library, she'll be satisfied."

I winced, thinking about the tone of the email and the not-so-thinly veiled threat of her taking further action.

"What if she isn't?" I asked.

"We will cross that bridge when we get there. For now, I want you to remember that you're a wonderful teacher and librarian. Focus on doing your job." She offered me a smile, which probably wasn't as reassuring as she intended, then headed out.

I followed her to the door, watching as she turned down the hall toward the front entrance, where students would be pouring in any second. Across from me, Jimmy stood with hunched shoulders and his hands in his pockets. "What happened?"

I gave him the shortened version. "She's going to set up a meeting to hopefully tide Mrs. Brooks over."

"Are you okay?" he asked, closing the distance between us, and I shrugged, biting my lower lip to keep it from quivering. He rubbed my back, kissed the top of my head. "It'll be all right. Kaplan's got your back."

I sniffled and fixed my hair, dragging my middle fingers

under my eyes to make sure my makeup didn't smudge. "How do I look?"

He tipped my chin up, so I could glimpse his full megawatt smile. "Cute as a button. Speaking of..." He leaned away from me, letting his gaze wander leisurely down the length of me, a lewd curl to his lips. After finding out how much he liked it at our radio interview yesterday, I wore the pink sweater he was so fond of and paired it with a cherry-printed knee-length skirt. "I don't know how you pull it off," he said, running his hand along my shoulder and arm, settling at my waist. "This supercute yet supersexy thing. I legit never knew I had such an obsession with flouncy skirts and buttons."

He shrugged and shook his head as if bamboozled after watching a magic trick, and I sniffled out a laugh. He pointed at me with a wink, clearly happy he'd gotten me to smile.

He bent with the clear intention to kiss me, but a stampede stopped him, and I settled for a high five before he spun away from me.

"Yo, yo, yo, Jae-sung. Good morning." Jimmy and Jae-sung completed their handshake as the other students lined up behind the little boy with the Spider-Man backpack.

Shandi waved at me from her spot along the wall. "Morning, Miss Hart."

"Morning, Shandi."

"My dad says he signed up to be a library volunteer. He's going to come in to be a surprise reader!"

I laughed. "Well, then it's not much of a surprise, is it?"

Shandi giggled into her hands, her pigtails swaying with the movement. "Guess not."

I offered her a smile and a wave to the rest of Jimmy's class then ducked back inside the shelter of the library. The one place where I'd always been safe from the outside world, but now the outside world was coming for me.

CHAPTER TWENTY-TWO

Jimmy

I could tell Claire was freaking out. She squirreled away in her room during her lunch break with Meredith and didn't respond to the *hilarious* video I'd sent her of a kid running over another with one of those Power Wheels Jeeps. So it didn't surprise me when she slumped into my room at the end of the day.

"Hey, I'm sorry, but I don't really feel great. Can I take a rain check for coming over today?"

I hurried to the door and hauled her into me, hugging her tight. She didn't reciprocate, keeping her arms down at her sides. "Do you want to talk about it?"

She shook her head.

"I know you said you want a rain check for coming to my house, but what if I come to yours?"

She stayed quiet, though her hands crawled up my torso, her fingers curving around to my back.

"We can relax, cuddle..."

"That's what you said yesterday, and it turned out to be much different."

I smiled against her hair. "You complaining?"

"No," she groused then buried her face against my chest.

"But, I promise, no sex. Or, maybe, just a little sex."

She pinched my ass. And not in a nice way.

"Ouch. Okay. No sex. Strict cuddling. Or!" I gripped her shoulders, holding her at arm's length. "You said you like doing face masks, right? Let's do face masks and a whole self-care night."

She snorted. "What do you know about self-care?"

"Nothing besides the kind that involves X-rated videos and my hand. But I want to do what you want to do. Please? I hate seeing you upset."

She prevented me from kneeling on the floor when I shifted my foot back. "Fine, fine," she mumbled, accepting another hug when I opened my arms. This time, she wrapped her arms around my neck, so I could hear her clearly when she said, "You and your literal begging."

But with the hint of amusement in her voice, I knew I'd have her laughing by the time the sun went down. I squeezed her tight and kissed her forehead. "I'll bring dinner."

Two hours later, I arrived at Claire's door with sushi. She gestured to the low table in the living room, and I set out the rolls, sweet potato tempura and California roll for her, and a dragon roll plus something called the dynamite roll for me. I dragged a hand through my hair, wet from the rain. "It's supposed to thunderstorm tonight." I plucked at my T-shirt, stuck to my shoulders and chest. "And I would like to reiterate, those steps out there are a deathtrap."

"You're so dramatic," she said, her back to me as she grabbed two glasses of water. By the time she turned around, I had my T-shirt stripped off. She stopped, her gaze zeroing in on my chest.

"My shirt was soaked," I said in explanation, and she wordlessly handed me the glasses in exchange for the drenched ball of cotton. I took off my jeans too because wet denim was the absolute worst, and she hung them and my shirt over chairs at the eat-in counter then dropped down next to me, both of us leaning back against the couch. Me in my black boxer briefs, her in leggings and a T-shirt.

We kept the television off as we ate, the only sound coming from the pitter-patter outside. And it was excruciating.

Knowing she needed peace and quiet, when all I wanted to do was tell her how Mariah needed new brake pads or about the adorable baby at the sushi place. Or, I don't know, how I needed to beatbox or something. Anything to expel some energy. Unknot the tension floating around Claire.

I didn't know how she did it. How she was able to stay so still and quiet all the time. Like she enjoyed it.

When I was upset, I usually went for a run. But that was out of the question with the storm brewing outside.

"We have to do something," I said, freeing the words like I'd been holding my breath for the last half hour.

She merely aimed a half smile in my direction.

"I can feel your nerves, and it's making me…" I wiggled my arms and legs.

"Come on," she murmured, taking my hand in hers to tug me into her small bathroom. "Sit," she ordered, and like the good doggie I was, I sat. Riffling through a drawer, she found a few tubes and small bottles, setting each one on the counter. "I have charcoal, green tea, pink clay, this one for anti-aging, and this one," she said, pointing to the last white tub, "is an intense hydrating mask. Which one do you want?"

I leaned over to snag the black tube. "You put charcoal on your face? That can't be healthy."

"Yeah, it's really good for blackheads. Reduces your pores too."

"But… Don't you need pores?"

She laughed, my favorite one, accompanied by a head-shake. "Yes, but it makes them look smaller."

I nodded as if that made any sense and put the tube back down. "I don't know. You pick."

She tapped her finger on her lower lip, taking the assignment seriously. "Do you have dry, oily, or combination skin?"

"Uh. Dry?" I *did* use a separate face wash from my body wash after Sam yelled at me for not moisturizing enough. Although I almost never remembered to actually use the lotion she'd arranged to have delivered to my door every few months. That was why a dozen bottles now lived under my sink.

Claire picked up the small white tub and dipped two fingers into the goop. I closed my eyes as she swiped what felt like a big dollop on my forehead and spread it all around my face.

"Smells nice," I said, and she hummed in agreement.

"You only need a little bit," she told me, although it felt like she slathered on a lot more than a little bit. "After we're done, we'll put a moisturizer on too. How does that feel?"

I opened my eyes to find her bent at the waist, mere centimeters from me, and I curled my hands around her hips to yank her closer to me. "Good." Then I pursed my lips, careful not to smudge the gloopy stuff. She met my kiss with a stifled laugh. "Which one are you using?"

She screwed the lid back on the white tub and reached for the small green bottle. With the cap off, I saw it looked like a tiny green dome, and she wound her hair up on the top of her head then slid a stretchy elastic headband around her head before painting her face green like she was coloring with a face crayon.

"Now what?" I asked when she finished.

"Now we wait."

I nodded, but instead of sitting still, I inspected everything in her bathroom. The towels, her brushes, her shampoo, conditioner, and razor. "Where do you keep all your headbands?"

"In my room. Some girls have jewelry stands. I have a headband rack." She picked up a nail file. "Why do you like them so much?"

"I told you," I started, sitting back down on the closed toilet lid. "I don't know why. I just do. They make me think you're prim and proper, when we both know you're not," I said with an over-the-top wink. She rolled her eyes, the corner of her lips twitching. "Can I take this off yet?"

"One more minute."

I let out a breath and dropped my head back, my eyes on the ceiling, where I spotted a small stain. Like water damage.

I didn't know how much I trusted this landlord of hers. First, the metal steps of death and now water damage. What if she had mold in here?

"You have to get out of here," I told her.

She froze, raising her gaze from where it'd been focused on her hand while she filed her nails. "What?"

I pointed to her ceiling. "That might be mold."

"It's not mold."

"How do you know?"

"Because it's been there since before I moved in. There was a leak in the roof, but they patched it."

I raised my hands, point proven. "Exactly. And they never did anything to fix your ceiling. Half-assed job if I've ever seen one."

"Jimmy." She put her file away and closed her medicine cabinet.

"Don't sigh my name like that. You know what it does to me," I said, coming up right behind her, grinding my hips against her so she could feel the half-aroused state of my cock. She ducked out of the way when I attempted to kiss her neck.

"Time to wash it off." She turned the taps and held her fingers under the water until it was a temperature she liked. She washed the green gunk off her face and moved over so I could clear the white cake mixture from mine too. We shared a towel to dry off, then she squirted a pea-sized amount of moisturizer into my palm, instructing me to rub it over my face and throat.

"You know. I like doing this." I caught her eyes in the reflection of the mirror. "It is pretty relaxing. Plus, my skin feels so soft." To prove it, I nuzzled my cheek against her neck, and she gave in to a laugh.

I wanted to collect each one of her smiles and giggles. Display them on my mantel like awards. *See this? I won these.*

Before I had any time to formulate an acceptance speech, Claire was leading me out of the bathroom and into her bedroom.

It was everything and nothing like I expected. It was plain beige, like the rest of the place, and she didn't have any photos or art on the walls, which was kind of disappointing. I bet if she were able to, she'd have this room looking like some Pinterest board. Although, her bed was covered with 14,597 pillows, and two different rugs were draped on top of each other in a weird yet cool way. One white and fuzzy and the other patterned with stripes of pink and navy. The curtains on the window and her bedspread matched, and a random thought about how she'd decorate my house raced through my brain before I could catch it.

She opened her window a crack, allowing the sounds of the still-faraway thunder to enter the space. She leaned over, her hands on the sill. "I love rain," she whispered. "It calms me down, and I always love how it smells just before a storm." Then she turned to me. "Don't you?"

I'd never thought about it, but... "Yeah."

She offered me a small smile and hopped onto the bed, shifting the mountain of pillows to grab the top book from the stack on her bedside table. It was a historical romance, of course.

"You going to read to me, Miss Hart?" I asked, making a home next to her.

"You want me to?"

"Yeah, but you have to fill me in first."

She adjusted a pillow behind her head then removed her bookmark. I huffed when I read it. "Fictional boyfriends do it better? Ma'am."

She snatched it back from me. "What?"

"Fictional boyfriends do it better? Do what better? Sex? Relationships?"

"You sound so offended," she muttered behind her book.

I crossed my arms. "Your fictional boyfriends have never once brought you dinner and then put on a face mask."

"Correct."

"They've also never provided you orgasms."

She tipped her head. "Not literally, but they do provide good fodder for the imagination."

With a grumble, I rolled on top of her so that she squeaked out a laugh, but I refused to move even when she batted at me. "You're so soft and warm."

"How can I read to you if you're on top of me?"

I scooted down, settling the lower half of my body in the space between her open legs. And yeah, it would have been real easy to put my mouth there, but instead, I held on to her like I was gripping my favorite pillow and nestled against her stomach, the valley between her breasts the perfect spot for my head. "Like this."

She let out an annoyed exhalation, yet her fingers still combed through my hair, my favorite thing.

"So, fill me in. What happened in the book so far?"

"Emma's a seamstress, and she shows up at this duke's door, asking to be paid for the wedding dress she made for his fiancée. But said fiancée dumped him."

"Bummer," I murmured with my eyes closed.

I felt Claire nod. "Yeah, so the duke decides he's not going to pay her, but he is going to make a deal to marry her."

I tipped my head up, meeting Claire's eyes. "What?"

She nodded excitedly. "He can see she's poor, and he's in need of an heir, so he offers to marry her. She'll get taken care of, and he'll get his heir."

"This sounds familiar," I mumbled. Not that I'd offered Claire marriage because I needed an heir, but I did offer her a deal. A relationship in exchange for money. What the hell was I thinking?

I'd treated Claire like a pawn. I didn't deserve her.

As if she could read my mind, Claire dragged the tip of her index finger across my forehead and down my nose to my lips. "It's okay. Remember, it's a romance. They'll always end up together."

Even though she was referring to the couple in her book, I couldn't help but think she was talking about us too. Would we always end up together? I didn't know, but...

I was pretty sure I wanted to.

"Okay, you ready? You have your listening ears on?"

I smiled into the curve of her breast. "Yeah. I'm ready."

"Chapter ten," she began in a soft, lilting voice, and I breathed in complete contentment as the storm raged outside. The faraway thunder oddly comforting, the slight breeze from her cracked open window even better.

In no time at all, my alarm was going off from where I'd left it in the living room. "Guess it's time for me to go home," I husked, too warm and cozy in her bed.

Claire's gaze flickered to her door then back to me, those eyes of her like two teardrops. "I know you have your brother's class in the morning."

I nodded, slow to swing my legs over the side of her bed. She had a really great mattress, and though all the pillows were kind of a hassle, I didn't want to leave the cocoon of her bed.

"But," she hedged, and I turned over my shoulder.

"Yeah?"

"Would you...maybe want to stay?" She bit into the corner of her mouth, and I reversed course, even as my cell phone still blared from her living room.

"You want me to stay?" I drew my thumb under her bottom lip, tugging her lip loose from her teeth, tapping my favorite freckles. "I'll stay."

She nuzzled her cheek into my hand, and I leaned in to kiss her sweet mouth. The sweetest mouth I'd ever had the pleasure of tasting.

And only then did I hop out of her bed for my cell phone, where I'd left it in the pocket of my pants, still draped over the chair in the kitchen. I returned to her and plugged it into her charger after texting Mike that I wouldn't be in attendance tomorrow. There was no way I was getting out of this bed until I absolutely had to.

In her bathroom, we brushed our teeth together once she found me an extra in the back of her closet. And to my utter *delight*, I discovered Claire Hart wore matching pajama sets to bed. Little scraps of silky material. Her choice tonight was tiny shorts that barely covered her ass and a tank top that did nothing to hide the outline of her hard nipples. The material was tie-dyed like rainbow sherbet, and I couldn't help myself. I lowered the strap over her left shoulder and sucked on her skin.

She tilted her head to the side, allowing me more room to work, even as she said, "I only want to sleep tonight, okay?"

"Mm-hmm."

She spun around to face me. "I'm serious. I need…" She glanced to the bed then back at me. "I need you to cuddle the shit out of me."

"Yes!" I hooted and flung myself on her bed, holding my arms open for her. She took her time, pulling the comforter back, setting all one hundred thousand of her pillows on the floor, then finally scooted against me. She rested her cheek against my bare chest, her fingers toying with the bit of hair between my pecs, and I played with a few of her strands, winding and unwinding them around my finger. "Can your fictional boyfriends do this?"

"No." I felt her smile against me. "No, they can't."

"So, who does it better now?"

"You do." She placed a kiss against my shoulder then set her chin on her hand and met my eyes. "You're the only boyfriend I've cared about like this. The only one I've let into my quiet space."

I knew how hard it was for me to open up. It had been almost thirty years until I'd found someone I wanted in my bed, so I knew how difficult it was for Claire to let me into her comfort zone. My little loner.

"Thanks for permitting me entrance."

She laid her head on my shoulder. "Thanks for keeping it down."

"You're welcome. You should know it wasn't easy."

"You're ridiculous."

I kissed the crown of her head. "And you're perfect. Alexa, lights out."

"I don't have my lights connected to Alexa."

"Hey, Google—"

"Don't have that either."

I wrenched my head to the side to catch her attention. "You mean you physically turn your lights on and off?" At her nod, I sighed. "What is this? The nineteenth century?"

She rolled away and hit a switch, which turned off her bedside lamp as well as the decorative string lights along the top of her wall. She snuggled back against me, fitting in so right along my side, I was tempted to her ask her if I could stay forever. Instead, I placed a possessive hand on her ass and tucked my nose into her hair, inhaling deeply.

The last thing I comprehended before I fell asleep was her murmured words that sounded an awful lot like, "Love you."

But then again, I was already halfway into dreaming. Probably just my imagination.

CHAPTER TWENTY-THREE

Claire

I didn't sleep well, tossing and turning, fretting over the meeting. I accidentally kicked and poked Jimmy enough times that he eventually stuck a pillow between us, and even though he said he wasn't going to get up at his normal time, he was wide awake and left with a kiss to my temple as soon as his alarm went off.

I took my time getting dressed, planning out what I would say to Mrs. Brooks, wondering if I should prepare anything more than an apology and promise not to suggest any more books to Anna, as per Mrs. Kaplan's instructions. I doubled up on my deodorant but was too nervous to eat or drink anything and headed to school with sweaty palms.

Meredith was waiting at the library door when I trudged down the hall. She held up a plastic container from the grocery store filled with my favorite lemon squares. "Thought you could use a pick-me-up."

I accepted them and unlocked the library doors. "Thanks."

"How are you feeling?"

"Like I could throw up."

Meredith thunked her purse down on the counter. "I know the meeting is to appease this lady, and I know you're averse to, like, pissing anyone off, but you did not break any rules. You did what you thought was right, which was helping Anna. You're a good person. This meeting today does not negate that. It doesn't take away from how good you are at your job."

I sucked in a breath and booted up the computer, knowing my best friend was correct, but I was also terrified of getting in trouble. Schools were easy targets in political battles, and this was exactly the kind of thing that could be taken way out of context. But all I did was give a student the opportunity to explore books she might have been interested in. The books weren't purchased with school funds and didn't even belong to the school. I didn't treat Anna any differently than I would have any other student.

"It's all bullshit just to smooth things over," Meredith went on. "Say sorry and move on. It'll be fine." She slung her arm around my shoulders. "But more importantly, how are things going with your golden retriever?"

"You have a golden retriever?"

Meredith and I both whirled at Jimmy's voice by the door.

"Yeah, you," she said.

He pointed at himself. "I'm a golden retriever?"

I shook my head. "More like a... What kind of dog needs a lot of attention? A terrier?"

Meredith nodded, waving Jimmy in to join us. "Yeah. We had a Jack Russell growing up, and that motherfucker never left us alone for a minute."

I shot a look at my boyfriend, but he only slid my coffee in front of me then wrapped his arms around my waist from behind me. He laid a peck on the side of my neck. "I do like belly rubs, long walks, and when people throw a ball to me."

I spun around in his hold and raked my fingers through his unruly hair, scraping my nails along his scalp, and he lifted his foot off the floor, shaking it slightly. I rolled my eyes and pushed him away. He staggered back, grinning like the terrier he was before offering me a soft kiss on the mouth.

"Things are obviously going well for you two." Meredith took a sip from her travel coffee mug. "I'm so happy for you," she said sarcastically.

"Hassan has yet to fall for her charms," I explained to Jimmy.

"Well, he is just coming out of a divorce," Jimmy noted.

She raised her Yeti. "Exactly. He needs a rebound."

"Which is you?" Jimmy guessed. When she ticked her brow meaningfully, he tipped his head side to side. "I mean... Not to say you have to give up on Hassan, but I've recently discovered the wonder that is being in a committed relationship, and I've got to say, I really like it."

Meredith shook her head, her long blond ponytail swinging. "You two have been together literal days."

Jimmy cocked his head back and slanted his gaze down to me. "That's it? No, it's been, like, a year."

I elbowed him. Although, I couldn't disagree. Being together for a matter of days had already felt much longer. Maybe because we had known each other for years. It wasn't a difficult transition to make.

"It's been a week," Meredith corrected. "Or, a month, depending on when you consider the beginning."

Jimmy shrugged. "Doesn't matter when. Only that we're together now."

I met his eyes, reveling in the security of his arm around me, his fingers tightening at my waist.

Meredith gagged. "Great. Let me go lie down in traffic."

"You could have this too, you know," he said to her back as she stalked toward the doors.

"No thanks!"

"We should set her up with one of your brothers," Jimmy suggested once she turned down the hall.

I snorted. "None of them could handle her."

"What about Ryan?"

I brushed the idea away. "They'd be terrible together."

"Yeah, but they don't have to date. Just bang."

"I'd rather not hear the word 'bang' in reference to one of my brothers, thank you very much."

He shifted so he was behind me, bending slightly, forcing me to put my hands on my desk. His breath was hot on my ear. "What about in reference to you?"

I angled my head, giving him access to my neck, but even as my skin pebbled with goose bumps and my heart rate sped up, I was in enough trouble as it was. "Don't do that here."

He squeezed my hips, straightening up to his full height and kissing my head. "Sorry, sorry. Got carried away." Striding around the counter, he tossed me a half smile. "Hey, don't worry about the meeting, okay? It'll be fine."

Jimmy crossed the hall to begin his day, while I felt mired, unable to complete any tasks. Each hour passed slower than the last, my patience and sanity wearing thin, so that I threw my lesson plans out the window and let the kids play computer games in the lab. It wasn't the best coping mechanism, but whenever I was really nervous, I became short-tempered, and I didn't want to take out my problems on the students.

When the final bell rang, I expelled a breath and slumped into my chair. The day for the students ended at 3:15, and until the buses and parent pickup vehicles were gone, it was usually about 3:30. Teachers were expected to stay until 3:45, but most cut out as soon as the parking lot cleared. Though today, instead of exiting out the front or side doors, which led to staff parking, they walked down my hall, to the doors that led out to the opposite side of the lot, to the playground and field.

They sent me sympathetic smiles and hopeful "Have a good weekend!" greetings. They knew. They all knew. Probably because of Meredith. Or Jimmy. Most likely both.

I didn't have the courage to wait by the door for my visitor, so I sat at one of the tables, in the uncomfortable blue chairs, like I was waiting for my execution.

"Hey."

I lifted my attention from my fingers twisted in my lap to Jimmy at the door.

"You have nothing to worry about."

I tried to smile but couldn't.

"After this is over, we'll celebrate. Voting begins at five."

I'd completely forgotten about the contest since all this had arisen with Mrs. Brooks. It was actually a relief to think about something fun and silly as opposed to the foreboding doom and gloom.

Jimmy knocked twice on the doorframe and winked. "Half-price apps?"

I laughed, and it felt wonderful to loosen up the tight web of anxiety in my chest. "Sure."

Mid-fist-pump, he rolled his head to the side, his attention on something, or rather someone, down the hall, and my stomach took a nose dive. He smiled at them, though it wasn't at all real. Closed-lipped and tight, he offered a tiny head bow and a quick glance in my direction before he backed away, mouthing, "I'll be right here."

Then Mrs. Kaplan appeared in the doorway with Mrs. Brooks, a tall, slender white woman with shoulder-length blond hair and glasses.

"Good afternoon, Miss Hart," Mrs. Kaplan said in greeting,

a small smile for my benefit only since Mrs. Brooks couldn't see as she paraded to the table.

She sat down right across from me and crossed her arms, mouth set in a grim line. She was *pissed*.

And I wanted to puke.

"How was your day?" Mrs. Kaplan asked me, and I managed to keep my voice even when I answered.

"Good. Usual Friday."

"That's for sure," Mrs. Kaplan said, and I'd never been so grateful that she was my principal. Always even-keeled and encouraging. It was obvious she knew this meeting was going to be rough and was attempting to lift me up a bit.

It wasn't working.

But still.

It was nice of her.

"So," Mrs. Kaplan started slowly, sitting between Mrs. Brooks and me so we were all points in a triangle around the circular table. "Mrs. Brooks wanted this meeting to address her concerns," she said to me then turned to the woman staring daggers at me, "and we are all ears. As you well know, Mrs. Brooks, our students' well-being is of utmost importance, and we want not only Anna to know she is supported here, but you as well."

Mrs. Brooks was probably not much older than me, maybe less than a decade, but she made me feel like I was a child by simply raising her brow in my direction. I couldn't imagine what it was like for Anna to live with her. Completely intimidating.

She focused her narrowed eyes at Mrs. Kaplan. "Well, you may think your students' well-being is of the utmost importance, but that is evidently not what your staff thinks. Not with the trash she's—" she swept her hand out in my direction "—giving them."

Mrs. Kaplan flattened her hands on the table. "As I said in my reply to you yesterday, Miss Hart did not mean to cause you any distress, but I think we should agree to be careful with the words we're using."

"Oh." Mrs. Brooks huffed indignantly. "That's what we're here for? So you can tone-police me?"

"No, not at all. We are here to listen to all your concerns, and they will be addressed, but I think we shouldn't be calling books trash." Mrs. Kaplan's voice was firm but gentle, though it only set Mrs. Brooks off more.

"Don't patronize me, and I will kindly ask you not to tell me how to feel and talk." She turned her rage on me. "The book you gave my daughter is *trash*."

"Did you read it?" I asked, my own hackles rising. I knew I was here to apologize and smooth the waters, but if the woman insisted on making more waves, I wasn't going to let myself be drowned.

"No, I would never read something as disgusting as a book grooming young kids."

I covered my eye roll with my hand.

"Did you see that?" Mrs. Brooks shrieked. "She just rolled her eyes at me."

Mrs. Kaplan sent me a reprimanding look, and I lifted my hands. "I'm sorry, but a book about kids fighting aliens in space in not *grooming* children. Whatever that even means."

"Grooming children to become perverts and—"

"Mrs. Brooks," Mrs. Kaplan cut in, "that is not at all the messaging in the book, and—"

"Did *you* read the book?" Mrs. Brooks asked, her voice rising. "Did either of you read it?"

"Yes, I did. I read all the books I recommend to the students," I said, leaning into the table, unable to keep my voice from wavering now. I was angry and appalled and *disgusted.* "There was nothing inappropriate in the book. If you read it, you would know."

"All I had to do was look at the back of the book to know it was filth. Girls liking other girls, that's grooming. You're giving these books to kids, teaching them about sex, and expecting them to turn into—"

"There was absolutely no sex in the book, and I would never suggest a book with sex in it to an elementary school student."

"I think we need to slow down," Mrs. Kaplan suggested. "Let's lower our voices and discuss what we can do to move forward. Miss Hart..."

I took a breath and tried to find an ounce of the previous guilt I'd felt about causing Mrs. Brooks worry, but I couldn't. I had no sympathy for her because she didn't deserve it. She was accusing me of being something I was not. "I apologize for suggesting Anna read a book you didn't approve. I won't suggest any more."

"No, you won't. Because you clearly do not know what is appropriate and what isn't." Mrs. Brooks gestured around the library. "All of these books should be examined, see which ones are inappropriate. Who knows what else you're stocking here."

"I can guarantee you all of the books in this library are age and content appropriate," Mrs. Kaplan said.

"Then where did my daughter get her books from?"

"It was a Little Library book," I explained, even though I could read the tea leaves on this. The woman would not be satisfied until she burned everything to the ground. "We keep books in the box outside of the school for any student or parent who wants to leave or take a book. Those books are not approved by anyone, but I monitor them, and I can tell you they are also age and content appropriate."

"I can tell you they are not!" she shrieked. "If I went out there right now, I can just imagine what garbage I'd find."

"I really wish you would stop referring to books as garbage," Mrs. Kaplan injected, and I could tell she was swiftly losing her tolerance.

"I can tell you you'd find the diary of Anne Frank, some Dr. Seuss books, and a couple of graphic novels," I said, ticking the books off on my fingers.

"Graphic novels?" Mrs. Brooks sputtered, pushing her chair away from the table as if she was about to sprint from the room. "You're admitting to giving children graphic content?"

This time, I didn't try to hide my eye roll. In fact, I wanted this idiot to see it. "Graphic novels are comic books."

She was undeterred by the truth, standing up so she looked down her nose at me. "You are a disgrace to the education system. What you're doing here? Indoctrinating these children with your liberal ideas and grooming them for disgusting behavior, it should be illegal!"

Mrs. Kaplan stood up too. "Mrs. Brooks—"

Suddenly, "No Scrubs" by TLC boomed from across the hall, and all three of us whipped our heads toward the door. The entrance to the library was empty, but it was obvious where the music was coming from.

Mrs. Brooks thrust her finger in my direction as she shouted over the music at Mrs. Kaplan. "What are you doing to discipline her?"

"Miss Hart and I have spoken about refraining from suggesting books to students, and we will remove the books you are concerned about from the Little Library."

"Well, I already did that for you. I threw that filth in the garbage, where it belongs."

My jaw hit the floor. Not that I was surprised, but it wasn't hers to throw away. I had purchased the book and put it in the

Little Library. Even if she wanted it removed, it rightfully belonged to me.

"I want that Little Library taken down, and I want all these books—" she arced her long-nailed finger around the library again "—gone through."

"No," I said immediately.

"Mrs. Brooks, each of our library books has to be approved and—"

"Are you going to go through each of these books?" I asked, taunting her now. "You're going to read and approve each one on the shelf?"

"Don't look so smug," she gritted out between clenched teeth, her jaw set, that finger still pointed at me. "I'm not done with you yet." Then she threw her purse over her shoulder and marched out of the library, tossing out one last bomb. "You'll be hearing from me again. After I speak to the superintendent!"

CHAPTER TWENTY-FOUR

Claire

My hands trembled as I reached for the counter to balance as I hobbled around it to sit in my chair.

"Claire." Mrs. Kaplan followed me, my name like an echo in the quiet library after Mrs. Brooks had taken her volume and indignation with her. And TLC had been silenced. Now it was just me and my simmering rage and overwhelming mortification. "You look a little pale."

I took a sip from my water bottle to clear my throat of the clawing emotion stuck there. My nose stung, and I blinked back the tears I'd held in through that meeting.

Mrs. Kaplan rubbed my shoulder. "That did not go as I'd hoped."

I sniffed out a sarcastic laugh. "No."

"Listen, you have my support one hundred percent, but I want you to contact Aggie."

Aggie was our school's union rep, and I nodded, accepting the tissue she handed me.

"And I think it would be best if we took down the Little Library," she said, and I understood the decision but still hated it.

"Okay."

"It isn't going to help...with whatever war Mrs. Brooks wants to wage, but moving forward, I do not want there to be any opportunity for someone to misconstrue what you or anyone on this staff does."

I blew my nose. "Okay."

She frowned, like a mother who knew her child was in the wrong but still wanted to comfort them. "You're an excellent teacher, and we're lucky to have you on staff. What you did, finding a book for a student, is not wrong. Offering anyone a suggestion to read a book is not innately wrong. But we do need to be very careful and aware of what different people find offensive. Ultimately, the guardians of our students need to make the decisions about what content these children consume. I know you know this."

I nodded, both defensive and chastened. "I do."

"But what Mrs. Brooks said to you today was wholly inappropriate and out of line. You do not deserve to be spoken to that way, and I will fight on your behalf."

"Thank you."

With one last squeeze of my shoulder, Mrs. Kaplan headed to the door.

Leaning my elbows on my knees, I dropped my head to take a few deep breaths. Never in my life had I experienced anything like that. I'd never had to defend my job. I'd never had to defend books. And with Mrs. Brooks's threat hanging in the air, I was afraid I'd have to defend *myself*.

I believed Mrs. Kaplan would fight on my behalf. I believed that reason and kindness would always win, but I didn't live in a fantasyland, and I knew what was happening in some school districts in other parts of the country. I knew what other librarians experienced, and I didn't want to face it. For the first time in my life, I actually feared for my job.

But beyond that, I felt bad for Anna. If she was exploring

the queer spectrum, she certainly was not finding support at home, which I assumed was why she'd come looking for books in the library in the first place. This poor child, she was the one suffering. She was the one who would be hurt by her mother taking away her ability to find comfort and solace in people like her, fictional or not. Yet instead of helping her daughter, Mrs. Brooks found a target in me. In books.

It was completely irrational and irresponsible. But what did I know? I was just a librarian.

With an infuriated huff, I sat up, grabbed my things, and started for the door, intent on locking up, but paused with the key in the lock when I heard Jimmy's irritation-filled voice.

"Well, I'm sorry I disturbed the meeting, but ridiculous behavior deserves to be drowned out by equally ridiculous behavior."

"I get why you're upset. Really, I do," I heard Mrs. Kaplan say. "But you cannot get involved in this."

"I'm already involved."

"This has nothing to do with you."

"If Claire is involved, so I am. Isn't that what you always say? A win for one of us is a win for all of us. We're all building a community here."

Mrs. Kaplan made a tsking noise like she didn't like her words being used against her. "Yes, that is what I say, but this situation has the potential to explode."

"And I'm not going to let Claire go through it alone," Jimmy nearly shouted.

"She will not go through it alone. She has my support. She has all our support."

Jimmy grumbled something I didn't catch, and Mrs. Kaplan responded with a curt, "We will take care of it, and I would advise you to keep your head down and finish out the rest of the year on a high note. If you get involved with this, it will most assuredly cost you Teacher of the Year."

"I don't care," he said immediately and clearly, and I spun my head around toward his door. "I don't give a shit about some award. That woman basically threatened Claire's job, her livelihood. If I have to choose between a stupid award and Claire, it's no choice at all."

Jimmy was a lot of things, attention-seeking and prone to hyperbole, but he was also honest and always followed through on his promises. So his easy and quick declaration to give up his chance at a prestigious teaching award was a *very* big deal.

And I knew, in that moment, I loved this man. This ridiculous, absurd, over-the-top man who would do anything for the people he loved, and I assumed I could be included in that incredibly lucky group now.

Mrs. Kaplan tutted. "There are procedures and policies in place. Let the administration handle this."

Jimmy didn't answer, and after a few moments of silence, Mrs. Kaplan's steps sounded closer to the door, and I snapped back into action, pretending I was in the middle of leaving. Mrs. Kaplan offered Jimmy one last warning. "Remember what I said." Then she rounded the corner of his room, spotting me. She smiled gently. "Have a nice weekend, Claire."

I waved and waited until she disappeared down the hall, toward the main office, before walking across the hall to Jimmy's room. He was pacing the length of it. On a pivot, he raised his dark gaze to me. His brow was pinched, shoulders high and rigid, hair a mess like he'd run his hands through it all afternoon, and my heart nearly about leaped out of my chest.

He stopped mere feet from me, his eyes raking over me as if searching for battle wounds. "Are you—"

"'No Scrubs,' really?"

He propped his hands on his hips, a reluctant laugh leaving him as he shook his head. "I heard her yelling at you. I heard everything, and I…" He shrugged. "I had to do something."

"It pissed her off more."

"Good."

"Is that your plan? To hang around her any time she tries to make noise and…what? Make *more* noise?"

"Didn't think that far ahead."

I closed the distance between us, but with how his body was so rigid with tension, I refrained from touching him. "I heard what you said. To Kaplan."

His throat worked on a swallow as he focused his attention beyond my shoulder, in the direction of the door. He scratched at his dark stubble and took a deep breath, his nostrils flaring, before meeting my gaze again. "Mrs. Brooks is a really shitty person, and you suggesting a book to her kid that she didn't like should not equate to steamrolling you. It's bullshit and stupid and—"

"I know. The irony, her thinking I'm brainwashing her kid when she basically wants to get rid of all the books in the library. She wants *If You Give a Mouse a Cookie* investigated."

Jimmy heaved out a sigh, and for the first time ever, he didn't have any comebacks or jokes readily available. This whole thing was really working on him.

And his defense of me was really working on *me*.

It made me feel supported and brave and like I could actually fight back.

"I heard what Kaplan told you about the Teacher of the Year award," I said, and he made no move to speak, so I continued. "She's right. You can't get involved. If this—" I gestured vaguely behind me "—becomes a big problem, which I can pretty well guess it will, you can't get involved."

He opened his mouth, probably to express what he told Kaplan. That he was already involved.

I cut him off. "The award is important to you."

The look he gave me was filled with such disdain, I actually shrank back a little. "You must think so little of me." He rubbed his fingers over his forehead and cursed quietly. "You think I care more about winning an award than I do you?"

I lifted one shoulder. No, I didn't believe that. But also, he was really competitive. Winning things was basically 75% of his personality. "Teacher of the Year is a big honor."

The angry fire in his eyes faded, and he dropped his hands to his sides, his voice low and ragged. "So, what? You're saying you don't want me to fight this with you?"

All the emotion that I'd been holding in for the past hour— the past day—came crashing down on me, and I covered my face as my tears streaked down my cheeks. I didn't want anyone to have to fight with me. I didn't want to fight, period. I shouldn't have to defend what I did, I shouldn't have completely false accusations thrown at me, I shouldn't have to argue with people who refused to see reason and logic. And I certainly didn't want anyone, especially Jimmy, suffering consequences because of something I did.

"I'm saying I don't want to drag you down."

"Come here," he murmured, curling his arms around me, urging my face to his chest. With one hand tangled in my hair and the other stroking my back, he held me for a minute, continually brushing his lips over my temple, whispering words about how it would all be okay.

Once I caught my breath and my tears slowed, I tilted my head, noticing wet spots on his shirt. I rubbed at them then at the throbbing behind my temples.

"Feel better?" he asked, and when I shook my head, he curved his palms around my jaw, his thumbs wiping the last of the wetness off my cheeks. "You're not dragging me down. We're in this together. It's you and me." Then he gently took my lips between his. More than a kiss, it was a promise. He spoke his next words against my mouth. "If you go down, I go down." Then he slanted a crooked smile my way, mischief lighting his eyes. "But I don't think anyone should be going down, unless it's me on you."

I thumped at his chest weakly, and he laughed. I did too. I needed him to keep me centered, help me to remember, even when things seemed horrible, I wasn't alone.

"Speaking of, let's go back to my place," he suggested, his hands trailing down my arms. "Let me de-stress you."

I didn't know if the headache was from crying or from tension, but either way, I felt ready to fall over. And his bed sounded really nice right now.

He tugged me to his desk to gather his backpack and keys then led me back toward the door and locked up, all one-handed.

"You afraid I'll run away?" I teased.

"Hm?"

I held up our linked hands.

"Oh, huh." He appeared clueless, as if he hadn't realized he had dragged me back and forth. In answer, he simply kissed the back of my hand.

We parted in the parking lot, where he told me he was going to run to the store, which was fine because I wanted to go home and pack a bag. I didn't think it was a wrong assumption to make when I tossed in an extra toothbrush and a few pieces of clothes to leave at his house.

After receiving a text letting me know I should come in through the garage, I arrived at Jimmy's house to find him opening a box of wine in the kitchen.

"Classy," I said, and he grinned.

"Yeah, I thought so." He pointed to the various packets of face masks with the box of lemon-flavored Italian ice cups in his hand. "I tried to get you all your favorite things. We could do whatever you want, watch a K-Drama and get drunk on wine, do the face masks, drink more wine, eat so much Italian ice we get a brain freeze...whatever you want."

I didn't have to think about what I wanted.

"I want you."

"You got me, baby," he said as he put the ice away in the freezer.

"No." I crossed into the kitchen and put my hand on his forearm. "I mean, I *want* you."

He froze mid-reach for the box of wine, his gaze dropping down to my mouth, eyes widening in understanding. Without another word, he took my hand in his and towed me to his bedroom. "Are you on birth control?"

"I get the shot."

Over his shoulder, he cringed at me. "A shot?"

"Yeah, every few months. I used to be on the pill, but—"

"You stick a needle in your arm every few months?"

"Well, I don't do it," I said with a shrug, "but yeah."

He visibly shuddered, though all traces of jokes were gone as he turned to face me, both of us standing at the foot of his bed. "I have condoms, and just so you know, I was tested a few months ago. There is nothing I want more than to be with you and have nothing between us, but I'll do whatever you want."

His gaze was serious, his intent completely clear, and while I knew my sexual partners numbered far fewer than his, I also knew he was careful. He would always be careful with me.

"That's what I want too," I said, ringing my arms around his neck.

Then his mouth was on mine, his hands roaming every-where, grabbing at my backside, tugging on my skirt, inching up my shirt, squeezing my breast. "I thought you wanted to go slow."

"That was before I heard what you said to Kaplan today."

The sound he made against my ear sent shock waves straight between my legs.

"No one has ever made me feel the way you do," I said, reaching my arms up so he could lift my simple pale-orange T-shirt over my head.

My skirt came off next, pooling at my feet, and he stepped back, admiring me like my soft belly and big hips were his favorite things. He never hid his admiration of me, and I loved that he loved it.

"I would literally give you my entire paycheck to spend on more of these bras and underwear." He slid one finger inside the top of my panties, brushing along my hip. This set wasn't very cute, plain beige lace, yet it was an apparent hit with him.

"I'll take it into consideration," I said, backing up on his bed, watching as he shucked his polo shirt and pants.

"Take me shopping with you?" he asked, and I bit back a smile.

"I'll take it into consideration."

He rolled his eyes up to the ceiling, muttering, "So difficult," before crawling over me on the bed. "Tell me that bag you brought has stuff in it to stay all weekend." When I nodded, he sank onto his elbows, his mouth at the crook of my neck. "Thank god."

His skin was warm, and I wrapped my arms around his torso, running my fingers over his spine as he arched, moving to lick and suck along the tops of my breasts. He cupped one of them roughly, his fingers digging into the flesh. "I love how soft you are." His hand drifted down to my hip, and he grabbed me there too. "This right here? I'm going to dig my fingers into you so hard while I fuck you from behind, you're going to have marks for days."

"Yes," I moaned. I wanted marks. I wanted him hot and hard and panting for me. Because I was desperate for him. I reached down, cupping his erection over his boxer briefs, but he shot his hips back, tearing out of my grasp.

"Not yet. You know the rules. I go down on you first. Hands stay on the bed. You don't touch me until I tell you to."

"Or what?"

"Or I don't let you come." Then he bared his teeth along my nipple. Another arrow straight between my legs. He arched a brow. "Got it?"

Sufficiently warned and entirely too aroused, I nodded silently.

"Now." He moved back to the edge of the bed to remove my panties. He balled them up and tossed them behind his shoulder. "Let's see how many times I can make you orgasm before you're begging me for my cock."

A laugh strangled my throat as he yanked me down the mattress. He kneeled on the floor, and that was about all the warning I got before he clamped his hands down on my hips and his lips on my aching core. He licked the flat of his tongue up my slit a few times, almost as a warm-up, before using only the tip on my clit until my hips were writhing in his hold.

"Uh-uh-uh," he chided when my fingers found their way into his hair without my brain even telling them to. He backed away but spread my legs wider, his hands under each of my knees, allowing the cool air to shock my hot center. But only for one brief moment because then his mouth was on me again.

I fisted my right hand into the comforter that was barely clinging to the bed and my left into the sheet, and he rewarded me with some move that was a quick sawing motion back and forth across my clit. My back arched up, the wicked touch over-whelming every one of my senses. I might have even gone momentarily blind when he thrust a finger inside me, his mouth never letting up, and fire spread over me, coating my skin in a thin sheen of sweat. As he pumped his finger into me, the first orgasm seemed to go on forever, and my mouth went dry with how quick I was breathing. Like I was sprinting.

I'd never sprinted for anything in my life.

But Jimmy didn't stop. Didn't even acknowledge or brag about the first orgasm. He only removed his finger from me and dragged the wetness down the line between my cheeks. His tongue followed, and I sucked in a sharp breath at the sensation of his tongue at the place where no guy had been before. Before I could consider whether I should be embar-rassed or not, he pushed my legs together, forcibly rocking my hips up and down, his tongue sweeping along the length of me with each movement.

And even though it felt so, so good, a part of me thought he was doing this for himself now, maneuvering me this way and that like I was his personal plaything.

I didn't hate the idea.

Closing my eyes, I hummed my appreciation as he pried my legs back open, stretching my thighs wide, his tongue fucking into me. "Oh my god."

"Mm-hmm." He sucked on my clit.

"Do that again."

He did as I said, and my entire body shuddered in pleasure, another orgasm building low in my belly. He curled his fingers into me, pumping them with timed strokes of his tongue, and I reflexively reached my hands out for him, only to remember his rule at the last second, and dropped them back to the bed, riding his face as I clawed at a pillow.

"I'm so close," I whined, and all it took was one crook of his fingers and a graze of his teeth, and I was hurled into another universe. I didn't know up from down, light from darkness, only this man's hands clutching my thighs, whispering words against the bare skin of my shoulder.

I didn't know when or how he did it, but I found myself turned over on my stomach.

"I can't wait anymore," he rasped, wrenching my hips up. "I'll make it up to you later."

An exhausted laugh escaped my throat as I pushed to my hands, but he slid his palm along my back, settling it between my shoulder blades. "Get down."

His voice was husky, more of a growl than anything, and goose bumps raced across my arms and up the back of my neck. My scalp prickled as he wound his fingers into my hair, gently pressing the side of my face into the bed. "Don't move."

Slowly, I slid my arms up the mattress until they were straight and curled my fingers into the fitted sheet.

"Yes," he hissed behind me. "God, you're perfect." His fingers kneaded my ass cheeks, spreading them. He sucked in a breath. "So gorgeous like this."

I wiggled, unable to keep from arching my back, feeling empty without his fingers or mouth on me. "I need you," I said, my voice having never sounded so petulant before. "Please, hurry."

"Hurry," he repeated, amusement laced in the one word. "That's what I'm trying not to do here." One hand left me for a moment, and I felt him shift behind me, kicking off his underwear. I peeked over my shoulder, and he smirked. "You ready, baby?"

"Please."

He prodded the head of his cock at my entrance. "So polite." And then he was inside me, filling up the empty, needy space. He eased out and pushed back in slowly, his hips jutting up against my backside. "You're so tight." He groaned. "Jesus fuck, Claire."

For a moment, he didn't move, and I rolled my hips.

"Don't. Don't move," he bit out. As he promised, he dug his fingers into my hips to the point it hurt, but I liked it and exhaled harshly, rubbing my chest against the sheet, needing to release the tension cording through me.

He bent over, one hand in my hair, the other ghosting over my breast. He pinched my nipple, still covered by my lace bra, then found my clit, slapping it lightly. "I'll give this needy little pussy what it wants, but I need a second."

He nipped at my ear, soothed it with his tongue, and then the weight of him was gone. Standing up behind me, he took hold of my hips once again. Using his hard grip, he pulled out and pistoned back in, filling me to the hilt again and again, each time hitting the aching place deep inside me.

"Feels so good," I panted between my labored breaths. "Harder."

He grunted, his fingers biting into me, his hips working so fast our skin slapped together with every thrust, the headboard cracking the wall so hard I worried it would leave dents.

Jimmy didn't seem to care.

I didn't either.

Not when I was climbing higher and higher. I could barely breathe, barely think. Heat flashed, and I squeezed my eyes shut to the blinding light behind my lids, screaming into the covers.

Behind me, Jimmy jerked, his fast and even drives stuttering out of rhythm until he collapsed on top of me, both of us splayed out ungracefully. His sweaty chest pressed against my back, his legs between mine, hanging off the end of the bed, both of us breathing unevenly.

"Am I dead?" he asked after a minute.

"Not quite."

He rolled off me, grabbing a T-shirt from the floor to clean himself off before offering it to me, but instead of using his T-shirt, I stood and grabbed a few tissues on my way out of his room to the bathroom. He wolf-whistled after me, and I rolled my eyes even though he couldn't see.

"Don't roll your eyes at me."

I threw back my head and laughed. "You're ridiculous."

"I know, but that's why you love me."

It was true, but even after that otherworldly experience a few minutes ago, I still couldn't find the courage to tell him. Being with Jimmy was like being swept up in a tornado.

Everything between us had happened so fast, I was already swirling in space. And now with this situation at school, my life was spinning out of control. Knowing he had my back meant a lot, yet I wasn't ready to take that leap of giving away that last part of me. I needed time and space to be calm, to let my feet touch the ground.

After using the toilet and cleaning up, I made my way back into Jimmy's room and tossed my bra on the floor by my bag. He watched with rapt attention and an entertained half smile as I stepped into a pair of boy shorts I'd packed and helped myself to searching through his drawers until I found a shirt. It was a graphic tee with an old-school MTV logo on it.

He held up his hands as if taking a picture of me with an invisible camera. "You should never wear anything else except exactly this."

I tilted my head to the hall. "Let's go get drunk on boxed wine."

"Yes!" He shot up from the bed and pulled on a pair of shorts, following behind me. "Want to play a drinking game?"

I only snorted in response.

Jimmy

We didn't play a drinking game, but we did end up getting a bit tipsy on my couch after eating a dinner of turkey and cheese roll-ups and Italian ice. We probably should have included some carbs because Claire promptly passed out as soon as I put on my favorite Thor movie.

I covered her with a blanket, tucked her toes in against my thigh, and settled back against the cushion with one hand resting on her hip. She was so cute with her fists up under her chin, her long hair loose on the pillow behind her, I snapped a quick picture and posted it along with the link to the radio contest website.

The profiles were posted promptly at five for voting, and while Claire and I had looked at it, listened to the interview, we didn't talk much about it. I was afraid to.

Our sex had been phenomenal, life-changing, the best I ever had. Yet, as soon as we had time to decompress, I could almost see the gray cloud forming over her head.

The meeting with Mrs. Brooks had shaken her up. Hell, it'd shaken me up, so I couldn't imagine what she was feeling. All I wanted to do was keep her as comfortable as possible, and while winning the contest was important, it was another stressor she didn't need to worry about. But I would no doubt be checking the site on the regular.

Even though we couldn't see which couple was receiving the most votes, we read the comments people left. So far, the only ones posted about Claire and me were from my mom, Sam, Meredith, and a few coworkers, including Aggie and Marla, the fifth-grade teacher out on maternity leave and no longer on our softball team. Really, it was her having a baby that kick-started this whole thing between Claire and me since she'd joined the team to fill in for Marla and, therefore, gave me idea to submit us to the contest. I should probably send Marla and her baby some flowers. Maybe a fruit basket.

While I scrolled through my social media, a text from my mom popped up.

MAMA DUKES

Haven't heard from you in a while.

We talked like 2 days ago.

MAMA DUKES

Yes and I thought you'd call me to give me the lowdown about the interview.

MAMA DUKES

Instead, I had to listen to it with the rest of the world. I'm your mother.

I've been busy.

Not even a minute later, my mom called through FaceTime. With a wince to Claire, making sure the ringing didn't wake her up, I scooted off the couch and crept into the kitchen so I didn't disturb her.

"What's up, Mom?" I answered, setting the phone on the counter while I filled a glass of water.

"Can you move the phone? All I see is your belly button."

I picked my phone back up once I had my drink, and Mom smiled at me from where I could see she was sitting in my parents' backyard.

"There you are. Your belly button is cute, but not as cute as this face."

I always knew I was my mother's favorite, and I grinned at her.

"What have you been up to?" she asked.

"Eh, there's been a lot going on."

"A lot going on with your girlfriend, who you have yet to introduce me to? Jim, I don't know why you didn't tell me about her before."

"Before?" I stretched my neck, peeking around the door. I didn't have a direct eyeline down into the living room, but I could see her feet had yet to move from their position on the couch. "I told you as soon as we started dating."

Which was basically the truth. As soon as I left Applebee's that first afternoon, I had texted my mother and told her I had a girlfriend and we were entered into a contest.

"Yeah, but obviously you've had feelings for her for a long time. According to your interview."

"Yeah," I said on a sigh. Between my brothers and me, I was the one closest to my mom. There wasn't much I hid from her, and maybe that was because nothing ever seemed that important to me. But Claire was. She'd somehow become the most important person to me in a matter of weeks, days even, and I wanted to keep her all to myself. "I don't keep a diary and tell you every little thing going on in my life. I didn't even realize I had feelings for her until I was smacked in the face with them."

She shook her head. "Oh, my little dum-dum. So oblivious sometimes."

I chuckled. "Too right."

"From the interview, she sounds so sweet, but a bit of a

ballbuster too, huh?" Mom pointed her finger at me. "I think she's so good for you."

"She is," I said without equivocation.

"So, when can we meet her?" she asked.

"I'm not sure. There's a lot going on."

"With the contest?"

I rubbed at the back of my neck. "Yeah, and some other stuff."

"Like what?"

"Work stuff."

"What? With your award?"

"No, Mom. It has nothing to do with me." I set my elbows on the counter and leaned my phone on the wall so I could dig my fingers into my hair. "Some stuff went down at school with Claire, and she's really stressed out, so I don't think—"

"What?" My mom lowered her voice. "What happened?"

I didn't want to get into all the details with her, but I relayed the main gist of it. "She had a meeting with a parent today, and it didn't go well, and the parent is threatening to escalate it to the superintendent."

"Oh no. Is she okay? Is she in trouble?"

"Not right now, and I don't want to stress her out even more, okay? So, let's drop the meet-the-parents conversation until later. I promise you'll meet her. I want you to, but not right now."

"Yeah, sure. Okay," my mom said, but I heard footsteps approaching, and I stood up, meeting Claire's sleepy gaze as she shuffled to the kitchen.

I smiled at her, and she yawned, twisting her hair over one shoulder.

"Honey, all I see is your stomach again."

The whites of Claire's eyes became huge, and I held up my hand, explaining, "It's my mom."

"Who are you talking to?" Mom asked, and Claire's mouth opened, her hands shaking in front of her.

I bent so my mom could see my face again. "Claire's here."

"She is? Oh, I have to meet her. Claire, honey, where are you?"

"I can't meet your mom," she whisper-shouted. "I'm in my underwear!"

"But you look so cute," I teased, and my mother prattled on about something while I laughed at Claire's obvious freak-out. "Come on. Neck up only," I told her. Lifting my phone from the counter, I slung my arm around her, making sure only our heads were in the frame. "Mom, this is Claire. Claire, this is my mom."

"Hi, Mrs. Ewing."

"Claire! Hi! It's so nice to finally see your face. I keep asking my son when I can meet you."

She pinched my ass. God, her pinchers could do some damage. I frowned at her. "I was telling my mom that she will meet you. Maybe after school's over."

Claire nodded. "Yeah, everything's so hectic right now with the end of the year right around the corner."

Because my mom was a pro, she didn't let on to the little bit I'd explained about Claire's situation. "Of course. I'm just excited to see you and can't wait to meet you in person."

Claire raised her hand and then ducked away, scurrying down the hall to my bedroom, and I laughed, turning back to my mother on my phone screen.

"She's really cute," Mom said.

"I know."

"You seem to like her a lot."

"I do," I said.

"It's serious?"

I nodded. "Very."

Then my mother grinned. "Finally."

After ending the call, I strolled down to my room to find Claire digging through her bag, a number of items laid out on the bed already. I carelessly threw myself onto the mattress, jostling her things, and held my head up with one hand. "Whatcha up to?"

"I can't find... Here! Here it is." She held up toothpaste.

"I hope you know I own some."

"I know, but I use this kind. It's whitening for sensitive teeth."

I ran my hand up her thigh. "You've got sensitive teeth?"

"Yeah. I also wear a mouth guard at night so I don't grind them." She held up a small plastic container.

I squeezed her butt. "So hot."

"And..." She nibbled at her bottom lip. "I brought a few other things... I thought, maybe, I could leave them here. In case of emergencies." She was adorable.

"Sure. One never knows when they'll need an emergency mouth guard."

She dropped her gaze to a few pieces of clothing, and I went right for her underwear, bringing a pair up to my nose, sniffing.

"Oh my god!" She snatched them back, but I didn't fight her.

"They're clean."

Her cheeks pinked. "Of course they're clean!"

I sat up, wrapping my arms around her hips to draw her between my legs. "Can I go down on you?"

"You already did." She checked the time. "About four hours ago."

"So?"

"So?" She laughed, stepping out of my reach. "I'm going to brush my teeth and get ready for bed."

"Ugh. Fine." I trudged behind her to the bathroom, where I watched her line up her toothpaste and toothbrush and travel bottles of lotion and face wash. I wanted to tell her we could go to her apartment tomorrow to pack up all her stuff to bring over here, but I didn't think she'd be down for that. Plus, I needed to make sure this house would remain in my possession.

We'd know by the end of next week.

After we both brushed our teeth, and Claire made me put on some moisturizer, we tucked into bed. It was still early, not even ten yet, but Claire apparently liked to settle in early with a book. She had a different paperback than the one she'd read to me last night.

I took the book from her hands. The spine was cracked and worn, pages dog-eared too many times to count, and as I flipped through, I noticed some lines were highlighted here and there. "What's this one about?"

"He's in an Egyptian prison, and the only way out is to accept the proposal of this widow to help her find her missing brother. It's basically a lot of hijinks and running away from snakes and mummies, but it's so good because he's a himbo and she's this brilliant—"

"He's a what?"

"Himbo," she repeated slowly. "A bimbo but male. He's all brawn and no brain but so sweet."

"I like that. Himbo. You come up with that?"

"No. I..." Her brows narrowed as she accepted the book back. "I don't know who in Romancelandia came up with that term. But this guy is it."

I held my arm open so she'd cuddle into my side. "Did you finish the one from last night?"

"No, but this one's a comfort read for me, so I snagged it on the way out the door before I came here."

"How many books do you read at a time?" I asked, getting more comfortable before reaching for my iPad.

"I don't know. Sometimes only one, sometimes more." She nuzzled her head into the pocket of my shoulder, flipping the book open to a dog-eared page. "I know a lot of people like listening to books or reading on a Kindle or something, but I still like holding the paperback. If it's a new author, I usually request it from the library, and then if I really love it, I'll buy their entire backlist. Like this one? I own almost every book she's ever written."

While she read silently next to me, I screwed around on my iPad, watching ESPN highlights, reading funny tweets, generally doing the stuff I did late at night when I couldn't sleep. But soon, Claire stuck her mouth guard in and twisted in my arms with a quiet good night.

I kissed her head, and just like that, we had a bedtime routine.

I was pretty sure Claire was my comfort read...or whatever you called the human equivalent.

I Googled it. There was no such term. I'd need to invent one.

Claire

I woke up hot. The skin on my neck damp, the comforter wrapped around my legs, and when I opened my eyes, it took a moment for me to orient myself. I wasn't at home. I was at Jimmy's house, and he had one arm banded around my waist, while he lay on his stomach, his head turned in the opposite direction of me. I smiled to myself, still in disbelief that we were together.

That I was waking up in his bed.

So much had happened since he'd kissed me last Sunday at my parents' house. Between our relationship and the book debacle at school, it felt like it had been a year, when only a week had passed.

My head was spinning.

And yet Jimmy, who was normally the one whipping up the storm, was my calm. He'd taken care of me yesterday. Hell, he had been this whole time. From sticking up for me at the very first softball game with Eric to reminding the waiter at Applebee's that I didn't like spicy food. He had always looked out for me.

But I didn't notice or even believe that someone like him

could actually want to be with someone like me. Yet, he was everything I'd ever wanted. He liked me for exactly who I was.

Mouth guard, freckles, big hips, introverted personality, and all.

With a quick drag of my hand along his back, I snuck out of bed to use the bathroom. As I was finishing up with brushing my teeth, Jimmy snuck up behind me, wrapping his arms around my middle.

"I didn't wake you, did I?"

He brushed my hair away and kissed the side of my neck. "Kinda. I suddenly noticed you weren't there."

"Maybe we need to get you a weighted blanket or something," I suggested, moving out of the way so he could brush his teeth.

"Tried it. Hated it. I'd rather have you lie on top of me." He met my eyes in the mirror. "Sit on my face."

I shook my head with a roll of my eyes.

"Baby, you know what that look does to me." He stuffed his toothbrush into his mouth and attacked me with pinching hands like crab claws until I squealed with laughter. I wiggled away from him and out into the kitchen in search of breakfast. His refrigerator was stocked well, shockingly enough.

When he joined me, his fingers absently scratching at his stomach, I waved my hand down the length of the door. "You like grocery shopping."

"Nope." He reached around me to open the freezer, pulling out frozen waffles. "I get mine delivered. Otherwise, I'd be there for hours and come home with nothing I needed and everything I didn't."

Smacking my butt on the way to the toaster oven, he held up the box of waffles. "You want?" When I nodded, he put as many as he could fit then set two plates down along with maple syrup. "Blueberry waffles. They're my favorite breakfast food."

"Noted."

He dragged me in front of him, pressing my back against the counter. "What's your favorite?"

"I like French toast. My mom makes a really good French toast casserole. That's my favorite."

He hummed into a kiss that tasted like mint toothpaste. I held on to his shoulders as his mouth trailed down my chin. When he sucked on my throat, a sharp breath left my lungs, and I already knew what he was going to ask.

"But you know what I could really eat?"

"My pussy?"

He jerked his head back, a goofy smile on his face. "How'd you know?"

"You're predictable."

"Really? That's not usually what I'm known for."

"I'd also suspect you don't ask to go down on every person you meet."

"That is correct," he said, gripping my waist to hoist me up onto the counter. "Pants off, Hart."

"Help me, Ewing."

With his eyes glued below my waist, he curled his fingers beneath the elastic of my underwear, and I planted my hands behind me to lift my hips. He slid the cotton down and off, and then his mouth was on me.

I doubted the linoleum floor felt good under his knees, but he didn't seem to care, given the soft sounds of pleasure he was making. He held me open to his kisses with his thumbs, his tongue licking the length of my slit.

I dug my fingers into his hair. "Why..." I blew out a breath when he flicked my clit. "Why do you like it so much?"

He did that humming motorboating move again, and I dropped my head back. "God, that feels so good."

"I like it because you like it," he said after a long pull of his lips.

"But I'm not the first woman who's let you do this," I finally got out between sighs.

He tipped his head up, gliding one finger inside, slowly twisting it in and out until I was writhing on the counter. "Yeah, but you're the first one who's never looked at me like I'm not a joke. Like I'm more than a good time." He licked the crease of my thigh. "Plus, you're the only one who's been so open with me. Usually, it's a means to an end, but you let me stay down here as long as I want."

I held his stare as he licked me, still twisting his finger.

"I'm no fool," I said, and he smiled against my flesh then sucked on my clit. I reflexively closed my eyes, but the fingers on my hips tightened.

"Look at me, Claire."

I leaned my weight back onto my palms, shifting my hips so I almost hung off the edge of the counter, and he compensated by wrapping his arms around me, holding me up. Nothing about this man was a joke. When it came to his heart, he was completely sincere. Silly puns and boundless energy aside, this man never failed to make me feel like I was the center of his world. Especially now, during this incredibly intimate act, one that had always made me feel uncomfortable, he made it about me.

"There is no one like you," he murmured, his finger stroking me deep inside. "The only woman I would give up anything for."

I couldn't answer, my chest rising with my rapid breaths, my palms slick on the counter.

"Before, I did this for myself." He spoke each word into my

wet skin. "But I'm doing this for you. To make you feel good. To show you that even though I'm not worthy of you, I will still worship you every day as long as you'll let me."

"Jimmy," I whispered, too lost in his eyes to say anything else, and just like that, my blood ran over, my heart exploding into tiny bits, only for him to put them back together. When my orgasm finally subsided, he stood and wiped at his mouth then placed a soft kiss to my jaw.

"Oh shit," he muttered suddenly, leaping to the side, where he pulled out our now burned waffles from the toaster.

"I didn't even hear the timer go off," I told him.

"Me either."

I offered him a fake smile. "Oops."

He threw back his head and laughed, and that was when I jumped off the counter and flung my arms around his neck, nipping at his Adam's apple. He smacked my bare ass. "Back to bed with you. I'll put some more in and bring them in when they're done."

I didn't need to be told twice, and I snatched my underwear from the floor on my way to his room. A few minutes later, he carried two plates of waffles and a glass of orange juice we shared. Then he rolled on top of me for "a midmorning snack."

The man was insatiable. Literally.

But this time it ended with him sliding his long, hard length inside me, smiling into the crook of my neck as he uttered words about how next time he wanted to lick syrup off my skin and take me to some soccer field where we could have sex under the stars.

"You'd like that, wouldn't you?" he asked, dropping to his side after finishing, wrapping his arm around my waist, gently squeezing my breast with his hand.

"I'd like to avoid being arrested for public indecency."

He flicked his hand in the air, like my stipulation was nothing. "We'll go during the summer, when it's still warm at midnight, and the only things still awake are the crickets and the stars."

Well, when he put it like that. "I would like that."

Sitting up, he scrubbed his hands over his hair and face, and I tugged on a few strands, pulling a curl straight then letting it bounce back. "You need a trim."

"I know. I keep forgetting to make an appointment." He grabbed his phone and typed something out. "I need to go for a run."

"Now?" It was almost eleven, and we had a softball game in a couple hours.

"Yeah. Want to come with me?"

"What part of me indicated I like to run?"

He looked over his shoulder to me. "Uh...no part?"

"Right." I got out of bed. "I don't run."

"What do you like to do?" he asked, stepping into clean underwear and a pair of shorts before following me into the bathroom.

I rolled my eyes at his lack of personal space.

"What?" he asked.

"I am peeing. I need to wipe."

His brow crimped. "Okay."

"Okay, so go away."

"Why?" He was genuinely confused.

I shooed him with the toilet paper. "Because!"

He refused to budge. "Because why?"

"Because people using the bathroom is private."

He waved off the notion and pivoted to check out his reflection in the mirror. "You're cute when you're shy."

I huffed. "I'm not shy."

He uncapped his deodorant and swiped it on. "If someone

asked me, I could describe your vagina to a forensic sketch artist. Color and length of your labia, how the inner left one is slightly larger than—"

"Oh my god!" I shrieked and threw the toilet paper roll at him. "You're the worst!"

He dodged the roll. "Like you couldn't describe my dick at this point?"

I could, but that wasn't the point. "I hate you so much."

He backed away, still grinning. "You love me."

I did, but that wasn't the point.

Once he finally left the bathroom, I finished up, washed my hands and face, and pulled my hair up in a bun. When I stalked back into his bedroom, he had on a shirt and was tying his laces. "So, you didn't tell me. What do you like to do for exercise?"

I plopped on the bed, grabbing my book. "I didn't tell you because you started talking about my vagina."

He squeezed my ankle. "It's my favorite thing."

"Everything is your favorite thing," I grumped.

"If it has to do with you, yes. Yes, it is."

I found the page where I'd left off reading. "I take an online dance class."

His eyes lit up. "You do? Can I do it with you?"

"Absolutely not."

His smile dropped. "Why not?"

"Because it's fun for *me*, and I do it to feel good and have fun, and you're not allowed."

He accepted the answer and jostled my leg. "I'll be back in a bit. Gotta burn off some energy."

I waved and didn't feel at all self-conscious about hanging out in his house while he was out running his puppy sprints. In fact, I helped myself to some water with lemon, because he was the most precious boy for buying me fresh lemons, and made myself at home on his couch.

By the time he returned, he was a sweaty mess, and he showered before meeting me on the couch with a bowl of popcorn. I was lying on my stomach, and he settled his head on my butt, poking and prodding it like his personal pillow before finding a position he liked.

I rolled my eyes. "Comfortable?"

"Very." And we stayed like that almost all afternoon until we needed to head to the softball game. Me reading and him watching TV or playing a game on his iPad. Sometimes he'd inform me of any new comments on our contest post, or I'd show him whatever text came in on my family thread.

It was perfect.

I should've known it wouldn't last.

CHAPTER TWENTY-SEVEN

Jimmy

If I could've, I would've boarded the door to my house and kept Claire hidden away forever. Alas, I didn't think she would take well to imprisonment.

So, I let her go. But only because we had a softball game. She had to go home and change. Something about putting clothes on.

What a shame.

I got to the field early, as usual. I liked to be the first one, not only to check out the other team but to greet all our players. There was no coach or anything, but since Hassan and I had put the team together, I liked to be the one to make sure everybody was happy and doing well. And today, I personally made sure everyone voted for Claire and me. Shook everybody's hand, even held and kissed Todd Fisher's baby. It was a winning campaign.

When Claire finally showed up, I greeted her with a smack on her ass. She threw me one of her looks, and I slapped my hand to my heart.

Truly, those narrowed eyes did something to me.

"This should be an easy win today," I said absently to Hassan as we watched a few of the players from the opposing team. They were very clearly not here to take it seriously, as a few of them already cracked open beers. Not that I didn't appreciate having a drink, but I didn't think it was all that smart when balls would be flying around.

"All right. Same batting order as usual?" Hassan asked the team, and a few gave their agreement. Claire didn't, too busy talking with Meredith, who was basically our mascot at this point.

Once the game began, I took a seat on the bench, shooting the shit with my teammates but mostly sneaking touches of Claire's thigh. About halfway through, after we strolled off the field for the next inning, Claire picked up her cell phone when Meredith told her it was buzzing in her purse. Since it was my turn to bat, I didn't pay much attention until I was at first base and noticed Meredith on one side of Claire and Aggie on the other. All of them had their heads bowed over her phone, and I could tell by the set of her shoulders and how her throat was red, Claire was upset.

"Hey." I craned my neck up to get their attention. "What's going on?"

Meredith lifted her eyes, briefly shaking her head with a frown. Claire didn't move as Aggie spoke to her.

I kept my eye on them, not caring when Pete Schwartz hit a line drive right out to second. By the time I realized I needed to move, the baseman was already there, tagging me out and throwing to first to get Pete out too.

"Sorry," I mumbled as I jogged past him, although I didn't really care. "What's going on?" I asked as soon as I rounded the fence.

Claire barely spared me a glance. "Tozer emailed *and* left me a voice mail."

Bill Tozer was the superintendent. If he'd emailed and called Claire on a Saturday, it had to be serious.

"About Brooks?" I asked, and she nodded.

"He wants to meet with me on Monday. Said we have to nip this in the bud before it gets worse."

Aggie patted Claire's shoulder. "I'm sure he wants to take care of this right away because he knows it'll blow over pretty quick. You know how parents are, they get up in arms about something, but after a couple days, they settle down once they see it wasn't as bad as they thought."

"Right," Meredith said breezily. "And as far as I know, Tozer is a reasonable guy."

"Oh, absolutely." Aggie slid her arm over Claire's shoulders. "I know you're nervous, but it's better to get this taken care of right away. After next week, you won't have to worry about anything."

Although none of that seemed to comfort Claire, and I stepped in front of her. "Come here."

She stepped into my outstretched arms, and I kissed her head. "Aggie's dealt with Tozer a lot, so if she says he'll take care of it, he'll take care of it."

"Yeah, and I can always be there if you want me to," Aggie offered.

"Thanks," Claire mumbled into my shoulder. "I just don't understand why she's doing this."

"Because she's a miserable cunt," Meredith sneered.

"Meredith!" Aggie and I both exclaimed, though hers was much more admonishing than mine.

"What?" Meredith shrugged. "She's calling my best friend a groomer. She's a cunt."

"But do you have to be so loud about it?" I asked, laughing.

"Like you have room to talk," she snipped back. "You gotta call a spade a spade."

"All right, but let's try not to shout it out, huh? Come on, we gotta go get on the field," Aggie said, grabbing her mitt. She handed me mine as well as Claire's, though she appeared less than thrilled to continue playing.

"Buck up." I gave her a chuck under her chin. "You can do it."

She fought a smile. "Enough of the sportsball platitudes."

I directed her out to her position on the field. "The best offense is a good defense."

"What? I don't even know..."

"You miss one hundred percent of the shots you don't take."

She threw up her hands. "I feel like you're saying these things just to screw with me."

"There's no I in team." I shot her a finger gun with a wink as I walked backward to the mound, turning as she muttered something that sounded an awful lot like, "I don't know why I like you."

I grinned as I wound up for my first pitch.

As suspected, we won handily, though I didn't feel much like celebrating when Claire was in such a dark mood. I walked her to her car, my arm around her shoulders. "I suppose you don't want to come out for a drink?"

She shook her head, unlocking her car with her key fob, and I backed her up against the door, my hands at her waist. "You done people-ing for today?"

"For the weekend."

The weekend. I wanted to whine, but she caught my mouth in a kiss. A kind of kiss that was a little noisy, a little overeager. Enough to send all my blood pumping south, and my cock strained beneath my shorts. I leaned into her so she'd feel it.

"Are you sure?" I asked, running the tip of my nose along hers.

"Yeah."

"I'm not too excited about the idea of you going home by yourself to freak out over this."

"I know, but I need to decompress."

"All right." I circled my arms around her back, hugging her tight to me, and she breathed out a sigh against my shoulder, wrapping her arms around my neck. We stood like that for I didn't know how long, until my dick got the message. No playtime today.

"I'm obsessed with you, you know that?" I told her.

I felt her smile against me. "I'm obsessed with you too."

"And I'm sorry you're going through this bullshit."

"Me too."

"I love you."

She wrenched her head back, diamond eyes roaming over my face, shining with tears. "You do?"

I nodded.

"I love you too," she croaked, and I'd never heard a more beautiful sound.

Winding her hair around my fist, I tipped her head back, kissing the sweetest mouth I'd ever tasted, caressing the softest lips I'd ever felt, loving the best woman I'd ever known. She combed her fingers into my hair, sliding her tongue along mine, and my body started getting ideas again.

"Baby, I love you, but if you keep pulling on my hair like that, I'm not going to be able to let you go home. I'll bend you over, right here in this parking lot."

She loosened her grip, drawing her hands down my chest and stomach. "Thanks for understanding."

"Understanding what?"

"That I need time to myself."

I huffed. "You don't need to thank me. That's basic human needs stuff, but I feel like you should give me the name of every guy you've ever been with so I can kick their asses for being such dicknozzles to you."

She snorted. "You'll kick their asses?"

"I'll call my brother to do it."

She laughed, shoving me away to drop into her car. I bent when she rolled down her window and popped one last kiss on her mouth. "Text me later."

"Okay. What are you going to do for the rest of the day?"

I straightened and stepped away from her car a few paces. "Probably have our birth charts drawn up. Maybe buy a star and name it after you."

"I'm guessing that's really expensive, and you're supposed to be saving up to buy your house."

"True." I waved. "I'll go for engraved mugs instead."

She shook her head as she drove off past me. "You're ridiculous."

"But you love me!"

She stuck her hand out of the window. "I do!"

Which was why I was walking on air at Callaghan's. Untouchable as I loaded up the jukebox with Taylor Swift songs. Practically writing my wedding speech on a cocktail napkin.

Until my phone buzzed with a number I didn't recognize. I answered it anyway. "Hello?"

"Hi, is this Jim Ewing?"

"Yeah, it is."

"Hey, it's Jenny from 99.1, Stef and Matt's producer."

I leaned back in my chair. "Oh hey, what's up?"

"Well," she started and then said nothing for five whole seconds. I knew because I counted. "I was calling because there's been a lot of unusual action on the contest website."

My brow furrowed, not sure what that had to do with me.

"Really? Everyone I've talked to has been very positive about it. They all think it's a cool idea. And Claire and I had a lot of fun."

"I'm happy about that, but we've decided to disable the comment section."

Again, I felt like I was missing some connection. "Okay."

"Because there were a lot of comments on your profile."

"Oh?" That made my chest puff up a bit. I knew Claire and I could win. "That's great."

"Actually, it's not. The comments people were leaving were..." She paused again, and the hair on the back of my neck stood on end, a foreboding feeling oozing its way through my bloodstream. "Unkind, at best. At worst, they were...making claims about Claire that were..."

"Shit," I breathed out. "Was it about her job? Were they accusing her of..." I hated even saying the words out loud, so I didn't. "Illegal activity?"

"Yeah. It was some pretty terrible stuff. The first comment appeared about three hours ago, and it was like a pile-on after that."

I rubbed at my forehead. "Do you know who it was?"

"You have to log in to our website with an email address to enter any contests or, in this case, leave any comments, but no one is required to attach their name to their comment."

I shot up from my chair, earning curious gazes from my teammates, but I didn't pay them any mind as I threw a twenty down on the bar and trudged outside, where I paced the parking lot. "So, you shut down the whole comment section. For everyone?"

I felt like a dick for even thinking it, but I'd entered this contest for a reason, and I didn't want anyone to have an unfair advantage.

"Yeah, we shut it all down," Jenny explained. "Voting is still up. All rules still apply, but after we saw what was happening, we made the immediate decision to cut it off. It was obviously a coordinated effort to attack you guys."

I kicked at loose pebbles with a curse.

"I barely know you two, but you both work at a school together. There is no way either of you is doing what they were saying about you. It was all hateful jargon."

"Yeah, and I think I know what it's stemming from," I said, my hand in a fist at my side. "This is work-related, and..." I didn't want to get into the details, but I knew it was that asshole Mrs. Brooks.

"I'm so sorry to hear that," Jenny offered. "And I'm sorry this contest is shining a light on you both when you don't need it."

"Yeah," I mumbled, dropping my head back on my shoulders, wondering what the hell I should do.

"Do you want me to take you out of the contest?"

I cringed. No, I didn't want to leave the contest, but I also needed to protect Claire. "As long as the comments are disabled, there won't be any way for anyone to say anything anymore, right?"

"Right."

I bent over, one hand holding my phone to my ear, the other on my knee. "Then... I guess, leave it for now. I really appreciate you calling me about this."

"It was truly the least I could do. I hope everything works out for you two."

"Yeah. Thanks. Me too." I sighed and hung up, pocketing my phone.

This attempt at hurting Claire had failed, and if Mrs. Brooks was going to try again, she'd have to get through me first.

CHAPTER TWENTY-EIGHT

Jimmy

Monday, my ADHD was off the charts, and my second graders knew it. They ran roughshod over me, but my bandwidth was shrinking with every hour I didn't hear back from Claire. She'd come in this morning but left at lunch for the meeting with Tozer. She'd looked as worried as I felt.

She didn't even wear a headband today. Instead, she had all her hair piled up on her head.

I'd told her to text me to let me know how it went, but it was almost time for dismissal and there was still no text message.

"Shane." I shot my eyes to him, where he had one foot on his chair. The kid was a climber. "Both feet on the floor. And Pax, go get a tissue. Come on, dude."

Mrs. Jones, a one-on-one aide who joined us for the afternoons with Takoda, a special needs student, shot me a covert eye roll. Pax was constantly full of snot and germs. His parents sent him to school no matter what, but I swear to god, that kid was in the nurse's office at least twice a month every month.

"Rough day?" Mrs. Jones asked, and I nodded, lacing my hands behind my head as I leaned back in my chair since I'd long given up on any semblance of teaching for the last part of the day.

"Is it Claire?"

There was no use denying it. Everybody knew we were together at this point and what was going on with her and this supposed disciplinary action. "Yeah. I had a hard time concentrating today."

"Doesn't help that it's so close to the end of the year. It's like dealing with a pack of wild animals." She swept her hand out to the class, where the kids waited anxiously to be called for dismissal, some singing songs together, others laughing about whatever eight-year-olds found funny. Elliana attempted to open the birthday bag Declan had given out today, but I pointed at her.

"Hey, Ellie, that stays in your bag until you get home."

She frowned and pushed it into her backpack.

"Julian, go change the number on board," I instructed, and he bounded up, erasing the number 19 and writing a sloppy 18.

Four weeks of school left, not counting the few days of professional development that were always tacked on at the end of the year. But that was it, only eighteen days left with this bunch of hooligans. One more year of teaching tucked into my back pocket. A year when I was nominated for Teacher of the Year. I should have been ecstatic.

Should.

And yet I couldn't piece together even one iota of joy because all I could think about were the reasons Claire wasn't texting me back. She should've been out of the meeting by now.

"All right." I stood, clapping a few times. "Hi, my name is!"

"What?" my class shouted back.

"My name is?"

"Who?"

"My name is?"

"J. Ewing!" they cheered.

I gave Takoda a double high five before pointing to the door. "Car pickup, line up."

A few kids hopped in line at the door, and Mrs. Jones tossed me a wave, taking Takoda's hand to walk him out to the bus now since it took him a little longer.

"Mr. Ewing, you had a bad case of the Mondays today," Zeke informed me like I didn't know, and I huffed a laugh.

"You're telling me, kid." Then we slapped hands twice, bumped elbows, and exploded a fist bump before he made his way out the door to stand against the wall.

This was the routine. Every kid was acknowledged with their handshake to start and end each day. A few seconds that I could connect with each of my students, a chance to either start the day on a positive note or reinforce the fact that we had a new chance to make it better when they returned tomorrow. Once all the car pickups were in the hall, I went through all the bussed kids and then escorted everybody out to their respective exits.

And then I was done, back in my classroom, absently rolling my chair side to side, cell phone in my hand, waiting on Claire.

I hadn't realized how much time had passed until she appeared at my door, and I shot up at her quiet, "What are you still doing here? It's four o'clock."

I glanced down at my phone as if I'd find a message from her explaining everything. "You never texted me."

"I know…" She stayed at my door, leaning into the frame. "I… It was too much to text."

I closed the distance between us in a near sprint. "What happened?" Her breath shuddered like she'd been crying, and I curled my hand around her cheek. "*What?*"

She stared up at me from under heavy eyelids. She looked so tired.

"Want to come over and talk about it?" I asked, and her bottom lip trembled. She lifted her shoulder, dropping it like it weighed 100 pounds. "I'm sorry," I said into a kiss. "We won't talk about anything."

She snorted.

"Promise. I'll do all the talking. You can sit there and pretend you're listening."

She tucked her head against my throat, her laugh all watery.

"Ah, baby, I'm so, so sorry." I squeezed her tight. "What can I do?"

Her voice was a hoarse whisper. "I don't know. I came here to talk with Mrs. Kaplan and Aggie."

"So, the meeting didn't go well?"

"No." She backed away from me, rubbing the back of her hand along her cheek. "It was fine. Tozer did have my back. He explained to Mrs. Brooks that even though she didn't like what I did, it wasn't grounds for disciplinary action. I broke no rules of the contract. But she said what I did was immoral."

I mouthed a curse at the ceiling, knowing it wouldn't help anyone for me to lose my temper. But this lady was not only out of line but out of her mind.

"I apologized to her, but she demanded to have me investigated and said she was going to the school board."

"The school board? What does she think they'll do? You didn't do anything wrong."

She drooped against the doorframe. "She's apparently got a friend on it. Margo something or other."

I walked in a tight circle. If this friend was even half the troublemaker that Mrs. Brooks was, I suspected this whole bullshit circus was just getting started.

Then Claire did the worst thing she could've done. She covered her face with her hands and cried.

Sobs that racked her shoulders and broke my heart.

And I kicked the doorframe. Which did nothing except possibly break my toe.

"This is bullshit!"

"Oh, here you are," Meredith said, her voice unusually subdued. She frowned at me and my tantrum then wrapped her arms around Claire, urging her to sit down at one of the kid's desks. "It didn't go well?" she mouthed at me over Claire's head, and I shook my head.

"She's here to meet with Kaplan and Aggie," I explained, and Meredith nodded, smoothing Claire's hair.

"We gotta get you looking presentable. Head up. Look at me."

Claire lifted her face to her friend, and Meredith wiped under her eyes before digging into her purse, retrieving some tubes. "This is a little dark for you, but it'll have to do. Tilt your head back." Claire followed Meredith's instructions, and she swiped some beige stuff under her eyes and around her nose, blended it in then slicked pink gloss on her lips. "There."

Claire seemed like she couldn't care less. "Thanks."

"Where are you meeting?" Meredith asked, standing up, taking hold of Claire's hand.

"The office."

I shut everything down and followed them out, Meredith delivering a sort of speech that sounded a lot like the "We go to the mattresses" line from *The Godfather*, while Claire shuffled along like she was being led to the gallows. For my part, I tried to think of who I could call, who I could influence to make this all go away.

Maybe I needed to start thinking like Meredith and planting horse heads in beds.

In the hall of the main office, Meredith hugged Claire, kissed her cheek, and passed her off to me. "Want me to wait?"

Claire shook her head. "I don't know how long this will take."

"Okay, but text or call me later. Please."

She nodded, and I combed my fingers into her hair, forcing her to meet my gaze.

"I'm serious, Claire. I'm worried about you."

"I will. I'll call you later."

I settled for a short kiss and waved at Aggie as she turned the corner onto the main hall, slipping her arm through Claire's. My little warrior was in good hands, but that didn't make me feel much better. Not after I knew what Mrs. Brooks was capable of.

CHAPTER TWENTY-NINE

Claire

I didn't leave school until almost six o'clock. Aggie reassured me the union president had been alerted to the situation and there were no actual grounds for an investigation into me, immoral reasons or otherwise. Mrs. Kaplan spent some time trying to come up with solutions, like a written apology to the Brooks family from me and a new school- or district-wide policy explicitly stating there would be no personal book loans between staff and students. Although, that put teachers in the crossfire because a lot of them had personal libraries in their rooms for their kids. That was what we did—we gave our students the opportunity to read and learn.

Mr. Manaloto, the head of library and media services for the district, who was also in the meeting this afternoon, was on speakerphone the whole time, reminding me that while what I did, buying a book to put in the Free Little Library for a specific student, was not innately wrong, it could be misconstrued. As it was being deliberately done now, and the repercussions were wide. We all knew the ripples of one small decision—one which I thought would help a child—would be felt for weeks, months, and maybe years to come, if Mrs.

Brooks had her way. And not only for me, but for every teacher in this school. Possibly every student too.

The last board meeting for the year was scheduled for next Tuesday, and Mrs. Kaplan surmised that Mrs. Brooks would make some sort of presentation. Aggie had already planned on being there since she attended each meeting, but now she was going with the specific purpose of defending me, if it came down to it. The problem was no one knew exactly what Mrs. Brooks was planning, so we had no strategy to counteract it.

All I could do was "sit tight."

Which I had a hard time doing.

Not to mention my boyfriend.

"Sit tight?" he practically howled, traipsing from one end of my apartment to the other. He hadn't waited for me to text or call him. When I pulled up at home, I'd found him sitting on the "deathtrap" steps. I'd promptly fallen into his lap, needing a hug and a laugh.

But now that I'd processed the day and regurgitated everything the administrators explained, he wasn't happy. "So, what? You're supposed to wait until Mrs. Brooks tries to attack you again?"

"Yeah, I..." I froze with my mug of hot tea halfway to my mouth. "What do you mean *again*?"

"Well..." He circled his hands. "You know...her making threats and stuff."

I didn't believe that was the end of the story. Not with how he tugged at his hair then crossed his arms, only to uncross them, propping his hands on his hips. "What do you know that I don't?"

"Nothing."

"Jimmy."

"You know," he started, inching toward me with a sly

smile. "You've been so stressed. Understandably so, and I heard the best prescription for stress is—"

"If you say an orgasm, I'm going to dump this tea on you."

He backed away with his hands up. "I was going to say ice cream, but good to know that's where your head's at."

I glared at him, and he sighed, dropping his arms to his sides with a smack.

"There's... Okay... So..."

"Jimmy!"

He slumped down next to me. "Don't be mad at me."

"Not a great start."

"I know, but I didn't tell you because I knew it would stress you out more," he said.

I didn't often have a temper, but my skin heated with every second he didn't fucking spit it out already. "What! Just say it!"

He leaned forward, his elbows on his thighs, rubbing his hands together. "Jenny called me Saturday."

"Jenny?" I racked my brain for who that was and came up empty.

"The producer of Stef and Matt's show."

"Oh. Right."

He looked over his shoulder to me. "They shut down the comments section of the website because it was overrun with inappropriate remarks."

Even though I had no idea what he was about to say, my stomach sank. I started sweating. And my palms were suddenly wet. "About what?"

"You." He closed his eyes as if it was painful to admit. "Jenny couldn't even tell me exactly what was said. She didn't want to repeat it."

"Oh god." I had trouble taking a full breath, and I pushed up from the couch, waving my hands by my face. "I can't... I can't..."

"Claire." Jimmy stood up. "You have to breathe."

I sucked in air, but my throat closed off. My chest heaved, and yet I couldn't get any air.

"Breathe. You have to breathe." He demonstrated what I should do, his shoulders rising, his nose expanding, his lips pursing as he blew out a breath, but I couldn't do it. I shook my head back and forth, drowning on dry land.

"I..." My chest burned, my head swam. "I..."

"I think you're having a panic attack, Claire. Stop moving around. Stop." He stood in my path, gripping my shoulders hard. "Look at me. Focus on me."

I stilled my feet but couldn't stop flailing my hands and arms. I was drowning! I couldn't breathe!

"Look in my eyes. What color are they?"

"I-I-I..."

"Don't look anywhere else. Right at me. In my eyes." He held my face, showed me how to breathe again. "Tell me what color my eyes are."

I gulped in what little oxygen I could. "Brown. Hon...honey brown."

His mouth tipped up. "Good. Very specific. Now, my hair. What color is it?"

I flapped my hands by my chest, starting to feel my rib cage expand. "Dark brown."

"That's it? Thought it would be more detailed than that."

I inhaled through my nose. "Unruly."

"That's 'cause your hands are always in it."

I exhaled through my mouth. "You wish."

He nodded. "Absolutely, I do." Then he breathed with me, in and out. "Feel better?"

Still trying to calm down, I answered silently with a nod, my hands trembling slightly as I curled them together.

"Sit down. Let me get you some water."

I followed Jimmy's instructions and burrowed into the corner of my couch, keeping my hands under the blanket I pulled on my lap. He sat next to me, holding out a glass of water to my lips, and I didn't feel at all bad that he was treating me like a child. I was afraid I'd drop it with how bad I shook.

After a while, he skimmed his hand along my neck and shoulder. "That's why I didn't want to tell you. You already have so much going on, I thought..." He set the glass down on the table and rubbed my leg through the blanket. "I don't know what the right answer is."

"Me either," I said, my chest still tight. "I feel like no matter what I do, it'll be the wrong thing and make everything worse." When he opened his arms to me, I crawled into his lap, tucking my head under his chin. "I'm scared."

"I know," he said, his voice hoarse. "I know, baby."

We sat quietly for a few minutes until his fingers skated up and down my back. "Are you hungry?"

"Not really."

"You need to eat. How about some toast?"

"Fine," I grumbled, and he kissed my forehead, nudging me off him. He helped himself to adding a few pieces of bread to the little toaster in the corner. I watched him cut up a banana then slather the toast with peanut butter, placing blueberries on top. It was only when he set the plate in my hands that I saw how he'd created a smiley face on the bread. I smothered my laugh with a bite.

While we ate our dinner, he told me how the kids ran him ragged today, and that since his birthday was coming up in a few weeks, he had to decide what he wanted for his birthday meal, which his mom made every year.

"You'll come, right? Meet my family?"

"Yeah, of course."

"Then why do you look all pinchy?" He smoothed the pad of his thumb over my forehead.

"I have trouble thinking about tomorrow, let alone three weeks from now."

He sucked air in through his teeth then hoisted me up from the couch. "Come on."

"Where are we going? Self-care?"

"Since I'll be the one giving you the orgasms, I don't think we can call it self-care." Then his lips were on mine, his tongue licking into my mouth, cutting off whatever argument I had. I couldn't even remember it. I didn't want to.

I wanted to forget anything outside of us existed.

In my bedroom, he stripped me of my clothes, impatient and not particularly smooth about it. I didn't care. Because then it was my turn, and I couldn't get his clothes off fast enough, have my hands on his bare shoulders, his naked stomach against mine, the hot and hard length of him rubbing against me.

We fell onto the bed, and he kissed his way down the valley of my breasts, squeezing them on the way, licking around my nipples. He kept his hands there as his lips brushed along my belly, his shoulders shoving my legs up and apart so he could settle between them.

I wove my fingers into his hair, and he wasted no time feasting on me. I'd lost my guilt about not enjoying giving oral sometime between him begging to go down on me and him declaring he owned my pussy. When was that? Not even two weeks ago?

It didn't matter.

It made no difference whether it was two days or weeks or years. His hands and mouth were on me now. He was here, feeding me dinner, taking care of me, supporting me without even needing to be asked. And that was all I ever wanted. Someone who wanted me.

"I want you so bad," he said, plunging what felt like two fingers inside me. The fingers of his other hand pinched my nipple, plucking at the cord connecting the two points of contact, and I moaned as the first traces of release burst through the cloud of anxiety. I needed this, to forget about everything else going on and focus on this man.

He twisted his fingers, his tongue swirling against my clit. "Let go, baby. Let go of everything else but this."

And I did.

I squeezed my eyes shut to the onslaught of pleasure and gave in to the rush. With heated skin and hard-working breaths, I tugged on his hair. "Up here. Come up here."

He didn't try to fight me, maybe because he knew I needed full contact, and he draped his body over mine. His fingers, still wet from the evidence of my orgasm, coasted over my side, lifting my thigh to his waist as he kissed me, his lips and tongue salty with the taste of me. I circled my hips under him, needy and wanton, and he raised himself away from me to swipe his fingers between my swollen flesh then took hold of his cock, coating it with my arousal. His eyes met mine, sizzling with heat and desire. The only warning he offered me was a ghost of a smile before he drove hard inside me.

I wrapped my legs around him and kept my hands locked at the back of his head, holding him as close as possible so his thrusts slowed to rocks, our hips aligned so that even buried deep inside, he still stroked the spot I needed to get off. He licked and kissed my throat, his breaths heavy and hot against my skin, and *this* was my security blanket. We were so close, so tight together, I could feel his heart beating, and I wanted to stay like this. Just like this.

"Please," I begged, although I wasn't sure why exactly.

Please make me come.

Please keep me safe.

Please love me forever.

"I got you," he whispered into my skin. With one last kiss to my collarbone, he met my gaze, steady and unblinking. "I'm here. I love you."

My eyes stung with relief and ecstasy, his promise pushing me over the edge. Though, he quickly followed, his hips stilling as he groaned softly into a kiss. Looping my arms around his neck, I dabbed at my eyes but couldn't hide my sniffle.

He wrenched back. "What's wrong?"

"Nothing."

His eyes narrowed. Who was the grumpy one now?

I tried to pull him back to me, but with his hands planted on either side of me, he was immovable. "Why are you crying?"

"Because." I sniffed. "I love you."

He cracked a half smile. "And that makes you cry?"

"How much I love you does. It's sort of overwhelming."

"It is, isn't it?" Then he laid his weight on top of me, rolling both of us over so he was on his back.

"I should go to the bathroom," I told him, but he only held me tighter.

"Stay right here. For a few minutes."

We stayed like that for a lot longer than a few minutes, and I eventually fell asleep with my head against his chest, his heartbeat echoing in my ear.

When his alarm blared the next morning, Jimmy slipped away with a kiss to my forehead and a promise to see me later with coffee. I stayed in bed a little longer, colder now that he was gone.

I showered and chose an outfit to cheer myself up, a bright yellow skirt. With a fluttering white top and matching head-band, I could at least *look* like I was happy.

As promised, Jimmy met me in the library with my coffee and a kiss. Though my smile lasted as long as it took me to listen to a voice mail left on my extension.

"This is Caroline Getty, Isiah Getty's mom, calling to let you know you should be ashamed of yourself. I know what books you're distributing to the kids at school, and I'm appalled. I have already emailed his teacher to request that he not sign out any more library books from the school until the entire catalogue there is evaluated. And you, you will be punished. If not by the school and the district, then certainly by God."

I set the phone down gingerly as if it might rear back and bite me with any sudden movement. Across the hall, Jimmy's music was blaring, kids filtering in through the halls, but I couldn't move.

Never in my life had I ever been made to feel so... demeaned. Didn't these people have anything better to do with their lives?

Apparently not.

Because my phone buzzed with a notification. Someone sent me a private message on Facebook. I should have deleted it immediately, but some sick curiosity had my thumb tapping on the notification button. I rarely posted on my social media accounts. Lately, it had been more because of the contest, and I supposed that was my mistake.

Since that was how they found me.

The first message was from a complete stranger.

Disgusting criminal. You're done. You'll never work with kids again, let alone look at one.

I swallowed down the bile rising in my throat.

The next message came soon after, this one short but effective. **DIE GROOMER!**

I threw my phone in my bag and ran to the trash can,

where I threw up the contents of my stomach, the few sips of coffee and water from this morning.

As I sank down to the floor, frantically wiping at my mouth and face with a tissue, Jimmy's happy music floated my way, lyrics about love being easy. But I couldn't find even a tiny part of me to enjoy it. All I felt was cold, hard fear.

There was nothing I could do to stop it from overtaking me. All I could manage was containing it so it wouldn't spread to anyone else.

This wasn't a fight I wanted or thought I could win. I only hoped I would still be alive when it was all over.

CHAPTER THIRTY

Jimmy

Claire was a zombie. And every day, it got worse. From phone calls to emails, Mrs. Brooks sent her flying monkeys after Claire. As Jenny had told me on Saturday, it felt coordinated. Like this had been planned out already, a hostile takeover of the school, and these people were only looking for a patsy. Apparently, Claire was it.

I asked if I could stay over at her house Tuesday, but she refused. Said she needed time to herself, but I didn't think that was a good idea. I didn't want her to spiral out. Yeah, I understood she needed time to process and be alone, that was part of who she was, but now was not the time to close herself off. Each morning, she came in later and later, the dark circles under her eyes growing.

Meredith informed me Claire wasn't eating during their lunch breaks, and every afternoon, she continued to decline my offer to take her out to dinner or come to my house. She wouldn't let me stay over at her place either.

She was icing me out.

She was icing everyone out.

Thursday, I found Meredith in her little corner classroom, where she brought students to one-on-one or small group instruction. I sat opposite her at the round table, both of us at a loss for what to do.

"She's scared she's going to lose her job," Meredith whispered even though the door was closed. It was the quietest I'd ever heard her.

Might have been the quietest I'd ever spoken too. "I know, but Aggie said that isn't going to happen. And all the administrators are behind her."

She raised her hands. "Fear isn't rational."

I spun my cell phone in circles on the table. A metaphor for my life. I was spinning in circles too. "I don't know what to do."

"I know what I'd like to do. Go to that bitch's house and give her a piece of my mind."

"You and me both," I mumbled.

"She's a terrorist. Whipping up all this bullshit. You know—"

My phone buzzed, and I flipped it over on the table, an unknown number, though it looked vaguely familiar. When I answered, it was Jenny again. A second phone call in a matter of days. This couldn't be good.

And it wasn't.

"I wasn't supposed to call you," she said in a hushed tone. "But I had to. I couldn't not."

Meredith stared at me with a frown as I scrubbed my hand through my hair. "What is it?"

"You're not going to win the contest."

"Oh." I exhaled a shaky laugh. I'd been holding my breath, prepared for something much worse. "Well, it's not the best news, but—"

"All week, the station has been inundated with phone calls and emails about you and Claire."

There it was.

My stomach churned, and I reflexively looked around the room as if Claire would pop up at any moment. This was one more attack on her, and again, I wanted to shield her from it.

"What?" Meredith mouthed, and I put my phone on speaker so she could listen in.

"The station is washing its hands of the whole thing with a canned response. But I had to let you know, this is a personal attack against the both of you. They were all really...vehement."

I rubbed the heels of my hands against my eyes, and when I blinked my lids open, this was still my god-awful reality. Shitty people doing shitty things for no good goddamn reason. "Yeah, I can imagine."

"I'm sorry that all I have is bad news, and I'm really sorry if our contest has somehow incited this."

"I appreciate that, but it didn't. It's my fault."

Jenny made a sad sound and then said, "Okay, well, I'll let you go. And, again, I'm so, so sorry."

"Thanks," I said and hung up to find Meredith watching me with hawk eyes. "What?"

"How is this your fault?"

I shrugged. "I signed us up for the contest. Claire didn't even know about it. Didn't want to do it, and now she's getting attacked publicly."

She slapped her hand on the table. "This isn't your fault. It's not Claire's fault. The fault lies solely with Vanessa Brooks and her minions. Whatever anyone thinks of Claire giving a book to a student they think may or may not be appropriate, that does not give them the right to harass her. She doesn't deserve what is happening to her now. Neither do you. Now stop sulking because we need to be there for her."

I inhaled a big breath and leaned back, staring up at the

ceiling for a second to stop my mental train from running off the tracks. "You're right. You're right."

"I fucking know I am." She stood with a flourish and pointed to the door. "Now, get out. I have students coming in five minutes."

I headed down to the music room to pick up my class. I tried to get a peek at Claire in the library as the kids filed into my room, but she had the door closed, and I hated I couldn't see her. She wasn't letting me in.

She wasn't letting anyone in.

In the evolved part of my brain, I comprehended that she was doing this for self-preservation, but in the lizard part of my brain, I was angry. It was selfish and stupid, but I was annoyed she was treating me like she was everyone else. When I was her boyfriend. I was special.

And that made me feel like even more of an asshole. Because this wasn't about me.

My lizard brain always wanted to make everything about me.

Stupid asshole lizard brain.

At the end of the school day, I ran right across the hall, where I found Claire banging books around.

"What's wrong?" It was a dumb question. I knew what was wrong.

She didn't look up. "They're trying to get me fired."

"I know, but they can't. Aggie—"

Another book slammed onto the counter. "Aggie was the one who alerted me to the fact that there's a petition going around. Two thousand signatures and counting."

"A petition?"

Slam. "They're signing it to give to the board."

"I don't understand. That's not—"

Slam. "Margo Stetler, she's Vanessa Brooks's friend on the board, promised if they get enough signatures, there will be an investigation."

"One person can't overturn policy. She isn't—"

One more book hit the counter, and she finally met my gaze, blazing with anger. And I was glad of it. Anger was better than the dead eyes I'd been gazing into all week. "It's not just Margo or Vanessa or whoever. It's a whole movement. It's a huge group. And it's not only local. They have the support of people from all over the country. They have pamphlets and YouTube videos and Facebook groups with directions on how to get me fired. How to get anyone who they think is a threat fired. For simply doing their job."

And as fast as a match burned out, so did Claire.

"I was only doing my job," she whimpered, slumping into her seat, and I kneeled down in front of her, taking her cold hands between mine. It was warm in the school building, yet she was shivering.

"Let me take you home."

She shook her head, sniffling, and I reached for a tissue.

"You have to let me take care of you. You can't keep going on like this."

"You can't do anything," she told me from behind the Kleenex.

"Yes, I can."

"I mean, you *can't*. It's already bad enough. You can't get involved in this too."

"Claire, I want to help. I don't care—"

"And I'm telling you!" She pushed me away and stood up, her rolling chair sailing backward so it crashed into the wall. "This is not about what *you* want. It's about *me* and my job. Stop acting like you can do anything."

I wheeled back like she'd slapped me. I kind of wished she had instead of informing me she didn't want my help. I stayed rooted on the floor as she marched around me, and I didn't turn to watch her go as she said, "I have a meeting I need to get to."

At a loss, I eventually forced myself up and returned to my room to lock up. I drove straight to my parents' house, where my mom was in her favorite place, the backyard. She'd taken early retirement from her administrative assistant position in a veterinarian's office and was now a part-time coordinator for a travel company, which basically meant she worked from home on her laptop, helping to set up group tours through Europe and Asia.

"Hey, honey. I didn't expect you today."

"Yeah." I plopped down in the chair next to her.

Since semi-retirement, my mother had also taken up a homemade happy hour. She passed me a mason jar of something with a few pieces of fruit floating in it.

"It's sangria. Delicious."

I helped myself to a healthy gulp then passed it back to her. It was sweet, and I could probably down a trough full of the stuff, but I doubted getting drunk was advisable at this stage in the game. Drunk Jim was liable to make a few phone calls of his own. And that wouldn't help anyone.

She eyed me. "What's wrong?"

"I, uh..." I stretched my legs out in front of me and crossed my arms over my chest. "I don't even know where to start. It's a mess."

Mom tipped her head to the side. "What is?"

"Work." I dropped my head back to my shoulders, the springtime sun bright on my face. "Claire."

"What happened? Everything was fine when we talked on the weekend."

"Yeah, and it's all sort of...come apart since then."

Concern creased my mother's face, and she leaned forward, tugging on my arm so I'd face her. "What's going on?"

I shifted in my chair, relating how this whole disaster started with Claire offering to find books for Anna to read and ending with the latest development of the petition.

"Good god." Mom huffed. "What's next? Throwing books in a bonfire?"

"I think so," I muttered. "I honestly think that's what they want. And the worst part is, most of these people harassing Claire don't even have kids at the school. They don't live in the district."

"Don't they have jobs? Hobbies? What are they doing all day?"

"Trolling," I said, my hands in fists because the more I talked about it, the angrier I got. "And Claire is... She's not doing well. She won't talk to me or her best friend. She looks like..." I closed my eyes, picturing the dark lines under her eyes and the glow gone from her skin. "I'm worried about her."

My mom took hold of my hand, forcing me to relax my fingers. "Of course you are. It's a terrible situation."

That was the sum of it. This was a terrible situation.

"I don't know what to say, honey. It's awful, and I'm sorry she's going through this. I will help in any way I can."

I nodded my thanks.

"Do you want to stay for dinner? Dad'll be home soon, and I have chicken marinating."

"Yeah." I rubbed at my forehead. "Might as well."

I tapped my phone to text Claire, let her know I was thinking about her, but I got sidetracked by a notification. I had a direct message from someone.

I was confused at first, seeing the picture of Claire and me. The one from the softball game that I entered us into the contest with. The one I kept forgetting to print out and buy a frame for. It was followed up with other pictures, all of photos I'd posted of Claire or the two of us together, but each one was edited, drawn over with giant red slashes and derogatory names. But it was the very last message that had me flying up out of my seat.

Once we find out where your bitch girlfriend lives, she's dead. Then your next.

I couldn't even make a joke about the bad grammar. Terrorists didn't care about homophones. They only cared about scaring people into submission.

Mom sat up. "What is it? What's wrong?"

The words stuck in my throat, my skin crawling with fear and disgust.

"Jimmy, what is it?"

I handed my phone over, and my mom gasped. "This is a threat. You need to go to the police."

At least, I thought that was what she said, but I was already striding to my car.

Mom ran after me. "Where are you going?"

"To Claire's."

"You're in no condition to drive." She yanked on my arm, but I was hyperfocused. I didn't care about anyone or anything else except Claire.

"I have to see her. I have to get her out of her apartment." With one goal in mind, my voice was completely emotionless. "She can't stay there."

"Jimmy, I'm not letting you—oh, thank god. Look, your dad just pulled up."

She tugged on my arm again, her other hand waving frantically at my father. He stepped out of the car, a worried expression on his face. It struck me in that moment, how out of the three of us boys, I was the one who looked most like our father, and I could almost see what I looked like to other people. See the anxiety on his face clearly reflecting mine.

Before he even asked, Mom provided a quick summary. "Jimmy's girlfriend is in trouble at work, and he received a threatening message. They said they were going to kill Claire and he was next."

"You *what?*" my father practically roared.

"Now he wants to go get her," Mom said. "But I—look at him, Bren. He can't drive like this."

"The hell I can't," I snapped, and my father snatched my car keys from my hand.

"No." Then he wrapped his arm around me and pulled me into him. "You're not going alone."

And because I was nothing if not the baby of the family and unable to contain my emotions, I broke down and cried. Right there. On the front lawn of my parents' house.

My parents basically called a family meeting with Adam driving over and Mike phoning in. They all spoke at and over me while I stared off into space. Mom shoved food into my mouth while Dad told me to write down everything I could remember as evidence to take to the police. Adam confiscated my phone to report the threat, lot of good that would do. And, of course, Mike stayed silent and seething.

I appreciated their desire to help, but all I wanted to do was see Claire.

But she wasn't answering any of my texts or phone calls. At some point around nine, when my texts remained on unread and my calls went straight to voice mail, I told my parents I had to leave.

I drove straight to Claire's and knocked on her door like the frantic maniac I was. When she finally answered, I pulled her straight into my arms. "Why didn't you text or call me back?"

"I'm not really in the mood to rehash anything. And I don't want to talk."

"Okay, so?" I held her at arm's length, annoyed. "I was worried about you. You can't just not respond."

She ducked away from me, her oversized T-shirt hitting midthigh, her hair knotted up at the back of her head. "I turned my phone off. I..." She dropped down on her couch. "I'm exhausted and frustrated and...oversensitized."

"I get it, but I really wish you'd have talked to me."

"I don't want to talk." She laid her head on a pillow. "I don't want to do anything but sleep. I'm so tired."

I sat next to her, curling my hand around her head. "Can I stay here with you?"

Her lids that were halfway to closing opened back up to me. "I don't have the energy."

"Please? I'm freaking out."

She pushed my hand away. "You're freaking out, huh?" she said, monotone. "Must be hard for you."

"Claire, come on. I don't want to fight."

"I don't either. I want you to leave me alone, so I can sleep."

I turned away from her, struggling with the decision to tell her about the threat or not. In the end, she had to know, so we could figure out what to do about it. "I got a message, a threatening one about you."

"Shit," she cursed quietly and sat up, moving next to me, her leg pressed up along mine.

I watched her, waiting for more of a reaction. "I thought you'd be more upset."

She sighed. "That's one of the things I've been in these meetings about."

"What are you talking about?"

"I got the first one a few days ago."

I shot up. "Jesus fucking Christ, Claire. Why didn't you tell me?"

"Because..." She glanced up at me, eyes glinting with unshed tears. "It's not exactly pleasant."

"I don't care. I told you, I'm here for you. I don't want you carrying this burden alone. You can't!"

"Don't yell at me," she said evenly.

I knew I shouldn't have been shouting at her. It wasn't angry at Claire. I was angry at all those fuckers who were threatening her. I was angry at Vanessa Brooks and her other asshole friend on the school board, but I felt like I was fighting a shadow. I couldn't yell and scream and punch them.

"I love you, Claire. I love you so much, and you're pushing me away. You're pushing everyone away."

"Oh, well, sorry I don't know how to handle someone trying to fire me, which is the best-case scenario. Worst-case, they want to hang me. Maybe you should write down directions so I could follow them better."

I gritted my teeth. "How many threats were there?"

"I don't know." Her shoulders curled as she pressed her hands together, sticking them between her knees like she was trying to be as small as possible. "About two dozen."

"Fuck, Claire." I yanked at my hair, spinning in a circle. "Fuck!"

"Can you please be quiet? I don't need to get kicked out of my apartment on top of all this."

"Good." I propped my hands on my hips. "Pack your stuff. You're going to stay with me."

She huffed. "What? No."

I bent so I was eye to eye with her, but she avoided my gaze. "You're coming to stay with me."

She shook her head, staring at the floor. "This is exactly why I didn't text or call you back. I can't deal with you flying off the handle." When she finally met my gaze, she looked so, so tired. "This is hard enough without me having to put up with your tantrums and chaos."

I wrenched back, running my hand over my hair, not sure what to say back. I supposed there wasn't anything to say. It wasn't as if I hadn't heard it before, that I was too much.

Too much and yet not enough.

Too much energy.

Not serious enough.

But that didn't matter to Claire. At least, I thought it hadn't. Until now.

Until it counted, then I went back to being the clown, the life of the party, the guy who could make her laugh but not help when she cried.

"Okay." I breathed out until my lungs were hollow. "All right. I guess I'll... I'll see you tomorrow."

Then I walked out.

CHAPTER THIRTY-ONE

Claire

As soon as I said it, I knew I shouldn't have. It was awful. I loved Jimmy, tantrums, chaos, and all. That was *why* I loved him. Because he was predictable in his unpredictability. Because no matter what, I knew he would always help me see the bright side. He would always put me before anyone or anything else, and yet I pushed him away.

As the world crowded in around me, I pushed everything and everyone else out. I pushed and pushed and pushed, and now I was left alone in my apartment.

Right back where I started.

I slept like I had every night for the past week, which was to say, not at all, and when I turned my phone back on, my email numbered in the hundreds, which was nothing new. As per Aggie's suggestion, I'd deleted all of my social media apps from my phone so I wouldn't be plagued by the constant notifications, and even though I knew people were probably still trying to bully me, I wasn't tempted to read any of it. The school district had all the evidence of it anyway. But what did worry me, more than anything before, was the number of missed calls. When I pulled up the log, I saw area codes I'd never seen before. So many, it was a red blur as I scrolled. And my voice mail box was full.

I played the earliest one from Jimmy. He'd called and left a message asking me to call him back. "Please, baby, I'm really worried about your safety," he'd said, and I collapsed back against the wall, my eyes filling with tears.

I was so sick of crying. That was what I hated most out of all this.

These people, they made me feel pathetic.

And stupid.

Proving exactly how stupid and much of a glutton for punishment I was, I pressed my thumb on the little play symbol, listening to the next message.

"Hey, you dumb bitch, we're coming to get you fired. See you at the school board meeting."

And the next.

"My name is Miranda Langley. I'm calling for Claire Hart on behalf of Mothers for Freedom. I wanted to let Miss Hart know that we will be using the full weight of our foundation to make sure she or anyone else like her cannot further push their woke liberal agenda on our children. We will be pursuing court action, so she should be prepared. Our kids deserve an education free of brainwashing."

And the next.

"You know what prisoners do to criminals like you who hurt children?"

And the next.

"Hi, my name is Joe Ackhurst, calling for Claire Hart. I'm a reporter with *Akron Today* and wanted to know if you had a statement to make about the accusations Mothers for Freedom have leveled against you. I'm interested in getting a quote before we run the article tomorrow."

And the next.

"I see you got your credentials from Kent State. I bet they'd love to know they have a groomer alumnus."

And the next.

"I hope you get fired."

And the next.

"You sick fuck."

And the next.

"Commie bitch."

And the next.

"Pedophile."

I didn't even get to listen to the other ninety messages because someone was banging on my door.

CHAPTER THIRTY-TWO

Jimmy

When Mrs. Shubert, the substitute for Claire, walked into the library, I darted right to Kaplan's office, bypassing Greta and her attempts to stop me.

"Did Claire call out?"

Mrs. Kaplan looked up from her seat at her desk. "She did."

"Did she say why?"

Kaplan dropped her attention back to her computer screen. "No."

"Is she—"

"Jim, I'm sorry, but I don't really have time for this. I have a meeting I've got to leave for at the admin building in a few minutes."

"About Claire?" I guessed, and she nodded. "What are they doing about the threats?"

She assessed with me a brief sweep of her eyes, but I wasn't going to leave until I found out what they were doing. She must have understood that in how I took up the space in her doorway, feet spread, arms crossed.

"We escalated it to the police, but they suggested first for Claire to block those people and/or delete her accounts. Social media has a lot of gray area when it comes to the law. The threat has to be explicit, and it would be taken more seriously if it was off social media. They can't do much about internet bullying."

"Internet bullying?" My jaw hit the floor at the utter fucking ridiculousness of that response. "That's horseshit!"

"Look, Jim, you need to calm down."

"No!" I flung my hand out in the direction of the front doors of the school as if those sociopaths were standing there. "Some of these people could be really dangerous. The police have no way of knowing who would follow through with their threats. They need to find these people."

"I know." Mrs. Kaplan stood up, pulling at her shirt. "I fully understand why you're so upset—"

"Do you? Because I don't see you doing anything. Claire isn't here. She could be hurt. One of these freaks could be trying to get her right now!" My mind spiraled, and I was being hauled right over the cliff. "They could have her right now!"

"Mr. Ewing, you need to lower your voice," Kaplan said curtly. "I am doing everything in my power to help Claire, and you standing here screaming is not helping the situation at all."

"Someone messaged me yesterday," I told her before she could feed me any more "sit tight" bullshit. "Saying once they find my girlfriend, they'll find me next."

"Screenshot it and send it to me."

"I will, but I've already blocked and reported the person, and made my profile private. What are the police going to do now?"

She closed her eyes for a moment, took a deep breath, then offered me a tight smile. "I don't know, but I am doing everything in my power to support and guide Claire through this. My advice to you is to keep your emotions in check. You need to *act* rationally, not *react* emotionally."

"Easier said than done," I muttered and stalked out of her office.

This was what Claire had been dealing with all week, dead ends, being told to wait it out, not to react. Well, I was tired of wringing my hands. I needed to do something.

On my lunch break, I headed straight to Meredith's room. She had a student with her, but she handed him a couple of crayons and a worksheet before meeting me in the hall. "Have you talked to Claire today?"

"No." She kept her voice as quiet as mine. "I texted her a few times, checking in, but she has yet to get back to me."

I growled out my frustration. "This whole thing is getting way out of hand. She's in real danger. We have no idea what these people are capable of."

"I know. I know." Her eyes slid to the end of the hall and back to me. "Aggie told me there are rumblings about a big crowd at the meeting. She expects they'll be outside with signs and inside trying to disrupt it."

I barked out a single infuriated laugh. If all they did was disrupt the meeting, it would be the least of my worries. "We need to be proactive. They want to cause a scene, then I say we give it to them."

A single brow shot up, a Grinch-like smile curling Meredith's mouth. "You're exactly right."

"We need people," I said. "Lots of them."

"Yeah." She nodded, her ponytail swinging. "I can take care of that."

"T-shirts?"

"An army does need a uniform."

"A petition of our own, maybe?" I suggested because I was all out of ideas. I was only trying to fight fire with their fire.

"I don't know what our petition would be, but I bet a

microphone and a couple of people who could yell pretty loud would do the trick."

"Say." I stroked my chin, smiling for the first time in what felt like months. "You know anyone who could be loud?"

She lifted an innocent shoulder. "I'll have to think on that. You know me, quiet as a church mouse." Then she spun around and clapped her hands. "All right, buddy. You color in all the pictures with beach items?"

I pivoted and marched back to my classroom, encouraged that Meredith and I had a plan of attack, but I was still unsettled that I couldn't get a hold of Claire.

Maybe she was asleep.

Maybe she was pissed at me.

Maybe she was done and didn't want to see me.

It was that last thought that had me blaring Metallica, needing to get out of my head for a little while at least.

The afternoon crawled by, each minute closer to dismissal was a year long, and I was in the middle of a lesson about community helpers—the irony didn't escape me—when my classroom phone rang. I picked it up with my usual, "Jim Ewing."

But I wasn't greeted with any of the typical callers, like Greta from the main office or another teacher.

"Jimmy, it's Toni, Claire's mom."

My heart stopped, my vision blurred, every terrible thing that could happen to Claire racing through my mind. "Wh-what's wrong? Is she okay?"

"She's...."

I pivoted to the wall, pushing my fist into the painted white cement, feeling the individual flecks of grain dig into my knuckles while the world around me crumbled in the seconds it took Toni to finally answer.

"She's here."

I wilted, my hand on my knee, relieved and confused. "Is she all right?"

Toni lowered her voice like she didn't want anyone else to hear where she was. "Someone doxxed her. They have her phone number. Left her messages on her cell phone all night. We were at the police station with her this morning."

Heat flashed over me, and I saw red. The only thing holding me back from cursing and throwing shit around the room were twenty-two pairs of eyes staring curiously at me. "She's at your house now?"

"Yeah."

"I'm coming over. I'll be there as soon as I can." Then I hammered the phone down like it personally offended me. The kids jumped in their seats, and I tipped my chin to Mrs. Jones. "Could you... I need a minute."

She nodded, and I ducked into the hall, closing my classroom door behind me before I let out a silent scream, kicking and punching at air. Then I paced the hallway, from my dead-end corner with Claire's library, past the T, all the way to the other end where Mrs. Greene and Ms. Fitzpatrick taught other classes of second graders.

I had nowhere for all this energy to go. It swirled and doubled, threatening to explode inside me until bits and pieces of my brain and heart splattered all over these halls. Halls that were meant to protect and nurture. Halls that threw a good and kind woman to the wolves.

I had always believed education was the basic building block to society. An educated society was a progressive and healthy society. Schools provided opportunity and change and a chance to level the playing field for those who needed a step up. They were the place to teach empathy and acceptance, a place where kids learned not only to count and read but to be good humans.

Now…

Now all I felt was disillusionment.

After a few minutes of settling my nerves so that I was on simmer instead of boil, I opened my classroom door back up to find Mrs. Jones had finished the lesson and had started readying the kids for dismissal. I thanked her and crossed to my desk, not caring it was bad form to be on my cell phone while students were still here. I texted Meredith then my family group chat to let them know what had happened. The responses were equal parts concern and anger on behalf of Claire.

But it was Mike's texts to me alone that had the hair on the back of my neck standing on end.

POTATO HEAD

Most of these threats are baseless. Keyboard warriors who don't have the guts to actually do anything.

POTATO HEAD

But all it takes is one guy who thinks he's saving the world by attacking a librarian.

POTATO HEAD

If I were you, I'd invest in a good security system and buy a gun.

POTATO HEAD

I know you're adamantly against guns, but you need to learn how to protect yourself. You need to know how to protect Claire.

POTATO HEAD

Sam and I are coming.

POTATO HEAD

And I don't want to hear shit about it.

I sank into my chair, my legs suddenly too weak to stand.

Mike had been a Marine. He'd gone on countless missions to help and serve those who needed his protection. He'd given so much of himself, including his left leg, and if he was telling me this was bad, then it was *bad*.

Mrs. Jones gave my shoulder a squeeze, dragging me into the reality of needing to get twenty-two kids on the bus or in cars, and I forced myself up, high-fiving Takoda then completing the dismissal routine with each kid. For being a Friday, they were all oddly subdued, and I could only assume it was because they understood how upset I was.

Kids were smart. Much smarter than adults gave them credit for.

Once I saw them all off, I practically raced to my car, singularly focused on getting to Claire.

I didn't even fully remember driving to the Hart Farm, but half an hour later, I turned onto the long gravel drive. I didn't bother knocking, just burst through the front door.

Toni, Scott, Evan, and Rosie were there, staring wide-eyed at me for the intrusion. I didn't care.

"Where is she?"

"Back room," Toni said, but Scott stopped me with a hand on my chest, the laid-back demeanor I'd been acquainted with long gone.

"Those assholes have taken everything away from her."

"I know," I gritted out.

"Her safety, her security."

I heard Toni squeak out a whimper, but my eyes were locked on Claire's dad. "I'm not going to let anything happen to her."

He nodded once, and I rushed off to their living room. She was curled up on the couch, a blanket pulled up to her chin even though it was over eighty degrees today, her gaze off in space somewhere, eyes glazed over.

"There's my little lemon drop."

She startled, her head dipping down so her attention landed on me, and her face crumpled. I immediately sank down on the couch and scooped her up. "I'm sorry. I'm so sorry for yelling at you last night. All I want to do is scream and yell and punch someone, but there's no one to take all my rage out on."

Her shoulders shook as she cried silently, and I kissed the crown of her head. "I'm so sorry, baby. I love you so much. Tell me what you want me to do. I'll do anything."

She sniffled, her tears soaking my shirt, her lips brushing my throat. "Take me home."

With a finger under her chin, I nudged her face up to mine and kissed her lips, salty with her tears. "Okay. Let's go home."

I tucked her under my arm, and with a promise to her mom that I'd call her later, I put Claire in my car and brought her home to my house. I knew that it wouldn't be my house for much longer since we'd lost the contest and the chance to find money for the down payment, but I didn't have time to worry about that now. Wherever I landed, as long as Claire was with me, I'd be home.

I brought her inside and right into the bathroom. She looked a mess and not in a cute way.

"What happened since I left last night?" I asked and reached her arms up to remove her shirt. She was dead on her feet, but I thought a hot shower would do a world of good.

"More emails. An article about me. And a lot of phone calls," she told me flatly. "Not very creative. Mostly die, groomer, die type stuff. And their spelling is atrocious."

I couldn't even crack a smile at her attempt to lighten the mood. "Not funny."

"Better than crying."

I bit the inside of my cheek until I tasted metal but kept my mouth shut, focused on one task at a time. The first thing I needed to do was get her cleaned up. I could deal with the other stuff later. Once I had her stripped down, I turned on the shower and dropped my clothes on the floor next to hers before helping her in.

I held her so the spray hit her back, and she melted into me, her head on my shoulder, her arms around my neck. I didn't have her fancy shampoo and conditioner, so I settled for using my all-in-one, wishing we were in another space and time, so she'd roll her eyes, tease me about my lack of proper skin and hair care.

"What happened at the police station?"

She sighed as I massaged her back. "Most of the calls were telling me what an awful human I was, but they did say they'd look into the credibility of the one or two actual threats. My parents contacted a lawyer, but I didn't have the bandwidth to pay attention to all the stuff about civil cases. Besides..." She shrugged, her words heavy with resignation. "I'm quitting."

"You're quitting?"

"That's what they want," she mumbled, her forehead on my collarbone. "And I just want this all to go away."

Nothing I could say would make any of this better, so I didn't say anything at all. Instead, I carefully washed every part of her, kneaded her tight muscles, and dragged my fingers over her scalp like she often did to me. And when I could tell she couldn't stand on her own two feet anymore, I shut off the water, helped her to step out of the shower before wrapping her in a towel and carrying her to bed. I put one of my T-shirts on her and found one of the extra pairs of underwear she'd helpfully left here. Then I slipped into a pair of shorts and tucked her into my side.

She yawned, and I drew my thumb across the wrinkle between her brows. "Go to sleep."

"I can't. My mind keeps going and going. It won't shut off. All I want to do is sleep, and I can't."

I kissed her temple, her cheek, her lips, and yet she still didn't close her eyes.

"I want to go to sleep and wake up and have this all be a bad dream."

I wrapped my arm around her middle and rolled us to our sides, her back to my chest, my knees behind hers, our fingers laced together. "You're home and safe. You can sleep now."

I held her close and counted her breaths until they turned so shallow I knew she'd fallen asleep, and that was when I tucked my nose into her hair and inhaled so deep my eyes stung with tears.

Because I would quite literally give up everything to make sure she was never harmed.

CHAPTER THIRTY-THREE

Claire

For how hyper and heated Jimmy had been last week, I couldn't believe how calm he was now. When I had told him how my landlord had knocked on my door yesterday morning, informing me he'd heard about everything going on and was not going to extend my lease agreement at the end of the month, Jimmy took it in stride. He simply kissed my forehead, retrieved his cell phone, and texted someone.

He'd been texting a lot.

His brother Mike and his wife, Sam, arrived early afternoon on Saturday. Jimmy pulled his brother into a hug. The two, though they had the same coloring, were night and day. Mike was thick like a tree trunk with a sleeve of tattoos and a beard. Jimmy looked like a noodle next to him. Sam, on the other hand, was bright, with mermaid hair and multiple piercings in her ears, a stud in her nose, and a few tattoos. She smiled at me as soon as she walked in the door, asking, "Can I hug you?"

Jimmy had apparently filled them in on everything going on, but even if he hadn't, it wouldn't have been hard to find. A single Google search would pull up multiple entries about me, including newspaper articles, social media posts, and the growing petition to get me fired.

Joke was on them, though.

I'd sent my letter of resignation in to Mrs. Kaplan and Mr. Tozer already. I had assumed Jimmy would fight me on it, but again, he merely kissed my head, told me he loved me, and went back to fiddling with his phone.

Saturday night, Jimmy disappeared with Mike, only to return a couple hours later with a few bags from my apartment. "I got all your clothes and toiletries but left your books. I was afraid to touch those and screw up your system."

It was the first time he'd smiled his old sunshine smile at me in a while.

Mike and Sam planned to stay the night, and I would've liked to hang out with them, but being here in Jimmy's house, I could finally sleep, and it was all I could do to stay awake.

Sunday found me cooking brunch with Sam while Jimmy and Mike ran errands. It didn't occur to me to ask about them; I was too exhausted to care. Making the decision to resign was not one I enjoyed, but I hoped it would make the harassment stop.

Sam compared it to giving in to a toddler's tantrum, but she also wasn't on the receiving end of that tantrum. When I described the phone calls and emails and direct messages, she put her arm around my shoulders, saying, "People can be real assholes sometimes."

Then she painted my nails while we watched *Twilight*, and honestly, I could see us getting along really well as sisters-in-law.

Especially when Jimmy grinned at us on his couch. "Sammy and I made a bet a few years ago, and if she won, I promised I'd name my firstborn child after her." He tipped his head in my direction. "That okay with you?"

I glanced between the two best friends, and Sam shook her head. "That was forever ago. You're not actually doing that."

Curious, I asked, "What was the bet?"

Jimmy gestured for her to answer, and her shoulders rose as she inhaled audibly. "I had an eating disorder in high school, a pretty bad one." She met my eyes. "Jimmy visited me at the clinic. Told me if I came home healthy and could keep steady at a normal weight for five years, he'd name his first-born after me."

"Well…" I shrugged, not at all surprised to hear this story. Jimmy was incredibly caring and would always do whatever he could to help, in his very specific Jimmy way. "Samantha was my favorite American Girl, and Samuel sounds like he'd grow up to be a scientist. So, I'd be good with either."

Sam stood up with an incredulous laugh then slapped Jimmy's shoulder. "You're lucky, you know that?"

"The luckiest," he said and bent to kiss me. "They're headed out."

I followed him out front, where Mike and Sam threw their overnight bags in the back of their car. Jimmy and Mike clapped hands and pulled each other in for a hug, then Mike slung his big arm around my neck. "Give 'em hell, okay?"

I nodded, although there wasn't really anyone to give hell to.

Sam hugged me, promising, "We'll see each other soon."

"For my birthday," Jimmy said.

Sam rolled her eyes. "God forbid anyone forget."

Jimmy socked her in the arm then kissed her cheek. With a quick "I love you" exchanged between the two, Mike and Sam were off, and Jimmy wrapped his arm around my waist.

"I really like them," I told him.

"The rest of my family wanted to come, my parents and Adam and his kids, but…" He slanted his gaze to me. "I thought it would be better for it only to be us."

Even though I wanted to meet his whole family, I was grateful it wasn't this weekend. "Thanks."

He squeezed my waist. "How's pizza for dinner?"

"Perfect."

It was while we were munching on our pizza in front of his TV that I remembered the contest had ended. I frowned. "I guess we didn't win, huh?"

"No."

"I'm sorry. It's my fault."

He tossed his slice down and wiped his hands. "It is absolutely not your fault. None of this is your fault," he said so vehemently, I had to blink away to the wall, my eyes blurring. "Claire."

It took me a moment to compose myself.

"It's not your fault."

"It is, though. None of this would've happened if..." I scrubbed the back of my hand across my nose, stuffy again.

"No. Not *if*. You did nothing wrong. Maybe..." He let out an aggrieved breath. "Maybe people just liked another couple more."

A smile threatened to break through. "It physically pained you to say that, didn't it?"

"Yes!" he moaned, falling into my lap.

I combed my fingers through his hair. "What are you going to do about the house?"

He stared at me upside down. "Find a new place. One for you and me. With two incomes, we won't have a problem getting a loan."

"I quit," I reminded him, but he tugged on my ponytail.

"Maybe you'll change your mind."

"I'm not going to change my mind." I huffed. "Besides the threats and invasion of privacy, I'm just plain mortified. How can you expect me to walk back into the school?"

"You're reacting out of emotion." He sat up again. "It's better to act rationally."

"Where'd you hear that from?"

"Kaplan."

"She did get her job for a reason," I said on a sigh. "She's been so kind to me. A lot of people probably would have folded by now, but she's really stuck up for me."

"Because, for the millionth time, you did nothing wrong." When I didn't answer, he knocked his elbow into my side and tipped his chin to my pizza. "You gonna finish that slice?"

I handed it to him and leaned back against the sofa cushion. "I'm taking tomorrow off. I said my last day would be Friday, but I might as well use up my sick and personal days."

He nodded. "Yeah? I'll take off too."

"You don't have to."

"I want to." He laid a smacking kiss on my cheek then tossed the television remote in my direction. "Where were we in that K-Drama?"

———

I should have known we weren't "taking the day off." Jimmy dragged me to my apartment to pack up the rest of my belongings. When I complained, he said, "Don't put off to tomorrow what you can do today," which was a very un-Jimmy Ewing stance to take, but I only had a few more days in there anyway. Figured, might as well.

After lunch, we ran some errands, including a stop at a print shop. When I asked him what was in the big box he placed in the trunk, he said, "T-shirts."

"For what?"

"Tomorrow."

"What's tomorrow?"

He flattened his mouth. "The school board meeting."

My stomach twisted. "What are you planning?"

"Not much." He shrugged. "We're calling in a counter-protest."

My brows shot up. "*We*? Who's we?"

He turned the ignition over and drove out of the parking lot. "Me, Meredith, Aggie, everyone."

"I'm sorry, *what*?"

He spoke as if this were an everyday event. "You thought we weren't going to do anything?"

I shook my head, blinking. "Am I... Am I in a different universe right now? Kaplan told me not to do anything."

"Correct. She told *you* not to do anything. She told me not to react emotionally. So, I'm acting rationally."

"By stirring the pot more?"

He pursed his lips. "No... I'd... I'd call it putting a lid on the pot."

Despite my best efforts at annoyance, a half smile curved my mouth. "You call a counterprotest putting a lid on it?"

"Yeah. We're going to silence them." He tilted his head in the direction of the trunk. "That box is full of a second order of T-shirts." Then he took my hand, lacing our fingers together. "I know you've felt alone. Like Brooks and her flying monkeys hold all the power, but they don't. We can fight this." He kissed the back of my hand. "And you know I never lose."

"Except for ten grand from a radio contest."

"Ma'am!"

And then I laughed, because no matter what, he was my sunshine.

CHAPTER THIRTY-FOUR

Claire

I didn't want to go. I wasn't going. In fact, I refused to leave the couch, latching my hands on to the cushions. A sit-in.

But then Jimmy called in reinforcements, and Meredith arrived. Together, they towed me out of the house, my supposed best friend smacking the cushion, which I still clung to, out of my fingers, and pushed me into the car.

"I'm not going," I said, even as Jimmy clicked my seat belt into place.

"You are," Meredith told me from the back seat.

I folded my arms. "I can't be in the same room as these people who hate me. Let alone look at them."

"So don't." Jimmy grinned. "Look at me."

"Your shirts are ridiculous."

Meredith pinched my arm. "Are not. I designed them myself!"

"I love it." Jimmy plucked at the bright-blue shirt with a comic-like female superhero on it. She looked suspiciously like me with bright-orange hair and a big butt. Over her head, bubble words spelled out, "Librarians are superheroes!"

"Yeah, stop being such a grouch," Meredith said.

I rolled my eyes. "I appreciate what you guys are trying to

do, but I already sent in my resignation letter. It's over. The bad guys won."

"It was only halftime," Jimmy said, and I groaned.

"Not another sportsball saying."

"Play through the final whistle."

"I threw in the towel."

"And I picked it up," he said, and Meredith cackled behind me like the traitor she was. "Now shut your adorable mouth up because we're not letting you give up without a fight."

Before I could argue anymore, he blasted "Tubthumping," quite possibly the worst song...ever. Yet Jimmy bopped in his seat, singing every single line.

"You know, everyone thinks this song's about drinking!" he yelled over the music. "But it's actually about political protests."

Meredith cheered behind me, and I was both appalled and filled with love when they sing-shouted the chorus together. They were an odd yet perfect team. I supposed people would say that about Jimmy and me too. The sunshine teacher and grumpy librarian, but we worked.

It was that confidence that had me opening my door on my own when we parked in front of the administration building. A huge crowd had gathered, most of them in matching blue T-shirts, cheering and holding signs like "Reading may cause kindness" and "Libraries are for everyone." They had to have numbered in the hundreds; some I recognized, but most I didn't. There were a lot of students, of all ages. I spotted Austin in the crowd with Shandi on his shoulders. They both waved at me.

I started toward the doors, but my family stopped me. My *entire* family, including Julie. Mom and Dad both embraced me, then my siblings piled on.

"What are you doing here?" I cried.

"Jimmy told us what he was planning," Mom said, and Ryan fist-bumped my boyfriend.

"You really thought we wouldn't be here?" Dad asked, running his hand over my head.

I turned to Julie. "How'd you...?"

"There're these things called planes. I bought a ticket." She arched her hand around the crowd. "Besides, this is news!"

I gave in to a soggy laugh.

Over my shoulder, I saw Jimmy beckoning another group. This one, his family.

I swiped at my eyes and quickly dampening forehead. I was sweating from all the fanfare, and now I had to meet his family on top of it?

He drew me into his side with an unrepentant apology in my ear. "They love you already." When I huffed, he kissed my temple. "Mom, Dad, I'd like you to meet my little trouble-making librarian."

His mom, tall and slender with a dark bob and shining eyes, took my hand in hers. "I am so happy to meet you. I'm also very happy to protest for you."

"Any woman who can keep our son in line must be worth protecting," his dad said, and it was obvious where Jimmy got his smile and humor from.

"Thank you for being here," I told them then waved to Jimmy's older brother, Adam. He held the hands of his two young daughters, with his wife, Lauren, on the other side. All four of them wearing the shirts. One of the girls—Amelia, I guessed—tugged on my hand, and I bent down to smile at her.

"Mommy said you work at a libary," she said, sweetly mispronouncing it.

I nodded, even though I wouldn't come Friday. "Yes, I work at a library,"

"I want to work at a libary when I get big."

I couldn't answer, my lip trembling too much, and Jimmy lifted both of his nieces for a hug.

And then our two families converged, greeting each other with handshakes and hugs.

"I'd say the meeting of the families is going well." Jimmy winked at me, and the absurdity of all of it—the protest, the counterprotest, our families meeting—hit me like a double shot of tequila. I couldn't stop giggling.

"Only you could find a purpose in the middle of a tornado."

He puffed up his chest, throwing his arm around me. "I feed on chaos."

Someone with a megaphone introduced themselves and their friends. It was a group of high school kids, and they each took turns reading aloud from commonly banned books like "And Tango Makes Three," a children's book about two male penguins and their chick, "The Bluest Eye," a classic by Toni Morrison, and "Nineteen Minutes," a book which depicts a school shooting.

Jimmy threaded his fingers with mine. "It started off as us wanting to support you, but it kinda blew up into a resistance campaign."

"You started a conversation," Meredith said on my other side, "about how important books and libraries are. No one wants to see books banned. No one wants to see librarians losing their jobs."

Out of the corner of my eye, I noticed a news van parked on the side street, where a reporter stood in front of a camera and light.

Jimmy followed my line of sight. "I didn't call them. They came on their own."

Meredith smirked. "But I did give them some quotes."

"Well, I could make this national news," Julie murmured, pulling her cell phone out to start filming.

Aiden nudged his glasses farther up his nose. "Don't you do fluff pieces?"

Julie kicked her foot out, nailing him in the shin, and Aiden hissed out a quiet curse, folding in half, right into Meredith's boobs.

"At least buy me dinner first," she said, and Aiden's face flushed bright red. Tristan patted his back while Evan and Rosie cracked up.

"Hey, we should head inside. They're about to start." Jimmy tugged me toward the doors. Our two families formed a barricade around us as we made our way through the crowd until the small group in front of the doors stopped us. They numbered in the dozens. Some of them wore red shirts which labeled them as part of Mothers for Freedom. One man with a big beard wore a hat that read "Fuck your feelings."

"These people don't understand irony," Jimmy mumbled, keeping me moving, but I still heard their taunts about "woke bullshit" and "Fire the groomer!"

Behind me, I heard Rosie tell someone, "Red's really not your color," and then Meredith said, "You spelled independence wrong. You should probably read more books."

Inside, it was standing room only, the tension palpable. The board members were already seated, and Vanessa Brooks was in the front row opposite them. When people spotted me, they whispered, and I only knew if it was negative or positive based on the shirts they wore.

A small fissure of hope splintered my rib cage at the ocean of blue.

Jimmy escorted me to the right side of the room, where there was an open chair next to Aggie. Jimmy and Meredith stood, both of them with their arms folded, gaze out, like my personal bodyguards.

"How you doing?" Aggie asked.

"Could be better."

"We're all here for you," she said with a squeeze to my shoulder as the bang of a gavel sounded, signaling the commencement of the meeting.

The president of the board, Tom Devine, started, "The last meeting of the school year is normally pretty quick, seeing as how it's wrapping up business, but I know a recent matter raised within the district has caused quite a stir. We will discuss it, but first, we need to conduct usual business. I ask everyone here to respect whoever is speaking and keep noise to a minimum. I do not have a problem throwing anyone out for disrupting this meeting. Now, Mrs. Candido, please take attendance."

The meeting crawled by, their agenda filled with mundane discussions of reallocation of funds for next year and a vote on whether they should change the policy for allowing the public to join the meetings via Zoom. Until finally it was time for public comments.

It was no surprise Vanessa Brooks had the first spot. She came armed with her petition, alleging it had over five thousand signatures. I bent over, my head in my hands, unable to watch, but I did hear someone shout, "How many of them live in this district?"

A gavel struck. "We will have respect and order here."

When it quieted, Vanessa Brooks spoke like her mouth was right against the mic, tinny and obtrusive. "The public has a right to know what books are in our schools. Our tax dollars cannot support any of this woke nonsense. These people are here to convince you—"

"We're teachers!"

"And students!"

"And parents!"

"And taxpayers!"

"Order!" Devine boomed. "I will shut this meeting down before I let it turn into a circus."

"Already is," Aggie murmured next to me.

"These people," Vanessa continued, "will try to convince you what Claire Hart did was acceptable. But let me ask you, what would you do to protect your child from a supposed educator giving them sexually explicit content?"

I lifted my head then because, even now, after all this time, she still hadn't bothered to learn what was in the books I'd suggested to her daughter. The willful ignorance was unsurprising and yet still astounding.

"We cannot sit by while our children are brainwashed. This is America, we have a right to dictate what is appropriate for our children."

Behind me, someone laughed. "You think she ever took a history class?"

"Or read a history book?"

"No," Jimmy said out of the corner of his mouth. "That's why we're here in this hell."

Vanessa handed the petition over to Mr. Devine then took her position back up at the podium. "I am formally requesting every book in the district be evaluated by a panel of parents to determine whether it is appropriate for the students."

"Okay," Mr. Devine said, "thank you for your comments. Your five minutes are up."

She sat, looking awfully smug, as Aggie rose to take her place. As she promised, Aggie described the amount of work each teacher individually did, including finding appropriate materials to meet each student at their level. "Miss Hart does that not just for one class, but for every student in the school. She has the full support of the union, and I would like to remind everyone here that she has not broken her contract. She is an exemplary librarian and teacher."

Aggie sat back down next to me with a smile. That was when I noticed Mrs. Kaplan. She seemed exhausted but was smiling at me, and though it wasn't clearly visible, I could see the collar of the blue shirt underneath her linen button-down.

For the next hour, so many people stood up to defend not only me but libraries and the ability of teachers to *teach*. At one point, Carol Monahan-Healy, Sam's mom, stood up to deliver a short but emotional speech about being a queer teacher. "I don't have framed photos of my family, like other teachers do," she said, her voice shaking. "I don't talk about my personal life, ever, because I'm afraid of this." She lifted her attention up from the paper she held to speak directly to the board. "A thinly veiled attempt at discrimination."

"How dare you!" someone shouted, and Devine hit his gavel, narrowing his gaze at the interruption.

"This is an attempt by a small group of individuals to weed out anything they don't like, anything they deem inappropriate, which, of course, we know means anything that is not white, straight, and cisgendered."

Boos rang out while we clapped on our side, and Devine hit the gavel again and again until everyone quieted.

"My students are all so young and full of curiosity and love, they would never judge me, but still, I don't talk about my personal life because of people who assume whom I'm married to affects my ability to teach. I can assure you it does not. My kindergarteners learn how to read and write and count to one hundred the same way now when I'm married to a woman as they did when I was married to a man. I implore you not to give in to the small number of voices calling for banning books. The loudest voices are not always the right voices."

When she sat to a chorus of boos, I stood to hug her and thank her for speaking. She smiled with tears in her eyes. "Some things are too important to stay quiet."

Then it was Jimmy's turn.

"My name is Jim Ewing, and I teach second grade at Lincoln Elementary. I have worked with Claire Hart for five years."

"And now he's dating her!" someone yelled from the red-shirted group. "He supports indoctrination!"

Jimmy simply smiled in the person's direction. "It's true. We are dating, so I think I'm uniquely qualified to tell you how much pride and passion she has for her work. I was with her the night she searched for those books which have led to the basis for this...exciting demonstration of our First Amendment rights, and I can tell you she takes her job seriously. She spent hours—*hours*—rummaging for a book that was age and content appropriate. I would ask you, when was the last time any of you—" he turned to the red-shirted group "—spent hours on one task for someone else? Then I would ask you how much you were paid for it? If it's more than zero, it's more than Claire was paid to go above and beyond for one student. I would also ask when was the last time you were sent a death threat for doing your job? Because Claire has received hundreds."

I closed my eyes to the well of tears, and I felt a hand on my shoulder, though I didn't know who it belonged to.

Jimmy finished with a simple, "I was told if I involved myself in this, I would lose my chance at winning the Teacher of the Year award. But here I am, standing with so many teachers and students, current and former, telling you what is happening is wrong. By giving in to the demands of that petition, you will not only be hurting students, but also teachers. And I highly doubt there are many, if any, who signed that petition willing to do our job. Thank you for your time."

He was met with a standing ovation, and I was pretty sure it was Ryan hooting like he was at a baseball game.

"That's it for public comments," Mr. Devine intoned as he flipped through the petition's pages then passed it to his left, where a woman with dark hair and glasses sat. It was Margo Stetler. One of the flying monkeys, as Jimmy liked to refer to them.

She lifted it up. "I motion to vote on the proposal."

Another man at the other end of the dais raised his hand. "Seconded."

"Shithead," Meredith grumbled.

Mr. Devine folded his hands. "Motion granted. Mrs. Candido, call the roll, please."

They needed a majority to pass, five out of the nine members to vote yes.

They had three.

CHAPTER THIRTY-FIVE

Claire

I couldn't move. Couldn't even speak. After the roar of celebration died down, and everyone turned to me as if they wanted to put me on their shoulders, I sat frozen. It wasn't until the room mostly emptied that Jimmy pulled me up out of the chair and slid a protective arm around my shoulders.

"It's over, baby." He kissed my forehead, my wet cheeks, my lips. "It's over."

Our families all congregated around me, telling me how happy and proud they were, but it was as if I was swimming underwater. I couldn't quite understand all their words. In my periphery, I noticed Meredith shepherding everyone away from me. My best friend, she was great.

"You ready to go home?" My boyfriend, he was great.

I nodded and stayed glued to his side, even as he stifled a frustrated chuckle at Vanessa Brooks, red-faced and pointing her finger at Tom Devine.

At the doors, Mr. Tozer stopped me. "Do you have a moment to speak, Claire?"

Mrs. Kaplan stood behind the superintendent, holding a folded piece of paper, and I met Mr. Tozer's eyes. "Yes?"

He took the paper from Mrs. Kaplan's fingers. "We received your letter of resignation."

My throat felt like glass, so I merely nodded.

"I understand if you would like to move on, but I would be happy to throw this in the shredder. No one would be the wiser."

"I..." I glanced at Jimmy then to Mrs. Kaplan. "I...didn't want to quit," I said honestly.

"Then don't," Mrs. Kaplan replied.

"I can guarantee your job with this district is safe," Mr. Tozer said. "And make no mistake, I may not have been able to be a part of the demonstration tonight, but I am on your side. I will be reviewing new policies about communication and privacy for our staff. The safety of our students and staff is our priority. I am so sorry for what you've gone through, but I promise I will be making changes so it cannot happen again."

Mrs. Kaplan reached out for my hand. "You're an integral member of our faculty. I understand why you would want to leave, but I am asking you to stay. The students need someone like you."

I rubbed at my forehead, weighing my love for my job, for my students, against everything that had taken place the last two weeks.

Two weeks?

Felt like two years.

But I hadn't wanted to quit. I had been cornered and did the only thing I thought would help, though now I knew I had more support than I realized. I met Mr. Tozer's gaze. "Shred it."

Jimmy's fingers tightened around my waist as Tozer nodded.

"I will see you tomorrow," I told Mrs. Kaplan, and she smiled.

"Looking forward to it."

Jimmy escorted me outside and through the crowd, ignoring the calls to talk or for congratulatory hugs. I needed to go home, and he got me there in record time.

We showered together then snuggled up in bed, and I stared up at the ceiling. "I can't believe any of this happened."

"Me either," he said, fiddling with his phone before fluffing his pillow. "Who'd have thought quiet little Claire Hart would make such a ruckus."

"Yeah." I took a deep breath for the first time in weeks. "You're the rabble-rouser."

"Rabble-rouser. I like that term."

I smiled against his shoulder. "I read it in a book."

"Speaking of…" He picked up a book from a stack on the bedside table. "We left off at chapter fifteen. They were about to do it in the parlor."

I cleared my throat, opened my mouth to read, but his phone buzzed. "Excuse me. Phones away, please."

A filthy grin slanted his mouth. "I love when you get all prim and proper on me." He palmed my breast then swiped his thumb over the screen. "It's Lucy."

I craned my neck to spy his screen. "Lucy?"

He tapped out a message. "She and her husband own this house."

"Oh, right."

"She's saying she heard about what happened and is hoping everything is okay."

"That's nice of her."

"Yeah," he droned absently.

"You're typing an awful lot just to say thank you."

"She's wondering if it's affected my plans to buy the house." He sent a message then met my gaze. "Has it?"

I shrugged. Now that I was keeping my job, it changed

things. "We do have two incomes. Should make getting a loan easier. That's what you said, right?"

"So, you're in?"

"I'm in."

He vaulted up, jostling the bed as he yelled out, "Alexa, play 'Believe' by Cher!"

I joined him, laughing and dancing and singing at the top of my lungs. This was going to be our house. This was going to be my life.

Never a dull moment.

After we fell down to the bed in a breathless heap, he rolled on top of me. "Guess that's our song, huh?"

"No. Absolutely not."

He cocked his head back, his hands on either side of my shoulders as he pushed up, hovering over me. "Why not? That's the song I played after you said yes to me the first time."

"So?"

"Soooooo," he said, all beleaguered, "it has meaning. Plus, it's a classic."

I rolled my eyes. "Everything's a classic to you."

"Fine. What's your pick for our song?"

I bit into my lips. "Um..."

"No suggestion, no say."

"Hey." I thumped his chest, but he lowered his weight onto me.

"Now, now. Please keep your arms and legs inside the ride vehicle at all times."

I wrapped my legs around his waist. "Or what?"

"Or I'll have to ask you to get off the ride." Then he flipped us, so he was on his back.

"What are you doing?"

His fingers bit into my ass, urging me forward. "Trying to get these things off."

I leaned over, lifting my leg to help him remove my under-wear, when all of a sudden, they ripped.

"Jimmy!"

"Oops." He was completely unrepentant.

I knocked his arm. "You did that on purpose."

"Yes. Yes, I did, and now I know why bodice-ripping is always in romance novels. I feel like a man, you know? Like a kill a bear, rip some panties with my bare hands *man*."

I clucked my tongue, staring down at the torn lace. He finished the job, ripping the other side off, so he could toss them aside.

"It's harder than it looks, though," he said with a shake of his head. "I think if you were wearing one of your other ones, like a sturdier kind of cotton, they wouldn't rip."

"Don't you dare try it on another pair."

"It's for science," he said seriously.

"You're ridiculous."

"And you love me. Now, get up here and sit on my face."

Well, I couldn't argue with that. It was the only way to make him stop talking.

Epilogue

Jimmy

I was still wearing the birthday crown my nieces made me when Claire and I walked into our house. It wouldn't become official for another three weeks, but we'd started to refer to it as our house as soon as I'd texted Lucy back the night of the protest.

Now that school was over, Claire and I had made plans to paint and decorate over the summer. She had already purchased 187 new pillows. But the first thing we did was hang a framed photo. Our very first picture together from the softball game. It was the beginning of our story, our weird and wonderful roller coaster of a story.

"That was a nice day," Claire said, slipping out of her sandals, her breezy sundress swaying with each of her steps.

"Mm-hmm." I snagged her wrist as she passed me, pulling her into my chest. She tilted her head back, her nose and forehead pink from the sun. And if it was possible, even more freckled. I kissed my favorite ones. "Dance with me."

"Alexa," she said, looping her arms around my neck, "Play 'Lover' by Taylor Swift."

"Mm. Good pick."

"Our song," she said, and I blew a raspberry.

"I love Tay-Tay as much as the next guy, but let's not be so conventional."

"There is nothing about you that's conventional. In fact, we could use some more conventionality."

I let my hands drift from her back to her butt as we swayed in the middle of our living room. "You'd hate conventional."

"No, I wouldn't. I'm boring, remember?"

"You're perfect," I said against her lips. "And you're mine."

"I'm yours," she agreed.

"Now, we only have to make it official."

"How much more official do you want? We live together, we work together, I have my own text thread with your mother."

"A ring," I said because while I had been browsing Pinterest the other day, I'd found the perfect one for her.

She huffed a laugh. "You need to slow down a bit."

"You're saying you'd say no if I asked."

She tipped her head to the side, giving me a *Come now, you bonehead* look. One of my favorites. Right up there behind the *I love you, you adorable idiot* eye roll. "It's a romance, so spoiler alert," she murmured, leaning up on her toes, "we end up together."

This girl.

I was obsessed.

"Let's go to bed," I told her, hauling her to the bedroom like the brute I was. "Time for my birthday orgasms."

"What makes birthday orgasms different from regular orgasms?"

I spun on her, pushing her down onto the bed. "I'm wearing a birthday crown."

"Right. Of course."

Then I sank to the floor, hiked her dress up to her waist, and yanked off her underwear. "Now, time for dessert."

"Happy birthday, Jimmy," she said, and I moaned my appreciation of my favorite flavor in the world, Claire Hart.

Soon-to-be Ewing.

My grumpy, boring, perfect librarian.

Acknowledgments

Indie publishing is a wild ride. Thank you, reader, for coming along with me.

I wouldn't be able to put out these books if not for the encouragement of my friends, especially Ellis Leigh and Brighton Walsh, and the help of my editors, Libby and Lisa. I'd especially like to thank my street team for helping me spread the work about my books. I'm forever grateful.

If you'd like more information about me, you can find it at: https://sophieandrewsauthor.com.

About the Author

Sophie Andrews is a contemporary romance author who writes steamy books that will leave you smiling. As a millennial, she's obsessed with boybands, late 90s rom-coms, and will always be team Pacey. When she's not writing, she's most likely trying to wrangle her children or drinking red wine. Or both at the same time.